CRIME FICTION

Crime Fiction provides a lively introduction to what is both a wide-ranging and a hugely popular literary genre. Using examples from a variety of novels, short stories, films and television series, John Scaggs:

- presents a concise history of crime fiction – from biblical narratives to James Ellroy – broadening the genre to include revenge tragedy and the gothic novel
- explores the key sub-genres of crime fiction, such as 'Mystery and Detective Fiction', 'The Hard-Boiled Mode', 'The Police Procedural' and 'Historical Crime Fiction'
- locates texts and their recurring themes and motifs in a wider social and historical context
- outlines the various critical concepts that are central to the study of crime fiction, including gender studies, narrative theory and film theory
- considers contemporary television series such as *C.S.I.: Crime Scene Investigation* alongside the 'classic' whodunnits of Agatha Christie

Accessible and clear, this comprehensive overview is the essential guide for all those studying crime fiction and concludes with a look at future directions for the genre in the twenty-first century.

John Scaggs is a Lecturer in the Department of English at Mary Immaculate College in Limerick, Ireland.

THE NEW CRITICAL IDIOM

SERIES EDITOR: JOHN DRAKAKIS, UNIVERSITY OF STIRLING

The New Critical Idiom is an invaluable series of introductory guides to today's critical terminology. Each book:

- provides a handy, explanatory guide to the use (and abuse) of the term
- offers an original and distinctive overview by a leading literary and cultural critic
- relates the term to the larger field of cultural representation

With a strong emphasis on clarity, lively debate and the widest possible breadth of examples, *The New Critical Idiom* is an indispensable approach to key topics in literary studies.

Also available in this series:

CRIME FICTION

John Scaggs

Routledge
Taylor & Francis Group

LONDON AND NEW YORK

First published 2005
by Routledge
2 Park Square, Milton Park, Abingdon, Oxon OX14 4RN

Simultaneously published in the USA and Canada
by Routledge
270 Madison Ave, New York, NY 10016

Reprinted 2007

Routledge is an imprint of the Taylor & Francis Group, an informa business

Typeset in Adobe Garamond and Scala Sans by
Keystroke, Jacaranda Lodge, Wolverhampton
Printed and bound in Great Britain by
TJ International Ltd, Padstow, Cornwall

British Library Cataloguing in Publication Data
A catalogue record for this book is available from the British Library

Library of Congress Cataloging in Publication Data
Scaggs, John, 1970–
Crime fiction / John Scaggs.
p.   cm. – (The new critical idiom)
Includes bibliographical references and index.
1. Detective and mystery stories, English–History and criticism.
2. Detective and mystery stories, American–History and criticism.
3. Crime in literature. I. Title. II. Series.
PR830.C74S28 2005
823'.087209–dc22   2004016596

ISBN10: 0–415–31825–4 (hbk)
ISBN10: 0–415–31824–6 (pbk)

ISBN13: 978–0–415–31825–9 (hbk)
ISBN13: 978–0–415–31824–2 (pbk)

To My Grandmother
Margaret Carter

CONTENTS

SERIES EDITOR'S PREFACE

The New Critical Idiom is a series of introductory books which seeks to extend the lexicon of literary terms, in order to address the radical changes which have taken place in the study of literature during the last decades of the twentieth century. The aim is to provide clear, well-illustrated accounts of the full range of terminology currently in use, and to evolve histories of its changing usage.

The current state of the discipline of literary studies is one where there is considerable debate concerning basic questions of terminology. This involves, among other things, the boundaries which distinguish the literary from the non-literary; the position of literature within the larger sphere of culture; the relationship between literatures of different cultures; and questions concerning the relation of literary to other cultural forms within the context of interdisciplinary studies.

It is clear that the field of literary criticism and theory is a dynamic and heterogeneous one. The present need is for individual volumes on terms which combine clarity of exposition with an adventurousness of perspective and a breadth of application. Each volume will contain as part of its apparatus some indication of the direction in which the definition of particular terms is likely to move, as well as expanding the disciplinary boundaries within which some of these terms have been traditionally contained. This will involve some re-situation of terms within the larger field of cultural representation, and will introduce examples from the area of film and the modern media in addition to examples from a variety of literary texts.

ACKNOWLEDGEMENTS

My thanks first of all to John Drakakis, whose help, support, encouragement, and advice throughout the process of writing this book, quite apart from getting me across the finishing line, have also taught me a great deal.

Thanks also to Liz Thompson at Routledge for her support and enthusiasm from the very early stages of this project, and to everyone at Mary Immaculate College in Limerick, Ireland, who contributed to this book, whether they know it or not. This includes the library staff, the Research Office, and my colleagues in the Department of English: John McDonagh, Gerry Dukes, Florence O'Connor, Glenn Hooper, and, most particularly, Eugene O'Brien.

I would also like to thank my family and friends, in particular my mother, Iris Scaggs, and the embarrassingly long list of people who, at some time or another, have had to listen to me ramble on about motive, means, and opportunity, all of which I now have in abundance to thank them: Hugh Widdis, Gavin Byrne, David Crann, Daragh McEnerney, Gary O'Brien, Kieran Cashell, Matt Cannon, and my friend and colleague, Brian Coates.

Finally, a special thanks to my fiancée, Alice Bendinelli.

INTRODUCTION

'Intellectual discourse is great, man, but in my business, violence and pain is where it's at.'

(Crumley 1993: 303)

It is worth noting at the outset that while the old adage that crime does not pay might well be true, crime has nevertheless been the foundation for an entire genre of fiction for over one hundred and fifty years. In fact it is the centrality of crime to a genre that otherwise, in its sheer diversity, defies any simple classification that has led me to adopt the title 'Crime Fiction' for this volume. Throughout its history, various titles have been coined to classify and describe the genre. From Edgar Allan Poe's 'tales of ratiocination', to the mystery and detective fiction of the turn of the twentieth century and the whodunnit of the period between the First World War and the Second World War, a focus on crime, but only sometimes its investigation, has always been central to the genre. For this reason, the majority of critical studies of the genre over the past twenty years employ the term 'crime fiction' to classify an otherwise unclassifiable genre, and this study will be no different. It does not attempt to seek or uncover a fundamental definition of the genre, but rather it examines how and why the genre is what it is today, and how and why it has developed and been appropriated in the ways that it has. In this sense, there are certain parallels between detection and literary criticism. Both are attempts to make sense of the here and now by examining the there and then.

However, it is not the intention of this study to straitjacket the genre either within an endless catalogue of sub-genres, or within a chronological approach that fixes such sub-genres, and their forms and themes, in time, and ignores the fact of their continual appropriation and reformulation by subsequent writers. The first approach, which might list the sub-genres of crime fiction alphabetically from the amnesia thriller to the whodunnit, is reductive, and serves only to lead the reader down a multitude of formal and thematic dead-ends. The second approach, what the structuralist linguist Ferdinand de Saussure might term a 'diachronic approach', is essentially historical, tracing development and change in the formal and thematic elements of the genre through time. There is in such an approach, however, a tendency to trace the development of the genre by establishing boundaries and identifying differences between a succession of sub-genres, each following the other like toppling dominoes to the present. As in the case of words in language, however, these subdivisions are arbitrary. The chapters in this study, therefore, examine broad categories that are not supposed to be viewed as mutually distinct, since one of the defining characteristics of crime fiction is its generic (and sub-generic) flexibility and porosity.

This reference to structuralism, and to Saussure, is not a casual one. Structuralist theory has a key role in the critical analysis of crime fiction, as it is a genre that is characterised by the way that it self-consciously advertises its own plot elements and narrative structures. Tzvetan Todorov, in a structuralist analysis that is one of the very first theoretical analyses of crime fiction, identifies a fundamental duality at the heart of crime fiction, and detective fiction in particular. In Todorov's analysis, the crime story contains two stories: the first is the story of the crime, and the second is the story of its investigation. This observation is an important one for this study, which similarly contains two stories. The first of these is the story of the development of a genre, or the story of the crime in Todorov's analysis. The second story can be traced in faint, tentative sketches and episodes throughout the first. This is the story of the investigation of a genre, or what we might refer to in a literary analysis as the critical and theoretical engagement with the genre that draws out the first story from the textual evidence of the novels and stories. These critical and theoretical engagements are numerous and varied, but the majority of the early influential critical analyses of the genre are structuralist in nature, and much contemporary criticism still uses this as its foundation.

Structuralist approaches do have their advantages, although they are limited, and this study will begin with a diachronic outline of the development of the genre in order to provide a framework within which to contextualise the key points of its broader analysis. However, its broader structure is not a diachronic or a chronological one, and instead the study identifies various ahistorical 'modes' that are mapped on to conventional, but ultimately reductive, sub-generic divisions for the sake of simplicity, not completeness. Like any literary text, individual works of crime fiction are built from the devices, codes, and conventions established by previous works of crime fiction, and they are therefore crucial to our understanding of these texts in the present. Like the detective, the literary critic retraces a chronological chain of cause and effect in order to make sense of the present, and the literary texts that it produces. Chapter 1, therefore, charts the development of the genre within a wider social and historical chronology, and flags the various modes to be discussed in later chapters by identifying the various contexts within which their devices, codes, and conventions first began to develop.

The first of these sub-generic modes is the one that most people, even those with only a vague familiarity with crime fiction, often identify as being representative of the genre as a whole. One reason for this is that mystery and detective fiction, which will be discussed in Chapter 2, represents the earliest consolidation of various themes, devices, and motifs within single texts. Another reason is that it has had more time than later developments of the genre to be appropriated by later fiction but also, more importantly, by other media, most notably film and television. What people remember about characters like Sherlock Holmes, or Hercule Poirot, are strong visual images: Holmes in a deerstalker hat smoking a pipe, Poirot with his waxed moustache and supercilious expression. The vividness of both of these images has more to do with the appropriation of mystery and detective fiction for both the large and small screen than it has to do with the number of people who have read the stories of Arthur Conan Doyle or the novels of Agatha Christie.

Similarly, the image of the hard-boiled detective in hat and overcoat with a gun in his hand is largely inherited from cinema and television.

Chapter 3 will examine the development of the iconic image of the hard-boiled private eye, and will suggest that of all the sub-generic modes examined in the study hard-boiled fiction is the most often, and easily, appropriated. In particular, this chapter will consider how the most truculently misogynistic and often racist sub-genre of crime fiction is the one that has been most frequently and successfully appropriated for ethnic, cultural, feminist, and gay and lesbian reformulations. This chapter will also consider the clear shift of focus from the rural idylls frequent in mystery and detective fiction to the grittily realistic 'mean streets' of the urban settings common in hard-boiled fiction within the context of a broader shift towards social realism in fiction as a result of the undeniably real carnage and disorder of the First and Second World Wars.

Chapters 4 and 5, respectively, will consider the debts that both the police procedural and the crime thriller owe to hard-boiled fiction, and will examine the two aspects of realism central to both sub-genres. The police procedural will be examined in the context of social realism, and this examination will consider how the procedural both engages with, and reflects, the realities of the contemporary multicultural world. The crime thriller, on the other hand, will be examined in the context of psycho-logical realism in order to suggest that a focus on the motivation for crime, and its after-effects, is not confined strictly to the twentieth century, but is at least as old as early-modern drama, in this way emphasising the ahistorical nature of these sub-generic divisions.

This emphasis on the ahistorical, and even *trans*-historical, nature of the broad categories outlined in this study finds its clearest articulation in the final chapter on historical crime fiction. This chapter will employ a post-structuralist analysis in order to examine the notion of 'histori-ography', or the writing of history, which lies at the heart of historical crime fiction, and, this chapter will argue, at the heart of crime fiction in general. This chapter will consider historical crime fiction not just as a re-engagement with and appropriation of history, but the genre of detective fiction itself. By way of conclusion, the discussion of historical crime fiction will be extended to encompass a discussion of the various postmodern appropriations of the genre as a means of highlighting the impossibility of what has always been central to crime fiction: the process of interpretation itself.

It is the indeterminacy of the interpretative act, and the parallels between detection and the reading process that allow postmodern crime fiction to underline this indeterminacy, that suggest various different ways to read this study. It can, and I hope will be, read conventionally from beginning to end, in this way first forming a picture of the broader social and historical development of the genre, and then inserting the discussions of the various sub-genres as the fine detail within the broader picture. It can also, and I hope also will be, read less conventionally from beginning to end in order to first form the broader picture, and then question the sort of mimetic representation or critical and theoretical approach that forms such a picture; in this way it will be possible to problematise the history of the genre, and of literary criticism itself, by recognising the ahistorical picture that runs across and through it. I imagine this sort of approach as being like looking at the Bayeux Tapestry and, to the horror of the curators, pulling out the threads that make up the figure of King Harold in order to follow them to the present in an attempt to understand the relationship between the Battle of Hastings in 1066 and the present moment of interpretation, and in so doing, to expose the tapestry's methods of representation. Pulling out the threads of the tapestry allows us to see it in a new way.

But there is another way to read this book, and different reasons for doing so. Those readers who are already familiar with the broader chronological development of the genre might decide to focus on specific chapters, as might those readers whose interest lies in a particular sub-genre. The variety of reading approaches that the book invites reflects, to some extent, the variety of readers who will find it useful. The book is primarily designed for students reading crime fiction at undergraduate level, and therefore in addition to providing a glossary of useful terms, it also builds its broader analysis, and the discussions in each chapter, from the ground up, starting with what the majority of criticism identifies as foundational points, and then outlining the various avenues that lead from these points. It is these more advanced avenues that will be useful for those who already have a good working knowledge of the genre but who for various reasons, such as further study or research, are seeking to refine that knowledge, or to develop it in particular directions. The bibliography provides the means for these readers to do so.

The book, in other words, is a means to an end, but, as crime fiction repeatedly demonstrates, in every end there must be a beginning, and just as it is the job of the detective to outline the relationship between beginning and end in order to make sense of the present, so too is it the job of the reader. To understand the devices, codes, and conventions of the genre of crime fiction in the present, in all of its various sub-generic manifestations, we must first identify its origins, and it is to these origins that this study will now turn.

1

A CHRONOLOGY OF CRIME

> Both the detective-story proper and the pure tale of horror are very
> ancient in origin. All native folk-lore has its ghost tales, while the
> first four detective-stories [. . .] hail respectively from the Jewish
> Apocrypha, Herodotus, and the Æneid. But, whereas the tale of
> horror has flourished in practically every age and country, the
> detective-story has had a spasmodic history, appearing here and
> there in faint, tentative sketches and episodes.
>
> (Sayers 1992: 72)

EARLY CRIME NARRATIVES

The general critical consensus is that the detective story begins with
Edgar Allan Poe, the 'father' of the detective genre. Crime fiction, however, of which Poe's detective stories form a subset, has a much earlier
provenance, and in order to understand contemporary attitudes to crime,
and to narratives of crime, it is necessary to outline the origins of the
genre. Dorothy L. Sayers, author of a series of novels featuring the much-
imitated, and frequently parodied, Lord Peter Wimsey, in her 1928
introduction to *Great Short Stories of Detection, Mystery, and Horror*,
published in 1929 in the United States as the first *Omnibus of Crime*,
identifies four stories as early ancestors of the genre: two Old Testament

stories, dating from the fourth to the first century BC, from the book of Daniel, one story from Herodotus, dating from the fifth century BC, and one story drawn from the Hercules myths.

In the story of Hercules and Cacus the thief, Cacus is one of the first criminals to falsify evidence by forging footprints in order to mislead his pursuer. Herodotus's story of King Rhampsinitus and the thief is often identified as the first 'locked-room mystery', in which a crime (usually a murder) is committed in a room which it seems is physically impossible for the criminal to have either entered or exited. In Herodotus's story, as in the story of Hercules and Cacus, the thief also tampers with the evidence of the crime to evade capture.

In the biblical story of Susanna and the Elders, in which Susanna has been falsely accused of adultery by two corrupt and lecherous judges, Daniel, in his cross-examination of the two men, exposes their perjury and exonerates the innocent Susanna. What most accounts of this story fail to include, however, is that under the laws of Moses the two men are subject to the same penalty that they had plotted to impose on Susanna, and are put to death. The story of Daniel and the Priests of Bel, like the story of Rhampsinitus and the thief, is an early prototype of the 'locked-room mystery', in which the priests of Bel claim that the statue of the Dragon of Bel eats and drinks the offerings that are made to him, while, in fact, they enter the temple by a secret entrance and, along with their wives and children, consume the offerings themselves. Daniel scatters ashes on the floor of the temple before it is locked and sealed, and the footprints left by the priests prove their guilt. As is the case with the story of Susanna and the Elders, accounts of the story of Daniel and the priests of Bel often omit the fact that the priests, their wives, and their children are all put to death as punishment for their crime.

Julian Symons, the British mystery author and critic, in reference to Sayers and other early twentieth-century commentators on crime fiction such as E.M. Wrong and Willard Huntington Wright, argues that 'those who search for fragments of detection in the Bible and Herodotus are looking only for puzzles', and that while puzzles are an essential element of the detective story, they are not detective stories in themselves (Symons 1993: 19). What sets the stories from the Book of Daniel apart from Herodotus or the Hercules myths, however, is the emphasis on punishment, more than on any true element of detection. The Book of Daniel, in particular the added episodes of Susanna and of the priests of Bel that are found only in the Greek version, is didactic in nature and emphasises right conduct, unlike the Herodotus story, for example, in which Rhampsinitus rewards the thief for his cunning and boldness by giving him his daughter's hand in marriage, implying that crime, at least in this case, really does pay.

The emphasis on right conduct, reinforced by the harsh punishments meted out in the stories from the Book of Daniel, is characteristic of most narratives of crime up until the mid-nineteenth century, including the stories of Edgar Allan Poe. The story of Cain and Abel can be read, in this way, as an example of how crime fiction, according to Stephen Knight, 'create[s] an idea (or a hope, or a dream) about controlling crime' (Knight 1980: 2). Cain murders his brother Abel out of jealousy, and is punished by God in two ways: he becomes an outcast, and he is marked by God so that all may recognise him for who he is, and, more significantly, for *what* he is – a criminal. This 'Mark of Cain' is a reassurance to all those who abide by the law, as it suggests that the criminal is always identifiable as 'other' than themselves. Furthermore, the identification of crime as a transgression of socially imposed boundaries has a dual purpose. In addition to identifying those who lie beyond the pale by marking them in some way, as evident in the biblical story of Cain, but also, for example, in Nathaniel Hawthorne's *The Scarlet Letter* (1850), the notion of crime as transgression also serves to establish the boundaries of acceptable social behaviour. Such boundaries are eventually codified in law, and in this way the social order is maintained, and a particular view of the world, or ideology, is further validated and disseminated.

The story of *Oedipus the King*, as set down by Sophocles and first performed in about 430 BC, draws together all of the central characteristics and formal elements of the detective story, including a mystery surrounding a murder, a closed circle of suspects, and the gradual uncovering of a hidden past. The city of Thebes has been stricken by plague, and the citizens turn to the king, Oedipus, who ended a previous plague and became king by answering the riddle of the Sphinx, to end the current plague and save them. He has sent his brother Creon to the Oracle at Delphi, and Creon returns with a message that the plague will end once the murderer of the former king, Laius, has been captured and banished from the city. Furthermore, the message states that the murderer is in the city of Thebes. Martin Priestman identifies the plague as 'a powerful image for [the] pollution of an entire society' (Priestman 1990: 23), and it is significant that this contamination can only be lifted by the banishment of the criminal, who, whether by virtue of his criminality, or otherwise, is identified as 'other', an outsider.

Oedipus, who as king of Thebes is an embodiment of the state and of authority, and who correctly answered the riddle of the Sphinx, employs the power of authority and his puzzle-solving ability to find Laius's murderer. When he asks Tiresias the seer about the murder, Tiresias answers that it was Oedipus himself who killed Laius, and when he hears a description of Laius's murder from his widow, and now his wife, Jocasta, he begins to suspect that Tiresias's claim is true. These suspicions are confirmed when a shepherd who witnessed Laius's death reveals that Oedipus is not a native of Corinth, but that he was delivered there as an orphan. Oedipus questions him to uncover his origins, and the shepherd reveals that Jocasta, reacting to a prophecy that her son would one day murder his father and marry his mother, ordered him to be put to death. The shepherd was charged with the task, but taking pity on the baby Oedipus, he brought him to Corinth as an orphan. In this way the truth of the prophecy and Oedipus's identity as the murderer are revealed.

The story depends formally, like much detective fiction, on uncovering the identity of Laius's killer. As in much crime fiction, until what is identified as the Golden Age between the two world wars, the criminal is an outsider. In the Oedipus myth, Oedipus is literally an outsider in that he is not from, or at least not believed to be from, Thebes, and therefore seems to have no conceivable connection to the crime. Significantly, after blinding himself on his discovery of the truth, he banishes himself, emphasising his status as an outsider by becoming an outcast as well, but in so doing, lifting the plague from the city and restoring the order that his 'unnatural' marriage to his mother, Jocasta, has disrupted. Oedipus's position as both the criminal and the force of law and authority is significant, and this doubling of functions reappears in later crime fiction, in particular in revenge tragedy and in hard-boiled detective fiction. Oedipus's appeal to Tiresias the seer is also significant. As a seer, Tiresias is somebody who sees the truth, and the structure of *Oedipus* foregrounds the search for truth that the figure of the seer embodies. Despite a plot which foregrounds a hidden secret at its core, and which is structured around the enquiries that uncover this secret at the end, Oedipus's enquiry is based on supernatural, pre-rational methods that are evident in most narratives of crime until the development of Enlightenment thought in the seventeenth and eighteenth centuries.

The revenge tragedy of the late Elizabethan and early Jacobean period, at the end of the sixteenth century and the beginning of the seventeenth, is situated at the cusp of the Enlightenment, and is structured by the overriding imperative of restoring the social order, as embodied in the act of revenge. The revenge pattern of injury and retribution creates a narrative in which the unity of justice and order prevails: the guilty suffer and are punished, and the crimes committed against the innocent are visited upon those who have committed those crimes. 'Revenge', however, as Catherine Belsey notes, 'is not justice' (Belsey 1985: 112). Ironically, it is in the absence of justice that the revenger pursues a course of action that is itself unjust, in an attempt to restore the unity and social order that justice promises. Furthermore, the tragedies of revenge are often structured around the fact that criminality has invaded the centres of justice. In *The Revenger's Tragedy* (1607), the duke is a murderer, just as the king is a killer in Shakespeare's *Hamlet* (1601), and it is this corruption at the heart of the structures of power and justice that signals to the revenger the overriding necessity of what Francis Bacon refers to, at the time of the first developments of revenge tragedy, as 'a kind of wild justice' (Bacon 1999: 11).

Gāmini Salgādo, a twentieth-century literary historian and critic with a special interest in early-modern criminal activity, outlines a five-part structure for revenge tragedy, based on the model laid down by the Roman scholar and playwright Seneca in the first century. Seneca's tragedies are bloody accounts of the downfall of royal families, and, significantly, the five-part structure of Senecan tragedy neatly parallels the narrative structure of much crime fiction, from the novels of Agatha Christie in the 1930s and 1940s in particular, to the present. The first part of the structure identified by Salgādo is the *exposition* of events leading up to the situation requiring vengeance, in revenge tragedy, or investigation, in the crime novel. The second part of the structure is *anticipation* as the revenger plans his revenge, or the detective investigates the crime. The third step is the *confrontation* between revenger and victim, followed by the *partial execution* of the revenger's plan, or, as is often the case with the detective's investigation in the crime novel, the villain's temporary thwarting of it. The final part is the completion of the act of vengeance, or, in the case of crime fiction, the detective's final success in bringing the villain to justice (Salgādo 1969: 17). Salgādo's model is a remapping and refinement of the structure of tragedy outlined by Aristotle in his *Poetics*. In Aristotle's outline, tragedy is governed by a unity of plot in which the narrative advances from beginning to end in an ordered sequence of cause and effect. While a unifying conclusion should tie up any loose ends, it can do so, in Aristotle's view, through the use of *peripeteia*, or ironic reversal, and *anagnorisis*, which translates as 'recognition' or 'discovery', and describes the moment when the hero passes from ignorance to knowledge. Such a movement from ignorance to knowledge is crucial to the narrative success of both revenge tragedy and crime fiction.

In *Hamlet*, a murder has been committed before the narrative begins, and just as the corpse is the starting point for much twentieth-century crime fiction, here, the ghost of the murdered king is the impetus for the action. The ghost of King Hamlet calls on his son, the Prince, to revenge his murder at the hands of his brother, Claudius, who is now king. Hamlet accepts his filial obligation, but before killing Claudius he takes the precaution of first proving his uncle's guilt, and his investigations, which correspond with the 'anticipation' in Salgādo's model above, constitute more than half the play. The primary means by which Hamlet establishes Claudius's guilt is his staging of 'The Mousetrap', a re-enactment of King Hamlet's murder. Claudius's reaction as his act of murder is acted out in front of him convinces Hamlet that he is guilty, and frees him to take his revenge. However, Hamlet's plans are thwarted when he inadvertently kills Polonius, the king's counsellor, in a case of mistaken identity that finds a parallel in the theme of personal reinvention that is central to much twentieth-century hard-boiled fiction. Hamlet is quickly dispatched to England with secret orders from Claudius to the English king to execute him upon his arrival.

Hamlet's accidental murder of Polonius is significant in two related formal aspects. By killing Polonius, and creating another revenger in Polonius's son Laertes, the same doubling of functions that characterises Oedipus also characterises Hamlet. He is both an *agent* of revenge, and therefore an agent of authority, and an *object* of revenge, and in this way he also mirrors Claudius's position in the play. Claudius, as king, embodies the forces of order and authority in the world of the play. However, he is also the villain, and it is this situation, in which those in power abuse it for their own villainous ends, which explains those narratives of crime in which the criminal is the hero, as long, that is, as it is clear that any crimes committed are committed against the villainous elite. Robin Hood is an example of the criminal as hero, but it is clear from narratives about criminals such as Robert Greene's 'cony-catching' pamphlets in the late sixteenth century, in which criminal con-men trick innocent 'conies', that in the late Elizabethan and early Jacobean period sympathy for the criminal was beginning to wane. As Knight points out, with increasing frequency these early-modern criminals are inevitably depicted as coming to a bad end (Knight 1980: 8–9). The ambiguous position of the revenger in the plays of William Shakespeare, Thomas Kyd, John Webster, Cyril Tourneur, Thomas Middleton, and William Rowley, and his inevitable death at the end of the play, seem to bear this out. By taking the law into their own hands, the revengers disrupt the very social order that they are trying to restore, and the response of the sovereign representative of order and authority, in the early-modern period of public execution that is the background to these plays, is swift and final. 'Besides its immediate victim', according to Michel Foucault, 'the crime attacks the sovereign: it attacks him personally, since the law represents the will of the sovereign' (Foucault 1991: 47), and it is for this reason that crime, in the period in which revenge tragedy flourished, 'requires that the king take revenge for an affront to his very person' (Foucault 1991: 48).

CRIME STORIES AS CAUTIONARY TALES

The violent and bloody spectacle of public execution, as a form of revenge in which the sovereign restores order and stability, also served as a warning, and similar warnings were an integral part of the broadsheet accounts of the crimes and punishments of major criminals which were common throughout the eighteenth century. The *Newgate Calendar* stories were the most common of these, and although the title was frequently used, drawing on the image of Newgate prison in the popular imagination, the first large collection of these cautionary tales gathered together under the title appeared in 1773. These stories, and stories like them, were cautionary tales in which the perpetrator of a criminal deed is captured, tried, and punished. Such collections were a response to the popular demand for bloody and shocking accounts of violent crime that spawned the tragedies of revenge in the seventeenth century, and they paralleled a similar demand in France, and elsewhere (Mandel 1984: 6). Like the tragedies of revenge, in which the revenger was executed, or anticipated their inevitable fate by committing suicide, the execution of the villain was an integral part of the popular accounts of the eighteenth century. As Knight observes, the warnings these stories provided were intended as a way of maintaining social order and personal security under threat from rising crime rates (Knight 1980: 10–13), but what is significant, as Knight further observes, is the reliance on pure chance to apprehend the criminal in these stories, rather than on detection and organised police work.

The same element of chance and coincidence that characterises the apprehension of the criminal in the *Newgate Calendar* stories is also evident in what is often identified as one of the most significant precursors to the detective novel: William Godwin's *Caleb Williams*, published in 1794. Caleb Williams, a promising lower-class youth, is taken under the wing of the aristocratic Falkland, and becomes his secretary. Subsequently, Falkland is publicly beaten by Tyrrel, another local squire whom Falkland accuses of ignoring the responsibilities that his position entails. Immediately after Falkland's public humiliation, and as a result of the importance he attaches to social standing and personal honour, he murders Tyrrel in secret, although in a plotting manoeuvre typical of detective fiction the novel does not immediately reveal he is the killer. Caleb, in an early example of investigation and deductive reasoning, establishes the facts of the murder and identifies Falkland as the killer. Falkland, however, realising that Caleb knows the truth, uses his position and influence to imprison Caleb, and, eventually, to discredit and humiliate him. At the close of the novel, Caleb eventually confronts his former master, and in the revised ending of the novel, which Godwin redrafted to replace the original ending in which Falkland once more outmanoeuvres Caleb, the confrontation kills Falkland.

After Falkland's death Caleb acknowledges his own complicity in his unjust persecution of Falkland as the result of his failure to accept his own social position as his master's servant. In this way, it is clear that Falkland embodies the ideology of a dying semi-feudal order in the importance he places on honour and social standing, while Caleb, by crossing the boundaries of class demarcated by such an order, embodies the concept of individual freedom that characterises Enlightenment thought and which led inexorably to the French Revolution in 1789, with its ideals of liberty, fraternity, and justice. Godwin's novel, in this way, is characterised by its essential conflict between Enlightenment ideas prevalent at the time he was writing, and evident in its radical questioning of political justice and its faith in rationality, and a semi-feudal, Christian ideology and Old Testament faith that wrong-doing will always be punished by God, regardless of individual action. The plot of the novel advertises its transitional nature in its depiction of crime in high places and the related notion of personal honour that is typical of Elizabethan and Jacobean revenge tragedy, and in its contrasting consideration of the power of the subjective, individual intellect to challenge such a system. The ending of the novel, however, mirrors the dilemma of revenge tragedy, and as Martin Priestman observes, 'the exposure of crime in high places must remain an act of rebellion which society cannot condone without fundamental disruption' (Priestman 1990: 12–13).

It is this ultimate rejection of the possibility of restoring the social order through the one-to-one conflicts between men that is structurally fundamental to much detective fiction. This makes Godwin's novel a problematic example of the form, despite his technique of working backwards to bring the narrative to its climax – a technique that crime fiction was later to adopt as its own (Knight 1980: 22). However, as a transitional text between pre- and post-Enlightenment narratives concerned with controlling crime, *Caleb Williams* illuminates the changing attitudes towards criminality, justice, and social order investigated in similar ways in the genre of Gothic fiction that developed contemporaneously with Godwin's novel. Where pre-Enlightenment thought looked to religious and sovereign sources to resolve legal and judicial issues, the undermining of religion and the monarchy that occurred as a result of Enlightenment questioning was to make such appeals redundant, and the Gothic novel was a site of conflict between pre-Enlightenment and post-Enlightenment ideas.

The Gothic novel is characterised by the disruptive return of the past into the present, particularly in the form of hidden family secrets and ghosts, and the narrative tension between the past and the present reflects the social and intellectual tension between pre-Enlightenment and post-Enlightenment ideas. There is also a clear parallel here with the 'hauntings' of later crime narratives, in which some crime in the past threatens the social order in the present, which the detective attempts to maintain or preserve. Fred Botting observes that while the Gothic novel, in its fascination with murder, intrigue, and betrayal, and in its presentation of diabolical deeds, 'appeared to celebrate criminal behaviour' (Botting 2001: 6), the horror associated with such criminal transgressions becomes, in actuality, 'a powerful means to assert the values of society, virtue and propriety', and serves 'to reinforce or underline their value and necessity' (Botting 2001: 7). In the Gothic novel the threat to the social order comes, significantly, from a pre-Enlightenment past associated with the tyranny and superstitious barbarity of the feudal order, which puts the characteristic trappings of the Gothic novel – old castles, evil aristocrats, and ghosts – into a markedly *post*-Enlightenment context, in which the haunting of the past in the present gives rise to the spectre of social disorder (Botting 2001: 2–3).

Paul Skenazy, in a discussion of Raymond Chandler, assigns the term 'gothic causality' to the hauntings that structure most crime narratives, in which 'a secret from the past [. . .] represents an occurrence or desire antithetical to the principles and position of the house (or family)' (Skenazy 1995: 114). Knowledge of this secret, in both genres, is the key to understanding the seemingly irrational and inexplicable events in the present, and it is this drive to make the unintelligible intelligible which characterises both Gothic romance and crime fiction. Characters protect themselves in the present by covering up their secrets in the past, and it is significant that in the Gothic novel, as in the crime story, '[i]n the skeletons that leap from family closets [. . .] there emerges the awful spectre of complete social disintegration' (Botting 2001: 5). Gothic plots, furthermore, employ delayed or regressive revelations to create what Skenazy describes as a 'double rhythm', 'moving inexorably forward in time while creeping slowly backward to resolve the disruptions and violence evident in the present' (Skenazy 1995: 113).

The 'double rhythm' of both crime fiction and the Gothic, of course, is clearly analogous to Godwin's technique of reverse composition in *Caleb Williams*, and the parallels between crime fiction and the Gothic novel are also evident in the development of the Gothic landscape in the eighteenth century from wild and mountainous locations dominated by the bleak castle, with its secrets and hidden passageways, to the modern city in the nineteenth century (Botting 2001: 2). The city, in both genres, is a dark, brooding place of threatening shadows and old buildings, a contemporary wasteland 'devastated by drugs, violence, pollution, garbage and a decaying physical infrastructure' (Willett 1992: 5). These are the 'mean streets' of the modern city that Raymond Chandler refers to in a famous description of the detective and his task of restoring a world that is 'out of joint' (Chandler 1988: 18).

CRIME FICTION AND POLICING

Caleb Williams and the Gothic novels of the same period are clear precursors to crime fiction, but according to Dorothy Sayers, in her introduction to *Great Short Stories of Detection, Mystery, and Horror*, 'the detective story had to wait for its full development for the establishment of an effective police organisation in the Anglo-Saxon countries' (Sayers 1992: 75). Her claim is borne out, at least in part, by the publication of Eugène François Vidocq's *Mémoires* in 1828, which highlights the shift evident in the first half of the eighteenth century from the robber hero to the policeman as hero.

In 1812, Vidocq, a former convicted bandit, became the first chief of the Sûreté, the detective bureau of the Parisian police force, and later established Le Bureau des Renseignements, the first modern detective agency. Napoleon's establishment of the Sûreté in 1812, and Vidocq's formation of the first private detective agency almost thirty years before the creation of Pinkerton's detective agency in the United States in 1850, were a clear response to rising crime rates in the late eighteenth and early nineteenth century. This rise in crime, which continued throughout the reprinting lifetime of the *Newgate Calendar* into the 1830s, coincided with the social and cultural upheavals that were a result of the Industrial Revolution.

In addition to shifting population distribution from rural areas to large, and often poorly planned and constructed, urban areas, the Industrial Revolution, as Ernest Mandel has argued, also precipitated the rise of capitalism and the consequent emergence of large-scale unemployment (Mandel 1984: 5). Mandel links this widespread urban unemployment to an increase in crime that by the beginning of the nineteenth century created a professional criminal class of a scale and ubiquity unknown in the previous century (Mandel 1984: 5). Like the 'cony-catchers' of the late sixteenth and early seventeenth century, this professional criminal class existed separately from the 'normal' social order of law-abiding citizens, who, with the rise of capitalism, increasingly had more material wealth to lose to the criminal. The inevitable response to the widespread emergence of the professional criminal was the birth of the modern policeman. In England, there was no professional police force, and soldiers were called in to uphold the law. In 1749, in response to increasing demand, freelance 'thief-takers' were organised, becoming known as the Bow Street Runners and taking their name from the location of their headquarters in Bow Street, an area that had suffered high levels of crime since as early as the 1630s. However, these thief-takers, who worked on commission, were accused (often rightly) of corruption, and of working with the very criminals that they were supposed to be apprehending. The Metropolitan Police Act of 1828 replaced them with the creation of the first municipal constabulary in the world, organised by Sir Robert Peel, a lawyer and former captain who had fought in the Peninsular War. These early policemen were first called 'Peelers', after Sir Robert Peel, and later became known as 'Bobbies'.

The development of police forces around the world from the beginning of the nineteenth century, in addition to being a clear reaction to the increase in crime, was also an inevitable result of eighteenth-century post-Enlightenment thought. Characteristic of the Enlightenment was the belief that the application of the power of reason would lead to truth, and this search for truth was integral to the improvement of human life. This faith in reason, which came to replace religious faith, was a development of scientific and intellectual rationalism, and sought to discover the natural laws governing the universe, and human society.

Modern police work, as it developed in the nineteenth century, was founded on the faith in knowledge, science, and reason that characterised the Enlightenment. Sir Robert Peel's belief that police records were indispensable for the effective distribution of police strength led to the widespread compiling of police records in Britain, and paralleled similar developments in France. The invention of photography in 1839 allowed for effective policing by augmenting these generalised records, recording in photographic form the evidence of crimes, and ensuring the accurate identification of known criminals. Photography also formed the basis for advances in identification techniques such as fingerprint identification, and the Bertillon system of criminal investigation, based on the classification of skeletal and other bodily measurements and characteristics, was officially adopted in France in 1888. Other countries adopted the system soon after, but it was quickly superseded by the Galton-Henry system of fingerprint classification, published in June 1900 and based on research published in the scientific journal *Nature* as early as 1880.

During the same period that science was first being pressed into the service of crime-solving, the first detective stories, in which the analytical and rational deductive ability of a single, isolated individual provides the solution to an apparently inexplicable crime, were being published. Edgar Allan Poe's 'The Murders in the Rue Morgue', published in 1841, is often identified as the first detective story, and in this, and the two Dupin stories that followed, Poe set the template for the crime fiction of the next century. 'The Murders in the Rue Morgue', which combines certain Gothic trappings with the rationalism of a post-Enlightenment age of science, is set in Paris, and Poe's choice of setting emphasises Sayers's claim that the development of detective fiction depended on the establishment of effective police forces (Sayers 1992: 75). As we have seen, the Sûreté was established in 1812, and Vidocq's *Mémoires*, which Poe had read and which Dupin refers to in the 'Rue Morgue', were published in 1828, the same year that Sir Robert Peel founded the Metropolitan Police in London. The first Day and Night Police in New York, however, were not established until 1844, in part, as Priestman observes, as a response to the public reaction to the murder of Mary Rogers, a murder which Poe fictionalised in 1842 in another story set in Paris, 'The Mystery of Marie Rogêt' (Priestman 1998: 10).

The Paris setting contributes to the formula that Poe's stories set out by employing existing police and detective forces as a foil to Monsieur C. Auguste Dupin's analytical genius. The formulaic device, which simultaneously identifies the dull and lacklustre mental faculties of the police force as a whole and the brilliance of the private detective as an individual, is further emphasised in 'The Purloined Letter' (1844), and clearly influenced later authors such as Sir Arthur Conan Doyle, writing at the turn of the nineteenth century, and Agatha Christie, whose heyday was the period of what is commonly identified as the Golden Age of detective fiction between the world wars. This device, furthermore, is clearly linked to the centrality to the detective story of the character and methods of the detective, which 'The Murders in the Rue Morgue' sketches in detail.

The narrator of the story, with whom Dupin shares a house and certain character traits, emphasises Dupin's eccentricity and his reclusiveness, describing their seclusion and their habit of refusing to admit visitors, and remarking that if the routine of their lives were known, they 'should have been regarded as madmen' (Poe 2002: 7). In particular, the narrator remarks on a 'peculiar analytic ability' in his friend (Poe 2002: 8), and provides an example that illustrates this ability in which Dupin seems to read the narrator's thoughts while they are walking through the city. The character of Sherlock Holmes clearly has much in common with Poe's Dupin, and Conan Doyle employs the same technique of describing the various logical steps in a feat of deduction that initially appears impossible to rationalise. Holmes carries off a similar feat of deduction in *A Study in Scarlet*, and, despite disparaging Dupin's abilities in the same story, he exhibits the same characteristics of reclusiveness, eccentricity, and penetrating analytic ability that are present, in varying degrees, in all the fictional detectives created in the one hundred years following the publication of 'The Murders in the Rue Morgue'.

In these hundred years or so, from the publication of 'The Murders in the Rue Morgue' in 1841 to the outbreak of the Second World War in 1939, both crime fiction writers, and the detectives that they created, seemed to endorse an undeniably patriarchal world-view. With only one major exception, this being Agatha Christie's spinster detective Miss Jane Marple, all of the fictional detectives of this period were men. Again, with very few exceptions, it is masculine heroism and rationality that solves crime and restores the social order, although various critics have read feminised male heroes such as Hercule Poirot as a challenge to traditional patriarchal structures (Knight 1980, Light 1991, Plain 2001). In general, however, the crime genre during this period was a particularly powerful ideological tool that consolidated and disseminated patriarchal power, and its voice was the rational, coolly logical voice of the male detective or his male narrator.

The character of the narrator, it is important to note, is as much a part of the formula laid down by Poe as the character of the detective is, albeit one that varies more with the development of the genre than that of the detective. The first-person narrator in the detective story normally performs three functions: they act as a contrast to the abilities of the detective, emphasising in the detective's genius a difference in degree, rather than a difference in kind; they act as recorders, not only of the story, but also of the physical data upon which the detective's analytic ability depends; and they embody the social and ideological norms of the period. These functions, and the formal significance of the relationship between narrator and detective, can be clearly seen in Conan Doyle's Dr Watson in the Sherlock Holmes stories, and in Christie's various narrators: Poirot's narrator Hastings in Christie's first novel, *The Mysterious Affair at Styles* (1920), and Pastor Clement in the first Miss Marple novel, *The Murder at the Vicarage* (1930), also perform, to a greater or lesser degree, these three functions.

The functions of the narrator emphasise the significance of logical analysis as both a thematic and a formal element of the stories, which Poe termed 'tales of ratiocination', and the mysteries posed in the stories, and the methods by which they are unravelled, emphasise this ratiocination. 'The Murders in the Rue Morgue', in which Dupin investigates the murder of a mother and her daughter, is an example of the locked-room mystery, in which a dead body is found in a room which is effectively sealed or locked from the inside. The locked-room mystery was a staple of Golden Age detective fiction, as were various examples of what is known as 'armchair detection', in which the detective (normally an amateur detective, rather than a professional) solves a crime through a process of logical deduction, or ratiocination, from the evidence that is presented to him or her by others. 'The Mystery of Marie Rogêt', in which Poe fiction-alises the infamous, and unsolved, murder in New York of Mary Rogers by transplanting the event to Paris, and in which Dupin solves the murder by reading the various newspaper reports describing it, is the forerunner of later stories of armchair detection, such as Christie's Miss Marple novels. 'The Purloined Letter' foreshadows most Golden Age detective fiction in its foundation on the idea that the apparently least likely solution is the correct one, and is a further example of armchair detection in which Dupin solves the crime and establishes the hiding place of the stolen letter of the title simply by listening to the police prefect's description of the situation. It is more significant, however, in its portrayal of a villain who is worthy, or almost worthy, of the analytic genius of the detective.

This villain, the Minister D- in 'The Purloined Letter', is a clear precursor of Conan Doyle's criminal mastermind and Holmes's nemesis, Professor Moriarty, although while Doyle's debt to Poe is clear, the line of inheritance between the two is not direct. In France, Emile Gaboriau created a series of loosely linked novels featuring two heroes: the amateur detective Tabaret and the police detective (and, later, inspector) Lecoq. The first novel, *L'Affair Lerouge* (1866), features Tabaret, the unprepossessing hero who is the forerunner for such amateur detectives as Father Brown, the creation of G.K. Chesterton, an early twentieth-century historian and journalist and a political conservative and Catholic. Other similar characters include Agatha Christie's Hercule Poirot, and, much later, television's professional detective, Columbo, and it is characteristic of such detectives that they initially appear unimpressive or ineffectual. In *L'Affair Lerouge* (in its English translation, *The Widow Lerouge*), Tabaret displays the deductive brilliance on which Conan Doyle clearly modelled Holmes's deductive genius, although, as Ernest Mandel observes of Gaboriau, 'social and political problems are far more prominent in his novels than in the stories of Poe or Conan Doyle' (Mandel 1984: 19). Such a distinction between Gaboriau and Doyle, however, ironically lies behind the obvious parallels in plot structure between Doyle's novels (rather than his short stories) and Gaboriau's. In Gaboriau, the investigation of the conflict in the Second Republic between conservative monarchist landowners and the liberal middle class, and the Oedipal struggles between fathers and sons, results in a split narrative, in which long sections describing events that have led to the current crisis are embedded within a framing narrative of investigation and deduction in the present.

The pattern is repeated in *Le Crime d'Orcival* (1866), *Le Dossier No. 113* (1867), and *Monsieur Lecoq* (1869), in which Tabaret reappears, but in which the leading detective is the police investigator Monsieur Lecoq. Lecoq, as a reformed criminal who has become a police detective and as a master of disguise, echoes the earlier Eugène François Vidocq in both character and name. Gaboriau is an important link between Poe and Doyle in the development of the genre, and Martin Priestman, in particular, has outlined Doyle's frequent borrowings from Gaboriau's novels (Priestman 1990: 83). Gaboriau's influence on the genre, however, is even more far-reaching than his influence on Doyle suggests. In his presentation of murders which have been committed to prevent the revelation of some scandalous past action or indiscretion, and in the frustrating failure of the hero to bring the criminal to justice due to the class difference between detective and suspect, Gaboriau also anticipates the hard-boiled mode as it developed in the hands of Raymond Chandler. Furthermore, in his portrayal of the honest professional, Gaboriau did much to salvage the reputation of the police in crime fiction and in the public imagination, and in this, and in his easy familiarity with police procedure, his novels can be identified as forerunners of a type of crime fiction that developed in the final decades of the twentieth century in which there was an emphasis on the police, and on police procedures.

In England during the 1850s and 1860s, Charles Dickens was also doing much to influence public opinion of the police force, which, since the early days of thief-takers and the Bow Street Runners, had been regarded with hostility and suspicion, particularly by the working class. The opinions expressed in his articles in *Household Words* on the Detective Department, established in 1842, are mirrored in novels such as *Bleak House* (1853) and the unfinished *The Mystery of Edwin Drood* (1870), both of which feature strong elements of detection. However, characters such as Inspector Bucket lack the deductive genius of Dupin or Holmes, and are more a model for the professional policeman, with his investigations comprising leg-work and a sound knowledge of criminality. Significantly, it is a fascination with criminality arising from a fear of the disruption of the social order that characterises both Dickens's journalism and his fiction. *Oliver Twist* (1838), which satisfies Dickens's fascination with the police force by featuring two Bow Street Runners, has been described as a 'Newgate Novel', emphasising, as it does, the moral that crime does not pay, and punishing the murderer Sikes with an accidental and providential hanging at the end of the novel.

Despite extolling the virtues of the police force, and satisfying a public (and private) fascination with crime in his novels, it is not Dickens, but his close friend Wilkie Collins, who is the author of what is generally identified as the first detective novel written in English: *The Moonstone* (1868). Although *The Moonstone* employs a technique of multiple and split narratives in order to pursue its subtexts of imperialism and social division, these various strands are important devices through which the central mystery of the theft of the moonstone (a valuable diamond) is ultimately resolved. It is the centrality of the mystery or puzzle of the moonstone, and its final solution, that qualifies the novel as a crime story in its purest sense, and, as in *Bleak House* and the later novels of Emile Gaboriau, the lead detective in the solution of the puzzle is a policeman: Sergeant Cuff. Cuff, like Gaboriau's Tabaret, did much to establish the tradition of the detective, from Agatha Christie's Poirot to television's Columbo, whose brilliance is concealed behind a mask of distraction or eccentricity. 'Cuff is', as Julian Symons remarks, 'a master of the apparently irrelevant remark, the unexpected observation. Faced with a problem and asked what is to be done, he trims his nails with a penknife and suggests a turn in the garden and a look at the roses' (Symons 1993: 50).

In the twenty-one years between the publication of *The Moonstone* and Conan Doyle's *A Study in Scarlet* (1887), which was clearly influenced by Collins's novel, the pattern of the detective novel in English had begun to form. The first detective novel by a woman was Anna K. Green's *The Leavenworth Case* (1878), which developed the figure of the private detective established by another American, Edgar Allan Poe. Fergus Hume's *Mystery of a Hansom Cab* (1886) was enormously successful, and it was the popularity of the detective novel that prompted Arthur Conan Doyle (from 1903, *Sir* Arthur Conan Doyle), an unsuccessful doctor writing freelance to earn more money, to turn to the detective story in search of increased sales. The result was *A Study in Scarlet* (1887), whose split structure, consisting of Holmes's investigations in the present, and an adventure story set in Utah which forms the back story to these investigations, owes a clear debt to the novels of Gaboriau. While not an enormous success, it did sufficiently well for Doyle to be commissioned to write another book for *Lippincott's Magazine* in America. *The Sign of the Four* (in England, *The Sign of Four*, which has since become the accepted title) was published in 1890, and its treasure theme and Indian sub-plot are ample evidence of Doyle's debt to *The Moonstone*.

While the second Holmes adventure, like the first, was not a particularly successful book commercially, the success of Sherlock Holmes as a character was later to be borne out by the phenomenal popularity of a series of short stories Doyle wrote featuring his fictional detective. Doyle based the character of Sherlock Holmes on a former teacher at the Edinburgh Infirmary, Dr Joseph Bell, who gave demonstrations of diagnostic deduction from which Holmes's analytic genius is clearly extrapolated. To this foundation, Doyle added elements of Poe, Vidocq, and Gaboriau to create the character of a 'consulting detective' who, like Poe's Dupin, is an analytic genius who displays various eccentricities and shuns society, and who also, like Vidocq, is a man of action and a master of disguise. Doyle then teamed the character of the remote intellectual genius with the loyal, honest, admiring, but less than brilliant narrator Dr Watson, who is the embodiment of middle-class morality in the stories.

The formula, which was fundamental to the first extended example of the single hero series, found success when Doyle submitted two short stories to *The Strand*, which led to a series of short stories being published monthly in the magazine, and then separately in an annual twelve-story book, the first of which was *The Adventures of Sherlock Holmes* (1892). The stories, in contrast with the first two novels, were an enormous success, and, in addition to making Doyle a wealthy man, they also endorsed and disseminated conservative middle-class attitudes towards crime and the maintenance of social order. That they first appeared in an illustrated magazine aimed at the commuting white-collar market is significant in this respect, and Martin Priestman's comprehensive analysis of the Holmes canon clearly outlines the conservative middle-class attitudes that the stories, and the magazine in which they appeared, endorsed:

> Of the forty-five punishable cases [in the canon], only eighteen actually end in the arrest and legal punishment of the main offender (that is, ignoring henchmen). Of the remaining twenty-seven, eleven end in the culprit's 'onstage' death or maiming, which is generally seen as providential. In seven further cases the culprits escape, only to be providentially struck down later. Finally, there are no less than eleven cases where Holmes deliberately lets the criminal go.
>
> (Priestman 1990: 78–9)

The ideology is clear. Crime will always be punished, either by the law or by divine providence. The only exceptions to this rule are the sins of the aristocracy, whom Holmes either cannot, or will not, bring to justice.

The last collection of Sherlock Holmes stories, *The Case-Book of Sherlock Holmes*, was published in 1927, by which time writers such as

G.K. Chesterton, E.C. Bentley, and Maurice Leblanc were already experimenting with the pattern laid down by Doyle in order to confound the expectations of readers accustomed to the conventions of the genre, and to comment self-reflexively on it. Leblanc's Arsène Lupin novels (*L'Arrestion d' Arsène Lupin*, 1905, and *Arsène Lupin, Gentleman Cambrioleur*, 1907), feature the Robin Hood-like Lupin, who steals from the rich and gives to the poor using a combination of analytic genius and disguise whose influences – Vidocq and Doyle, primarily – are clear. The first collection of Chesterton's Father Brown stories, *The Innocence of Father Brown*, was published in 1911, and Bentley's *Trent's Last Case* appeared in 1913, but by the time of *The Case-Book of Sherlock Holmes*, the inter-war period of detective fiction, known as the Golden Age, was already well established on both sides of the Atlantic.

THE GOLDEN AGE TO THE PRESENT

In Britain, the Golden Age has a convenient point of origin in the publication of Agatha Christie's first novel, *The Mysterious Affair at Styles*, in 1920, and the reign of the 'Queen of Crime' continued until long after the Golden Age is normally considered to have ended, in the wake of the Second World War. Christie's influence on the genre is enormous, and includes the development of the country-house murder which is synonymous with the whodunnit, as well as a willingness to subvert the pattern that she effectively created. However, even without her, the inter-war period is an especially bountiful one for crime fiction.

The Golden Age in Britain, in addition to Christie's contribution, was defined by three other authors. All of them were women, but they all chose to concentrate on series featuring a male detective, and the genre had to wait until after the Second World War before female detectives (other than Christie's Miss Marple) took centre stage. The first of these authors is Dorothy L. Sayers, who created Lord Peter Wimsey, the cultured, aristocratic, but slightly distracted detective who was to feature in twelve novels and various short stories and become one of the most imitated of the Golden Age detectives. Wimsey first appears in *Whose Body?* (1923), and develops as the series progresses. Albert Campion, the series sleuth created by Margery Allingham, first appears in *The Crime at Black Dudley* (1929), and initially seems to be almost a parody of the

Golden Age detective, and Sayers's Wimsey in particular. He is aristocratic and affected, but, like Wimsey, matures as a character as the series progresses, eventually taking a subsidiary role in such novels as *More Work for the Undertaker* (1948) and *The Tiger in the Smoke* (1952), the most highly regarded of Allingham's novels. The fourth member of the British quartet, Ngaio Marsh, was actually a native of New Zealand, but in 1934, at the time she wrote the first novel featuring her series detective, Roderick Alleyn of Scotland Yard, she was living in London, and spent most of the next seventeen years of her life travelling between New Zealand and England.

Two other Golden Age British novelists are worth mentioning in a short chronology of the genre. Anthony Berkeley (the pseudonym of Anthony Berkeley Cox) was the author of *The Poisoned Chocolates Case* (1929), and founded the Detection Club in 1928, whose members, including most of the major authors of the Golden Age in Britain, took the Detection Club Oath and swore to adhere to the rules of 'Fair Play' established in 1929 by Father Ronald Knox, a Catholic priest and crime-story writer, like Chesterton. The idea of fair play is grounded in the notion that the reader should, at least in theory, be able to solve the crime at the heart of a story of detection, and for this reason should have access to the same information as the fictional detective. In addition to founding the Detection Club, which still exists today, Berkeley also wrote under the pseudonym Frances Iles, most famously with the novel *Malice Aforethought* (1931).

The second novelist is Nicholas Blake, a pseudonym of the poet Cecil Day-Lewis who was appointed poet laureate in 1968. Day-Lewis used his friend W.H. Auden, who produced a number of essays on the detective genre, as the model for his series detective Nigel Strangeways, who first appears in *A Question of Proof* (1935). The second Strangeways novel, *Thou Shell of Death* (1936), uses a quotation from Tourneur's *The Revenger's Tragedy* as its title, and thus clearly identifies the ancestry of the genre that other Golden Age titles often echo.

Although the classic whodunnit is often considered a distinctly British form, in contrast with the 'American' hard-boiled mode, its practitioners in the United States during the Golden Age were numerous, and, in most cases, well regarded. In the classic whodunnit, character is usually seen as being sacrificed in favour of ingenious plotting, as the puzzle element, or the challenge to the reader to discover 'whodunnit' before the book reveals it, is emphasised. Hard-boiled fiction, traditionally, makes no such appeal to reason and logic, concentrating instead on the character of the detective in a plot normally characterised by violence and betrayal. John Dickson Carr, who also used the pseudonym Carter Dickson, was the undisputed master of one of the key forms of the whodunnit, the locked-room mystery, and in his most famous novel, *The Three Coffins* (1935, published in Britain as *The Hollow Man*), his detective, Dr Gideon Fell, delivers a long lecture on the form. Carr's carefully constructed plots emphasise the puzzle at the heart of the story, often at the expense of character development and credibility, and his novels feature many of the trappings of the Gothic that are often played down by other authors of the period.

Ellery Queen was the pen-name of two cousins from Brooklyn, Manfred B. Lee and Frederic Dannay, as well as the name of the series detective that they created. He first appears in *The Roman Hat Mystery* (1929), and by advertising the notion of a central 'mystery' this title, and the titles of the many novels and stories that followed, is a clear indication of the tradition in which the series was located. *The French Powder Mystery* appeared in 1930, and *The Greek Coffin Mystery* in 1932, and in all of the Ellery Queen novels there was an emphasis on the puzzle and on the notion of 'fair play' established in Britain by the Detection Club. Willard Huntington Wright, writing as S.S. Van Dine, had already prefigured the notion of fair play in his 1928 essay, 'Twenty Rules for Writing Detective Stories', which included the injunction that all clues must be clearly stated and described, and that the criminal must be uncovered through logical deduction. However, the novels he wrote under this pseudonym, featuring the pretentious, loquacious, and impenetrably erudite detective genius Philo Vance (who, according to the poet Ogden Nash, 'needs a kick in the pance'), do not always adhere rigorously to the twenty rules he created. Philo Vance, as with many detectives of the Golden Age, is clearly modelled on Sayers's Lord Peter Wimsey.

Another American novelist who began his detective fiction career in the Golden Age, with the publication of the novel *Fer-de-Lance* (1934), was Rex Stout. Stout created the detective Nero Wolfe in the fashion of such exalted and isolated geniuses as Sherlock Holmes and Dr Gideon Fell, but added a tough, street-smart assistant, Archie Goodwin, to the formula. The result, which blended the pattern of the classic whodunnit with elements of the hard-boiled mode in novels such as *The League of Frightened Men* (1935) and *Too Many Cooks* (1938), as well as later novels, marks Stout as a transitionary figure between two 'schools' that are normally seen as mutually distinct.

Hard-boiled detective fiction developed in the early twentieth century as a distinctively American sub-genre, and grew out of sources as diverse as the Western and gangster stories like W.R. Burnett's *Little Caesar* (1929). Such gangster stories, in which an individual from a disadvantaged background becomes rich and powerful from a life of crime, only to become a victim of the criminal world that created his success, sprang from the reality of the attraction of crime as an understandable career choice in an increasingly aggressive capitalist society. *Little Caesar* offers an account of the rise and fall of a Chicago gangster in the mould of the *Newgate Calendar* stories, and hard-boiled fiction placed the laconic, self-reliant hero of the Western genre into this urban world to create something entirely new. Under the editorship of Joseph T. Shaw, *Black Mask* magazine was largely responsible for the development of the hard-boiled school. Both Dashiell Hammett and Raymond Chandler, the foremost early practitioners of the school, published hard-boiled stories in the magazine before going on to write novels. The first of these, and still one of the best examples of tough-guy fiction, was Hammett's *Red Harvest* (1929), and Chandler always made his debt to Hammett clear. Chandler's *The Big Sleep*, featuring the P.I., or private eye, Philip Marlowe, appeared in 1939, and from this point on the pattern was firmly established. Ross Macdonald followed it, and broadened Chandler's horizons, in his Lew Archer novels which began in the 1940s, while writers in the same period, such as Mickey Spillane in his Mike Hammer novels, narrowed the formula to its barest essentials, with a tough, insensitive, overtly masculine, and sexist detective who solves crimes with a pistol and his fists, rather than through any deductive reasoning or application of logic.

Hard-boiled detective fiction, however, unlike the whodunnit alongside which it developed, survived the Second World War in a way that classic Golden Age fiction did not. One reason for this survival was the uncertain post-war world in which writers, and readers, found themselves, to which the calm certainties of the whodunnit were unsuited and in which they were no longer useful. A second, and more interesting, reason for this survival is the suitability of hard-boiled fiction for gender, ethnic, and cultural appropriation. An example of how hard-boiled fiction can be appropriated can be seen in the development of a feminist pattern from the hard-boiled mode, ironically the most defensively masculine branch of the genre. Feminist appropriation of the hard-boiled mode in the form of the female private eye novel began in earnest with the development of feminist theory in the 1970s, a decade which witnessed the publication of P.D. James's *An Unsuitable Job for a Woman* (1972), and which established the foundation for future development in the 1980s. In the same year that Sue Grafton published her first Kinsey Millhone novel, *'A' Is For Alibi* (1982), another female private investigator made her first appearance in print. Sara Paretsky's *Indemnity Only* (1982) is located firmly in the hard-boiled mode, and her series hero, V.I. (Victoria) Warshawski, is characterised as much by her gender as by her ability to inflict, and to endure, physical trauma. This feminist appropriation of an overtly 'masculine' mode was also foundational in the development of the lesbian detective fiction of Barbara Wilson, in novels such as *Gaudí Afternoon* (1990), and in the novels of Katherine V. Forrest. Unlike the novels of Paretsky, Grafton, and Wilson, however, Forrest's series does not feature a private investigator. Forrest's series character is Kate Delafield, a homicide detective with the Los Angeles Police Department, whose investigations are complicated by the sexism of her male colleagues, and by the mixed reactions of others to her homosexuality.

The Kate Delafield novels, in their examination of the procedures and personal dynamics of the modern police force, are also, to some extent, examples of the police procedural. The police procedural is a sub-genre of detective fiction that examines how a team of professional policemen (and women) work together, and for this reason there are 'purer' examples, such as the 87th Precinct novels of Ed McBain and television series such as *Hill Street Blues*, and those which, in their concentration on a single individual within the police force, are less 'pure'. A case in point would be the novels of Chester Himes featuring two black police detectives, Coffin Ed Johnson and Grave Digger Jones, which began to appear during the 1960s, the initial period of the development of the police procedural in America, which is generally identified as beginning with Ed McBain's first 87th Precinct novel, *Cop Hater* (1956). While the Coffin Ed Johnson and Grave Digger Jones series offers an effective platform for an examination of racial and ethnic issues during the period of Civil Rights movements in America, the attention paid to police procedure or professional teamwork is slight. What the series does have in common with the police procedural as it developed in America, and as it appeared on television in such series as *NYPD Blue*, is an urban setting, and this emphasis on the modern city is clearly drawn from hard-boiled fiction. The urban setting is frequently employed in contemporary variations on the procedural on television in *C.S.I.: Crime Scene Investigation*, *Third Watch*, and the distinctly post-modern *Boomtown*.

In Britain, the crime fiction of the 1970s is characterised, in part, by its lack of the aristocratic trappings of the pre-war generation. In the novels of Colin Dexter and Ruth Rendell, and the Inspector Dalgliesh novels of P.D. James, the detectives are not private investigators, as in hard-boiled novels, but professional policemen, and in this they clearly draw on the distinct development of the police procedural in America in the 1960s. However, similar to the American development of the police procedural, there are varying degrees to which those British novels featuring police detectives are actually identifiable as police procedurals. The principal reason for the development of the procedural might well lie in the search for realism that gives the hard-boiled mode its distinctive voice and characteristics. The police procedural, according to Peter Messent, 'seems to be supplanting the private-eye novel as "realistic" crime fiction' (Messent 1997: 12), and as James Ellroy, one of the foremost contemporary practitioners of the police procedural, observes of his own fiction:

> I consciously abandoned the private-eye tradition that formally jazzed me. Evan Hunter wrote 'the last time a private eye investigated a homicide was never'. The private eye is an iconic totem spawned by pure fiction [. . . .] The American cop was the real goods from the gate.
>
> (Ellroy 1994)

Significantly, novels like Ellroy's *The Black Dahlia* (1987) and *L.A. Confidential* (1990) are examples of one direction that the contemporary crime novel is increasingly taking. *The Black Dahlia* is a fictionalised account of a 1947 Los Angeles murder cast within the framework of the police procedural, and, while such fictionalised accounts of real murder cases are not new, it is the period setting that characterises this relatively recent development. *The Big Nowhere* (1988) and *L.A. Confidential* are set in the same period, and depend for their success, in part, on the depiction of a 1950s Los Angeles familiar to readers of the genre through Chandler. Walter Mosley has created a hard-boiled series of Los Angeles novels that begin in the same period, featuring the black detective Easy Rawlins, but historical detective fiction is by no means confined to this period. To quote only a few examples, Lindsey Davis has created a long-running series set in Ancient Rome, featuring the private informer Marcus Didius Falco; Ellis Peters has created an equally long-running series set in a twelfth-century monastery featuring Brother Cadfael the monk; Patricia Finney has written a number of novels of detection and intrigue set in Elizabethan London; Caleb Carr has written two novels set in New York at the end of the nineteenth century; and Philip Kerr has written three novels set in Berlin shortly before and after the Second World War.

The greatest benefit of the historical crime novel is its liberation of the genre from the search for realism that has, to some extent, caused it to favour the single, and sometimes narrow, path of the police procedural over that of the private investigator or amateur detective. Ironically, however, and as this study will later demonstrate, the historical crime novel is as much characterised by its search for realism as the police procedural, albeit an historical realism that foregrounds the narrative relationship at the heart of most crime fiction: the relationship between the past and the present. It should be noted that such developments in the genre in the 1990s were not restricted to historical crime fiction, and the most illuminating fictions of recent years have been those that construct the detective as a hybrid between the amateur and the professional. Such formal and thematic shifts should ensure a return to, and more importantly a renegotiation with, the early patterns of crime fiction that went on to define a genre, and this study will now outline these early patterns as they began to coalesce in the late eighteenth and early nineteenth centuries.

2

MYSTERY AND DETECTIVE FICTION

'It's called retrograde analysis.'
'What kind of analysis?'
'Retrograde. It involves taking a certain position on the board as your starting point and then reconstructing the game backwards in order to work out how it got to that position. A sort of chess in reverse, if you like. It's all done by induction. You begin with the end result and work backwards to the causes.'
'Like Sherlock Holmes,' remarked César, visibly interested.
'Something like that'.

(Pérez-Reverte 2003: 73)

RETRACING THE STEPS: THE ORIGINS OF MYSTERY FICTION

Those who take the short view of the history of the genre generally acknowledge four, or sometimes five, Edgar Allan Poe stories as marking the birth of mystery and detective fiction, or 'clue puzzles' (Knight 2004: 81). These are 'The Murders in the Rue Morgue', 'The Mystery of Marie Rogêt', 'The Purloined Letter', 'The Gold Bug', and, in a contentious fifth position, 'Thou Art the Man'. 'The Murders in the Rue Morgue' introduces the genius detective Auguste Dupin, who also appears in 'The Mystery of Marie Rogêt' and 'The Purloined Letter', and who, in the first of the stories, investigates an apparently motiveless and unsolvable double murder in the Rue Morgue. 'The Mystery of Marie Rogêt' is a thinly fictionalised account of the death of Mary Rogers, a New York shop assistant whose real-life murder was never solved. The details of the murder are transplanted to Paris, where Dupin proposes a solution to the crime based solely on his reading of newspaper reports. 'The Purloined Letter', the last of the Dupin stories, concerns the theft of a compromising letter from the Queen of France, and Dupin's recovery of it from the thief, a high-ranking minister. Of all of Poe's 'tales of ratiocination', 'The Purloined Letter' has attracted the most critical attention, from Jacques Lacan's famous 'Seminar' to Jacques Derrida's critical response to it. In contrast, the remaining two stories have received very little critical attention, the first of them, 'The Gold Bug', because it is generally viewed as merely a fictional outlet for Poe's academic interest in cryptography, and the second, 'Thou Art the Man', because it clearly parodies the mystery-story form whose outlines Poe had sketched only a few years previously.

What sets Poe's stories apart from the narratives of crime that predated them, according to Dennis Porter, is their narrative structure, in which the denouement determines, from the beginning, 'the order and causality of the events narrated' (Porter 1981: 24). 'It is only with the *dénouement* constantly in view', according to Poe, 'that we can give a plot the indispensable air of consequence, or causation, by making the incidents, and especially the tone at all points, tend to the development of the intention' (Poe, quoted in Porter 1981: 26). Both Poe's observation and Porter's structuralist analysis underline the central significance of the chain of causation in mystery and detective fiction, in which the final solution of an apparently unsolvable mystery depends on the 'primacy of plot' and the narrative importance of cause and effect (Porter 1981: 26) which characterise fiction of this type.

A mystery or detective novel, according to Porter, 'prefigures at the outset the form of its denouement by virtue of the highly visible question mark hung over its opening' (Porter 1981: 86). This 'question mark' encourages the reader to imitate the detective, and to retrace the causative steps from effects back to causes, and in so doing to attempt to answer the question at the heart of all stories of mystery and detection: who did it? Answering this question requires a reading approach that parallels the investigative process as a process of making connections (Porter 1981: 86), or of bridging gaps in the chain of cause and effect. The question mark hanging over the opening of the mystery or detective story is always the question of 'whodunnit?' – in other words, who committed the crime – and for this reason the term 'whodunnit' was coined in the 1930s to describe a type of fiction in which the puzzle or mystery element was the central focus.

The 'Golden Age' of the whodunnit, as the period in which the term was coined suggests, is generally identified as the period between the First and Second World Wars, although both earlier and later commentators on the form differ in this regard. Many of the Golden Age writers continued writing in the mode they established until well after 1939, and this underlines the fact that what most characterises mystery and detective fiction is its multiple, overlapping development and re-appropriation (Knight 2004: 86). Furthermore, much commentary (with important exceptions) views the Golden Age as a predominantly British demarcation, dominated (for the most part) by female authors. The major writers of the Golden Age include Agatha Christie, Margery Allingham, Ngaio Marsh, and Dorothy L. Sayers, and the period is generally acknowledged as beginning with Christie's *The Mysterious Affair at Styles*. The title of the novel, in its use of the adjective 'mysterious', like many novels of the period, identifies the centrality of the mystery element to the form, and in much criticism the term 'mystery fiction' encompasses the whodunnit alongside more Gothic adventure stories to which they are closely allied. More will be said of the significance of Golden Age titles later, but for the moment it is the matter-of-fact statement of some mystery or crime (usually murder) to be solved that is a clear indication of the primacy of plot over all other considerations that is typical of Golden Age whodunnits.

The general critical consensus regarding Golden Age fiction is that the plot is elevated above all other considerations (often including credibility), and that realistic character development takes a back seat to the construction of the puzzle. Stephen Knight identifies in Christie's fiction, for example, a 'shallow and naturalised' presentation of character, usually consisting of a few cursory assessments and surface details (Knight

1980: 124). Similarly, the motivations of the characters are simple and uncomplicated, allowing for a greater emphasis on the twists and turns of the plot and the extraordinarily complicated action. Similarly, the 'Great Detectives' of the Golden Age lack a certain depth of character, and their experiences, throughout the series, as well as in each individual novel, fail to promote in them any change or development. The exception to this (and there are always exceptions) is the character of Lord Peter Wimsey in the novels of Dorothy Sayers. While Wimsey undergoes a marked transition through the series from *Whose Body?* (1923) to *Busman's Honeymoon* (1937), Christie's Poirot, like the characters around him, is merely a collection of surface details: vain, fussy, fastidious, and Belgian, with a French accent suggested by repeated key phrases such as '*Mon ami*'. But it is *because* of this flatness of character, rather than in spite of it, that Poirot, like most of the other Golden Age detectives, is so memorable, and this is one of the key reasons for their popularity.

Knight goes on to describe the characters of Golden Age fiction as 'marionettes' (Knight 1980: 124), but it is perhaps more revealing to think of them as pawns in the larger game of the mystery plot in which they play a part. Certainly, by the end of the 1920s there was a view of the detective story 'as something having *rules* which could be strictly formulated' (Symons 1993: 104), and by 1928 the Detection Club had been founded by Anthony Berkeley (author of an acknowledged classic of the genre, *The Poisoned Chocolates Case*), reinforcing this notion. The Club was an organisation of British mystery and detective authors, and membership depended on taking the 'Detection Club Oath', in which members swore to adhere to the rules of 'Fair Play'.

'Fair Play' is the notion that a mystery or detective story should, in principle, at least, be capable of being solved by a careful and obser-vant reader. In 1929, the same year as the publication of Dashiell Hammett's *Red Harvest* in the United States, Father Ronald Knox, a Catholic priest and mystery writer who was eventually ordered by his bishop to stop writing mystery stories, codified the notion of fair play by establishing ten basic rules. Knox's 'Detective Story Decalogue' includes the following:

   I.   The criminal must be someone mentioned in the early part of the story [. . . .]

II.   All supernatural or preternatural agencies are ruled out as a matter of course [. . . .]

III.   Not more than one secret room or passage is allowable [. . . .]

VII.   The detective must not himself commit the crime [. . . .]

VIII.   The detective must not light on any clues which are not instantly produced for the inspection of the reader [. . . .]

IX.   The stupid friend of the detective, the Watson, must not conceal any thoughts which pass through his mind [. . . .]

X.   Twin brothers, and doubles generally, must not appear unless we have been duly prepared for them [. . . .]

(Knox 1992: 194–6)

The effect of the notion of fair play, and in particular Knox's codification of it in his 'Decalogue', is to reduce the novel to a level of abstraction comparable to that of a puzzle, or a game of chess. Besides appearing as an important motif of isolation in Chandler's fiction, in which Marlowe plays chess games against himself, the convergence of the chess theme and detective structures is significant (Lange 1998: 50). Arturo Pérez-Reverte, in the 1990 novel *La Tabla de Flandes* (translated into English as *The Flanders Panel* (1994)), foregrounds the parallels between the whodunnit and chess by featuring a game of chess depicted in a painting as the key to a murder. In order to solve the mystery, a process of 'retrogade analysis' is performed, in which the moves in the game are retraced with the characters being identified with pieces on the chessboard in order to finally identify the murderer. On the other side of the Atlantic, at the earlier end of the century, the author S.S. Van Dine's outline of 'Twenty Rules for Writing Detective Stories' (1928) echoes Knox's 'Decalogue' in almost every instance, and identifies the detective story as 'a kind of intellectual game' (Van Dine 1992: 189): a game, furthermore, with identifiable rules. This view of the detective story, however, reduces it to 'mere mechanisms' (Lange 1998: 50), but what is more significant is how Van Dine's rules, like Knox's 'Decalogue', refer at every point to the participation of the reader in the process of detection.

The idea of the mystery or detective novel as a kind of game in which the reader participates, and the corresponding clue–puzzle structure of the novels, 'invited and empowered the careful reader to solve the problem along with the detective' (Knight 1980: 107). It is significant for this reason that the methods employed by Christie's detectives, which will be discussed in more detail later, parallel the approach of the careful reader in their emphasis on close observation and orderly thought. The active participation of the reader in the whodunnit, therefore, might seem to echo the approach to those texts identified by Roland Barthes as 'writerly' texts. The goal of the 'writerly' text, according to Barthes, 'is to make the reader no longer a consumer, but a producer of the text' (Barthes 1975: 4), by constantly challenging the reader to rewrite it and to make sense of it by inviting the reader 'to participate in the construction of meaning' (Fiske 1992: 103). The difference between Barthes's writerly text and the whodunnit, however, is that, despite their participation, the reader does not create or produce meaning, but merely affirms the 'meaning' or solution set down by the author.

This does, however, emphasise the importance of the reader as consumer in mystery and detective fiction, and, in particular, in Golden Age fiction. Christie's consumers, for example, consisted of respectable, suburban readers (often women) who shared Christie's upper middle-class, property-owning, bourgeois ideology, and were keen to have it confirmed (Knight 1980: 108). However, it should be noted that the notion of the mystery or detective story as a kind of game or puzzle, and the central role of the reader as a consumer of both the text and the ideology it confirmed, are not purely Golden Age phenomena. Sir Arthur Conan Doyle, discussing the genesis of the Sherlock Holmes stories, makes a revealing comment about the genre that he is mostly responsible for creating:

> I had been reading some detective stories and it struck me what nonsense they were, to put it mildly, because for getting the solution of the mystery, the authors always depended on some coincidence. This struck me as not a fair way of playing the game.
>
> (Doyle, quoted in Knight 1980: 67)

Doyle's comment, of course, emphasises both the notion of fair play and the idea of the mystery story as a kind of game, and in this there are obvious parallels with Golden Age fiction. Just as there are parallels, however, there are also points of divergence, and the changes in the figure of the detective from Poe and Doyle to Golden Age fiction, and beyond, illustrate these divergences well.

REASONING MACHINES: THE FIGURE OF THE AMATEUR DETECTIVE

The significant parallels between detection and the reading process, particularly in the approach to the Golden Age whodunnit suggested by the notion of 'fair play', go some way to explaining the prevalence of the methodical detective – that is, a detective who employs a particular method. The emphasis on method is evident as early as Poe, who is largely responsible for creating the template of the 'Genius Detective' borrowed by Doyle in the creation of Sherlock Holmes. This figure of the genius detective, who is invariably depicted as a reasoning and observing machine, is often accompanied by a friend and colleague who, in addition to being the foil for the detective's genius, is also the narrator of the stories. This 'Watson' figure, so called because of the encapsulation of the role by Watson in Doyle's Holmes stories, becomes the eyes and ears of the reader, providing them with all the clues necessary to solve the mystery. In Poe's 'The Murders in the Rue Morgue', the story's narrator remarks on his friend Dupin's 'peculiar analytic ability' (Poe 2002: 8), and provides an example of how Dupin seems to read his thoughts. The example is important for three reasons. First, it prompts the narrator to demand to know 'the method – if method there is – by which [Dupin has] been enabled to fathom [the narrator's] soul' (Poe 2002: 9), in this way reinforcing the notion of the methodical detective, crucial to the series detective, of which Dupin was the first. Secondly, it identifies the two key components of Dupin's method: observation, which as Dupin remarks, 'has become with me, of late, a species of necessity' (Poe 2002: 10), and an awareness of causality, as Dupin outlines the 'larger links of the chain' in his feat of mind-reading (Poe 2002: 9). Thirdly, it sets a pattern followed by Doyle in which the story begins with a demonstrable example of the detective's method and genius, an example, furthermore, which sets him above and apart from the mean represented by his narrator which corresponds to that of the average reader.

The pattern is clear in Doyle's Sherlock Holmes stories. Holmes invariably provides an example of his deductive genius, as in 'A Scandal in Bohemia' when Watson, now married, pays him a visit and Holmes, after a moment's observation, notes to the pound how much weight Watson has gained since his marriage, correctly deduces that Watson is practising medicine again, and notes that in addition to 'getting [him]self very wet lately', he has 'a most clumsy and careless servant girl' (Doyle 1981: 162). Such feats of deduction lead his companion and narrator, Watson, to describe him in the same story as 'the most perfect reasoning and observing machine that the world has seen' (Doyle 1981: 161). Holmes's method, encapsulated in this description, clearly mirrors Dupin's, and the two detectives share a number of significant characteristics. Both are reclusive, and both have a private income that is sufficient for them to live in reasonable comfort without having to rely on their detective skills to support themselves. In this respect, they are amateur detectives, in the true sense of the word 'amateur', practising their profession more as a hobby than as a means of making a living like the professional private eye or the police detective of the police procedural. While there are dissimilarities between the 'Genius Detectives' of Poe and Doyle and the later Golden Age sleuths, in their amateur status they are the same. All of the most famous sleuths of the Golden Age were amateurs: Hercule Poirot, Miss Marple, Lord Peter Wimsey, Albert Campion, and others. Their methods, however, differ in many respects from those of the genius detectives Dupin and Holmes.

Holmes's method, in particular, is worthy of a detailed description. Doyle's inclusion of a chapter entitled 'The Science of Deduction' in each of the Sherlock Holmes novels, in which Holmes displays his analytic and deductive abilities, highlights the two central elements of Holmes's method: a scientific approach rooted in a Victorian faith in the accumulation and cataloguing of data, and rational and logical analysis based on this scientific foundation. Reinforced by Doyle's use of the term, such reasoning has normally been termed 'rational deduction', although as Knight observes, 'if Holmes really were finding patterns in facts he would be practising "induction"' (Knight 1980: 86): that is, the inferring of general law from particular instances. In fact, what the stories repeatedly demonstrate is that Holmes already knows what certain phenomena will mean in advance, and that by inferring particular instances from general law, he is actually practising deduction. The deductive approach clearly appeals to a sense of order, and Doyle's misnaming of Holmes's method is a significant indication of the anxieties about social order that his fiction was attempting to assuage (Knight 1980: 86).

Watson's outline of Holmes's character in *A Study in Scarlet* neatly summarises the importance of the accumulation of observable scientific data to Holmes's method. Watson describes Holmes's abilities in various fields, remarking that his knowledge of literature and philosophy is 'Nil', and his knowledge of geology is 'Practical, but limited', while his knowledge of chemistry is profound (Doyle 1981: 21–2). His knowledge of British law is 'practical', and what is clear from Watson's catalogue is Doyle's insistence on the practical application of science and knowledge in Holmes's method. Holmes is a man of science: specifically, a science based on the collection and analysis of data that is central to the world-view of the nineteenth century. Holmes does not, and cannot, deduce or induce in a vacuum. He interprets physical data through the framework of his Victorian materialist mentality (Knight 1980: 79).

Holmes's nineteenth-century scientific approach has been reinvented for the twenty-first century in the figure of 'Gruesome' Gil Grissom in the television series *C.S.I.: Crime Scene Investigation*. Computers and technology in *C.S.I.* allow for the development of Holmes's nineteenth-century science of the accumulation and cataloguing of data to an exponential degree, with national computer databases of fingerprints, DNA, tyre- and shoe-treads, chemicals, ballistics, and more. *C.S.I.*'s use of extreme close-ups and microscopic images, furthermore, echoes the attention to small details that is fundamental to mystery and detective fiction. It is Holmes's belief, as he expresses it in 'A Case of Identity', 'that the little things are infinitely the most important' (Doyle 1981: 194), and Doyle's stories, like *C.S.I.*, portray a material world of physical data. The Las Vegas setting of *C.S.I.* is crucial, for this reason, in relation to the overriding structural and thematic importance of materiality from Doyle, through the Golden Age, right up to contemporary manifestations of mystery and detective fiction. Las Vegas is the epitome of materialism. It is a gambling city, founded on the lure of easy money, and, in order to underline this, every episode of *C.S.I.* opens with an overhead shot of the city as a vast neon playground, and many of the crimes that the crime lab investigate have their motivation, like many of Christie's novels, in greed.

Greed and the desire for material wealth are frequently highlighted in *C.S.I.* Besides featuring as a criminal motive in many episodes, the crime-scene analysts themselves are frequently tested in this regard. Sara Sidle, in the episode 'Ellie', is the target for a Treasury Office sting operation involving counterfeit money designed to tempt law enforcement officers, while the character of Warrick Brown is addicted to gambling.

Furthermore, whereas Holmes, as an 'amateur detective', has a private income, Grissom and his team are paid professionals, although it is intriguing to note that in many ways they are not professional police officers either. They are crime-scene analysts, and although they carry guns and badges, they do not have the power to make arrests. This further marks them out as 'reasoning and observing machines', and in this there is an important distinction between Holmes and Grissom. Holmes is very much a man of action in the tradition of Gaboriau, often donning elaborate disguises in order to trail suspects or gather information, and the classic depiction of Holmes wearing a deerstalker hat underlines this view of the detective as a kind of hunter, further linking the figure to the hero of the American frontier romance tradition. Grissom, on the other hand, is uncomfortable in a world of action, and this is clearly suggested by his glasses, his distaste for violent physical activity, and his distinctive pigeon-toed gait.

One final difference between Grissom and Holmes, in particular, and Grissom and the genius detective, in general, is that the genius detective, from Doyle right through the Golden Age, required complex and brilliant crimes to solve. The Holmes stories, for example, rely ultimately on the existence of Professor Moriarty, but such crimes and criminals do not exist in reality, but only in the puzzle-plots of Golden Age fiction, and its imitators. As Holmes tells Watson in *A Study in Scarlet*, 'There are no crimes and no criminals in these days' (Doyle 1981: 25), after which Doyle created a string of crimes and criminals that was to last for four novels and over fifty short stories. However, Holmes, or Dupin or Poirot for that matter, would not be caught dead dirtying their hands investigating violent 'unplanned' street crime and gangsterism, despite its dramatic increase from the middle of the 1800s and into the twentieth century. It is significant that these are the very crimes that the hard-boiled detective and the police detective of the police procedural – both more straightforward and realistic crime-solvers – usually deal with. These are also the crimes that the *C.S.I.* team investigate, and their allegiance to the police detective of the police procedural in this respect is a significant one.

What is significant about Poirot and Miss Marple, however, is that in many ways they do not fit comfortably into the pattern of the genius detective in the mould of Dupin or Holmes. Their methods involve careful observation and common sense, and, in Miss Marple's case, a general abstraction of human nature from the particulars of the inhabitants of St Mary Mead. In this respect, like Grissom in *C.S.I.*, they do not need a master criminal to battle, all they need are clever crimes, or simple crimes that have been cleverly concealed, or simple crimes in which the detective's investigations are either wittingly or unwittingly complicated by chance or by human action.

ESCALATING CRIMES: FROM PURLOINED LETTERS TO MURDER

Crime, of course, is the motor of crime fiction, and mystery and detective fiction is no exception to this, although the nature of the central crime varied somewhat until the Golden Age. Through a process of escalation from the stories of Poe, and later the stories of Doyle, neither of whom concerned themselves exclusively with the crime of murder, murder became, inevitably, the most common crime investigated, and this was increasingly reflected in the titles of Golden Age novels. According to Willard Huntington Wright (writing as S.S. Van Dine) in 'Twenty Rules for Writing Detective Stories', 'There simply must be a corpse in a detective novel, and the deader the corpse the better. No lesser crime than murder will suffice' (Van Dine 1992: 190). This assumption, however, really only arose during the inter-war period, and it is significant that in the Sherlock Holmes stories, which set the pattern for mystery and detective fiction of the twentieth century, there is very little murder. In fact, as Knight crucially observes, in two of the first twelve Holmes stories, no crime at all is committed, and those crimes that do occur are targeted significantly at physical and concrete forms of property and wealth, such as bank deposits, coins, and jewels (Knight 1980: 88–90). What all of Doyle's crimes have in common, however, is that they threaten the dominant bourgeois ideology of respectable Victorian England, and the perpetrators of these crimes are anarchistic enemies of order, respectable people gone bad, or aristocratic villains (Knight 1980: 90–3).

Despite the violence associated with the crime of murder, which had become *de rigueur* by the Golden Age, Christie's inter-war fiction is characterised by its absence of violence, and by its curiously sanitised and bloodless corpses. It is not the murders themselves that are characterised by this lack of violence, however, but rather the manner in which fatal shootings, multiple stabbings, bludgeonings, and poisonings with acid are presented. In *The Mysterious Affair at Styles* (1920), the dying body of Mrs Inglethorpe 'arch[es] in an extraordinary manner' as those around her attempt to administer brandy, after which the victim simply falls back 'motionless on the pillows' (Christie 2001: 47–8). In *The Murder at the Vicarage* (1930), the description of death is even more sanitised, if not stylised by rhyme: 'The man was dead – shot through the head' (Christie 2002: 59). The corpse in Christie, and in much detective and mystery fiction after her, appears simply as a repository of clues, what Gill Plain terms 'a corpse-as-signifier' (Plain 2001: 32). This notion of the corpse-as-signifier is developed as the framework of contemporary reworkings of the clue-puzzle form by such novelists as Patricia Cornwell. The air-brushed depictions of violent death in Golden Age fiction seem at odds with Wright's assumption, echoed later and with a different emphasis by others such as George Orwell (1965: 68), that corpses are central to the detective novel, 'and the deader the corpse the better'. The corpse is only central to the detective novel whose central crime is murder, however, and perhaps one reason for this widespread assumption is the fact that the crime of murder, as one of the most extreme crimes imaginable, carried with it in most societies of the time the most extreme punishment: the death penalty. What is significant about crime fiction from its formalisation by Poe on, however, is that the punishment of the criminal is rarely, if ever, described.

The conspicuous absence of legal punishment in mystery and detective fiction, as opposed to the providential punishments occasionally meted out in Doyle's stories, is at odds with the nature of crime itself. Crime, as Dennis Porter observes, 'always occurs in a community', implying the violation of a community code of conduct and demanding a response in terms of the code that has been violated (Porter 1981: 120). In *C.S.I.*, Grissom draws an analogy between organised sports and this aspect of the judicial system. According to Grissom, 'Organised sports is the paradigmatic model of a just society. Everyone knows the same language. Everyone knows the rules. And there's a specific punishment handed out the *moment* someone tries to cheat. Instant morality.' Mystery and detective fiction, like organised sports, maintains and disseminates the ideology of 'instant morality' because it rarely, if ever, questions the community code of conduct. Particularly in the fiction of the Golden Age, the law and the system of legal punishment are invariably accepted as givens, and in this respect Porter regards fiction of this type as a repressive state apparatus (Porter 1981: 121). It is this passive, albeit unwitting, acceptance of the dominant social order disseminated in mystery and detective fiction that clearly identifies novels of this type, in Barthes's terminology, as *readerly* texts, despite the apparently *writerly* participation of the reader in the detective's investigative process.

A readerly text, according to Barthes, 'plunges [the reader] into a kind of idleness [in which] he is left with no more than the poor freedom to accept or reject the text' (Barthes 1975: 4). By accepting the text, and in doing so, recognising, confirming, and negotiating the dominant textual codes, the readerly approach can be allied with Barthes's idea of *plaisir*, in which there is pleasure 'in conforming to the dominant ideology and the subjectivity it proposes when it is in our interest to do so' (Fiske 1992: 54). In the case of mystery and detective fiction, it is the home-owning bourgeois reading public whose interest it is to see the dominant social order of which they are a part maintained, and their stake in it protected. It is in this way, rather than in any graphic depiction of the punishment of the death sentence, that detective fiction becomes what Foucault has described as the discourse of the law (Foucault 1980: 41), while others 'have regarded it similarly as the re-affirmation of the socio-economic order' (Willett 1992: 7).

This discourse of re-affirmation, however, evident in the tidy denouements of the puzzle-oriented mystery story, comes at a price. In *Discipline and Punish*, Foucault observes that publicising the investigative and judicial process, and putting an end to punishment as a public spectacle, created a judicial ideology characterised by constant surveillance. While the notion of control through surveillance is clearly embodied in hard-boiled fiction in the figure of the private eye, and is clearly manifested in *C.S.I.* in the use of video surveillance and national information databases, Miss Marple's surveillance, in many ways, fulfils the same function. Pastor Clement, the narrator of Christie's *The Murder at the Vicarage*, observes that 'Miss Marple always sees everything' (Christie 2002: 26), and in this way 'a spinster lady of uncertain age with plenty of time on her hands' (Christie 2002: 47) becomes in Christie's fiction the embodiment of Bentham's Panopticon. The difference between the Panopticon, however, and the constant surveillance of the new judicial ideology, is that the

Panopticon presupposes that the prisoners open to constant visual inspection from the tower at the centre of this model prison are guilty of some crime, whereas the objects of Miss Marple's gaze are nothing more than suspects and *potential* criminals, and in the textual Panopticon of detective fiction, it would seem that everybody is a suspect.

This assumption, however, is not entirely accurate. The murderer in most Golden Age fiction is rarely a professional criminal, and furthermore, to satisfy various narrative and ideological demands, he or she is invariably part of the same social group as the other suspects, all of which means that the butler rarely did it. When Wright, writing as S.S. Van Dine in his 'Twenty Rules for Writing Detective Stories', rules out servants as viable suspects, his reasoning highlights an important point. According to Wright, 'The culprit must be a decidedly worthwhile person – one that wouldn't normally come under suspicion' (Van Dine 1992: 191). Christie, as Knight observes, 'does not take the simple path of making the murderer a stranger, a foreigner or a servant' (Knight 2004: 91), and her most famous manipulation of the tenet that the culprit must be somebody who would not normally come under suspicion is in *The Murder of Roger Ackroyd* (1926), in which Poirot's stand-in narrator, Dr Sheppard, turns out to be the murderer. As both a doctor and the narrator of the investigation, Sheppard represents the two pillars of societal and textual reliability, and his identification as the murderer is therefore doubly threatening. Sheppard clearly demonstrates that the threat of social disorder comes from within society, and the reason for this is simple. By identifying the threat to the social order as coming from within, Golden Age fiction emphasises the necessity, embodied in the figure of Miss Marple, of a society that maintains the social order through self-surveillance.

MAINTAINING SOCIAL ORDER AND THE STATUS QUO

The Murder of Roger Ackroyd neatly summarises the central fear articulated in Golden Age fiction: that the threat of social disruption comes from within. In this way, Porter's structuralist observation that crime fiction 'is a genre committed to an act of recovery, moving forward to move back' (Porter 1981: 29) has a twofold application. It can be applied to the narrative structure of the whodunnit, in which the narrative moves forward towards its conclusion and resolution as the detective moves back into the past in an attempt to uncover what occurred there. Porter's observation, however, can also be applied to the ideological motivation to recover, or return to, a previous period characterised by stability and order. In Christie's fiction, this impulse to recover and reinstate the sort of order that existed in the past is a direct response to the disruption in the present caused by the crime of murder. For this reason, it is significant that Poirot's method consists of the observing and ordering of facts, because order, as Knight observes, is 'the overt method and the covert purpose of the analysis' (Knight 1988: 110). That is, it is Poirot's aim (and purpose) to restore order after it has been disrupted by crime, and this notion is given a twenty-first-century reinterpretation when Catherine Willows, in the pilot episode of *C.S.I.*, notes that 'We [crime scene analysts] solve. *We* restore peace of mind, and when you're a victim, that's everything.'

The notion of order is, by implication, bound up with the notion of social order, and it is significant in this respect that the resolution of the mystery in Christie, as in Gothic fiction, is often marked or accompanied by romantic resolution. Many of the novels end, not with a final solution of the problem, but with the final union of two lovers (Knight 1980: 116, Porter 1981: 186). In contrast, no romantic resolution is offered in hard-boiled fiction. Rather, the impossibility of romantic resolution parallels the impossibility of resolving the criminal problem and restoring social order, and it is for this reason that the tough-guy detective, despite his (and more recently her) well-concealed romanticism, is invariably single. The romantic resolution of Golden Age fiction is made possible, or, at least, is made more likely, by the fact that, unlike the private eye of hard-boiled fiction, the genius detective is always a respectable figure, who is not personally involved with any of the suspects. He (or she) has only the most tangential relationships which go no further than a broad concern to avoid unnecessary scandal about the upper middle class. This pattern of maintaining the upper middle-class status quo was established by Doyle, and to some extent even earlier by Poe in 'The Purloined Letter', but by the Golden Age it had become a naturalised feature of the form. 'Naturalised', in this context, refers to its acceptance as an ideological given, largely due to its dissemination in fiction.

This naturalised impulse to preserve the upper middle-class status quo explains the fact that fiction of this period from both sides of the Atlantic, in social terms at least, is set in comfortable upper middle-class and, more rarely, aristocratic country surroundings (Knight 2004: 87). The Golden Age fixation with the upper class, or the upper middle class, is further compounded in British fiction of the period by the fact that the physical and social settings are so isolated from post-war depression that it is as if the Great War had never happened: this, despite the fact that *The Mysterious Affair at Styles* makes direct, if fleeting, reference to the war by employing a wounded officer as the narrator and by locating Poirot in England as one of a group of Belgian refugees. In this social and historical cocoon, the victim, as Knight observes, 'has some wealth and authority', and most of the suspects 'will be relatives or close associates of the important dead person' (Knight 2004: 88). Furthermore, they will all have secrets to hide that make them viable suspects. However, in the hard-boiled mode the common man is more than just the hired help. In contrast with the Golden Age, the common man could be the victim, the villain, or the detective.

Christie's upper middle-class semi-rural village communities, while they provide the formal device of offering a closed society and a correspondingly closed circle of suspects, also reflect Christie's conservative social vision. Christie's inter-war fiction, in particular, and its country-house settings, 'are not a reflection of contemporary life, but a recollection of Paradise Lost' (Mandel 1984: 30), and for this reason they seek to exclude from the positively Edwardian world they create all the devastation of the Great War and the social and economic upheaval of 1920s and 1930s depression. In this conservative social vision there is a clear relationship with the fact that the success of Sherlock Holmes as a character lay in his ability 'to assuage the anxieties of a respectable, London-based, middle-class audience' (Knight 1980: 67). Watson, for example, personifies the positive qualities of Victorian middle-class masculinity: he is honest, loyal, and brave. These virtues emphasise the ideological significance of his position as first-person narrator, and, considered in this respect, Christie's narrators, who include pastors, doctors, and retired officers, serve a similar function.

If such observations applied only to Christie's fiction, it would be difficult to make broader statements about Golden Age fiction as a whole. However, these phenomena are not restricted solely to Christie. In the British school, the detectives of Dorothy Sayers, Margery Allingham,

Ngaio Marsh, and Michael Innes are all upper-class establishment figures, and they are all deeply implicated in the social order that they work to protect; indeed, Sayers's Lord Peter Wimsey is even a member of the peerage. Furthermore, unlike the relative outsiders the Belgian Poirot and the spinster Miss Marple, who, crucially, lies outside the conservative and patriarchal socio-economic unit of the family, the detectives of the other British Golden Age writers are all inside members of the social order that they participate in maintaining. Symons, for this reason, identifies the majority of the British Golden Age writers as right-wing conservatives, and although he is quick to state that this does not mean that they are anti-liberal or openly anti-Semitic, for example, he does point out that 'It would have been unthinkable for them to create a Jewish detective, or a working-class one aggressively conscious of his origins, for such figures would have seemed to them quite incongruous' (Symons 1993: 108).

In contrast with the British model of the Golden Age, Priestman suggests that the detective of the American whodunnit of the same period is characterised by a greater flamboyance (Priestman 1998: 25). S.S. Van Dine's Philo Vance, for example, who is clearly an Americanised version of Sayers's Lord Peter Wimsey, is pompous and almost aggressively erudite, and parades his Oxford education as part of his eccentric and quasi-aristocratic persona. Rex Stout's detective Nero Wolfe, who first appeared in *Fer-de-Lance* (1934), is a greedy, obese, orchid-loving Montenegrin-American beer-connoisseur whose reluctance, or, according to some, inability, to leave his New York home offers the opportunity for various feats of armchair detection carried out by proxy through his sidekick Archie Goodwin. Despite the flamboyance and eccentricity of their detectives, however, the social conservatism of the American strand of Golden Age fiction is clear, and in the stories of Van Dine, Stout, John Dickson Carr, and Ellery Queen there are 'no Radicals, no Southern Demagogues or home-grown Fascists' (Symons 1993: 108). However, in their use of the tough, streetwise Archie Goodwin the Nero Wolfe stories of Rex Stout are often identified as bridging the widely-discussed gap between the conservative and cerebral clue-puzzle of the British form and the urban realism of American hard-boiled private eye fiction.

SETTINGS AND SUB-GENRES

The broad, rule-of-thumb divisions between British and American Golden Age fiction, and between the clue-puzzle form and the hard-boiled mode, can also be identified in their characteristic settings. The modern city is generally recognised as the normal setting for hard-boiled fiction, while Golden Age fiction, at least in its British version, often features a rural or semi-rural setting. The earlier fiction of Doyle, as Porter points out, alternates significantly between the two (Porter 1981: 190), and in many ways the urban/rural divide allows for a comparison with a pastoral vision evident in English literature from as early as the Renaissance, and articulated significantly in revenge tragedy, in which the urban court setting is used to explore the theme of sexual and moral contamination. The rural setting of much British Golden Age fiction, in this way, is an important link to what Priestman identifies as the version of pastoral that they articulate, and which is emphasised in the term 'Golden Age' (Priestman 1990: 151). The characteristic desire of Golden Age fiction to restore or return to a lost order that, in all respects, is superior to the present world, reinforces this pastoral reading.

The setting of Golden Age fiction can also have important stylistic effects, such as the characteristic irony in the incongruity of murder in a pastoral setting. As W.H. Auden, an ardent fan of detective fiction, observes of the pastoral setting in his essay 'The Guilty Vicarage', 'the more Eden-like it is, the greater the contradiction of murder' (Auden 1963: 151). The shock of the incongruous is still deployed in contemporary variants of mystery and detective fiction, such as Colin Dexter's Inspector Morse novels and stories, in which murder occurs among the dreaming spires of Oxford. Dexter, furthermore, also structures his fiction around a Holmes/Watson relationship, with the grumpy, intellectual, opera-loving Chief Inspector Morse and his sidekick Detective Sergeant Lewis, who is unimaginative, but reliable and diligent. *C.S.I.* takes the notion of the shock of the incongruous a step further in the episode 'Scuba Doobie Doo', in which a scuba diver is found dead up a tree in the desert, miles from the nearest water source. Again, in this instance the physical setting is crucial to the formal operation of the mystery.

Porter's identification of how detective stories very quickly suggest or depict a scene in an implied space in the contemporary world significantly relates the fiction of the Golden Age, and its variants, to the realist tradition (Porter 1981: 115), and the central importance of realist spatial setting is evident in the almost obligatory presence of maps in Golden Age fiction. *The Mysterious Affair at Styles* features a map of the murdered Mrs Inglethorp's bedroom, and most of Christie's subsequent novels also feature maps, whether or not they are helpful to the reader. The use of maps, along with the use of titles that fix a particular event in spatial terms, can be seen throughout Christie's *oeuvre*. These include *The Mysterious Affair at Styles*, *The Murder at the Vicarage*, *Murder on the Orient Express* (1934), *The Body in the Library* (1942), *Death on the Nile* (1937), *Murder on the Links* (1923), and others. Similarly, maps of various kinds, including those of a topographical, meteorological, and geological nature, are central to the twenty-first-century investigations of *C.S.I.*

These points underline the importance of setting in Golden Age fiction, and its various descendants, in both socio-cultural and formal terms. Just as a character's social position is a crucial factor in his or her identification as a suspect, Christie's use of titles that refer to a particular location reinforces the central importance, in the same procedure of identifying possible suspects, of an objectified sense of place in the use of maps and plans as well as the importance of an objectified sense of time in the proliferation of times, clocks, timetables, and alibis, in the same procedure. It is for this reason that Knight suggests that the location of people in time and space is usually the central issue in Christie's fiction (Knight 1980: 120). Quite apart from their obvious importance in establishing alibis, the central presence of timetables, clocks, and chronology is also a marker of a modern, industrialised society: a modern industrial world often quite at odds with the pastoral idyll that the Golden Age longs for.

The various settings and locations of mystery and detective fiction also created various sub-genres. The most frequently visited of these include the country-house mystery and the locked-room mystery, in which various ingenious methods of committing murder in a hermetically sealed environment formed the core. The American writer John Dickson Carr, to the exclusion of all else, wrote variations on the locked-room formula, and in his most famous of these, *The Hollow Man* (1935, published in the USA as *The Three Coffins*), the detective Gideon Fell lectures at length on the various permutations of the form. Fell's lecture outlines an exhaustive list of these variations, including:

1) The murder which is not a murder, but rather a series of accidents and/or coincidences ending in what appears to be murder. The *C.S.I.* episodes 'Chaos Theory' and 'Random Acts of Violence' are examples of this variation.

2) Murder by a mechanical device already planted in the room.

3) The murder which is, in fact, a suicide intended to look like murder.

(Dickson Carr 2002: 155–63)

The locked-room mystery was immensely reassuring for the inter-war reading public, reducing the world, as it did, to self-contained, enclosed, manageable proportions and dimensions. The enduring popularity of this sub-genre is evident in its use in contemporary crime fiction and television, such as the *C.S.I.* episode 'Random Acts of Violence', in which a computer worker is found dead in a closed room which, according to his co-workers, nobody has entered or exited for hours.

The country-house murder, which may incorporate within it the locked-room mystery, has important structural implications. First, and most importantly, it limits the number of suspects to the guests, residents, and staff of the country house, or its substitute, as in the case of Colin Dexter's *The Secret of Annexe 3* (1986). Secondly, it provides a restricted setting from which the various suspects cannot leave, and into which new suspects cannot enter, providing a microcosm of the larger society which supports it and furthermore creating the social equivalent of the hermetically sealed environment of the locked-room mystery. *The Mysterious Affair at Styles* is a country-house murder, and marked the transition from the Holmes story to the whodunnit novel, making the sub-genre popular at exactly the time, between the two world wars, when the social structure that supported the setting and ethos was going into irreversible decline. Again, the popularity of the country-house mystery is evident in the number of variations on the restricted setting which it provided. One of these is the deserted 'haunted' house in the USA, where the lack of a landed gentry demanded that the sub-genre be modified. A contemporary cinematic appropriation of this would be the abandoned motel, built on an Indian burial ground, in the film *Identity* (2003), and it is the melding of the mystery and horror genres in contemporary Hollywood cinema that underlines the relationship between crime fiction and the Gothic which is clearly evident in Poe's *oeuvre*.

Another variation of the country-house sub-genre includes the snow-bound mystery, such as Christie's play *The Mousetrap* (1949), and Marsh's *Death and the Dancing Footman* (1941) and *Death of a Fool* (1956). The snowbound mystery combines elements of both the locked-room mystery and the country-house mystery, but is often too contrived for contemporary sensibilities. One variation that avoids the taint of contrivance is the idea of murder afloat – that is, murder on a boat or ship. This is a popular variation for a number of reasons, including the romantic potential that enables it to appeal to a larger audience. There are various opportunities for accidents, which complicate the plot and action, and can contribute to the shifting pattern of suspicion that is characteristic of mystery and detective fiction in general. The cramped, claustrophobic setting has atmospheric potential comparable to that of a more Gothic locale, and the isolated setting provides a limited number of suspects all confined to one space with no opportunity to leave or escape. Examples include Christie's more famous *Death on the Nile* (1937), as well as Nicholas Blake's *The Widow's Cruise* (1959) and Ngaio Marsh's *Singing in the Shrouds* (1958), and variations of the idea of 'murder afloat' include murder on a train, such as Christie's *Murder on the Orient Express*, which has itself been reinvented in a further variation for the twenty-first century. In the *C.S.I.* episode 'Unfriendly Skies' a man is murdered in the first-class cabin on a commercial airliner, and, in a further appropriation of Christie's novel, all the passengers in first class, including the stewardess, are guilty.

Country-house and locked-room mysteries, and their various derivatives, are still evident in contemporary crime fiction, although it is significant to note that British crime writers have been reluctant to revert to a structure and a form that is characteristic of a certain stereotypical view of a Britain which no longer exists, and which perhaps never did. The developmental relationship in British crime fiction between the Golden Age whodunnit and the police procedural will be discussed in a later chapter, but it is an American writer, Elizabeth George, who employs the most straightforward mapping of the whodunnit onto the procedural, in her Inspector Lynley novels. Without a trace of irony, in addition to being a Detective Inspector, Thomas Lynley is also the 8th Earl of Asherton, and in many ways can be viewed as an updated version of Sayers's Lord Peter Wimsey. This view of George's novels as 'updated' whodunnits is reinforced in *A Suitable Vengeance* (1991), in which Lynley's return to Howenstow, his ancestral home, with his bride-to-be provides an opportunity for a conventional country-house mystery when a local journalist is murdered.

In this, then, there seems to be an inversion of the typical, but misguided, view of a great divide between British crime fiction and American crime fiction, with the more cerebral whodunnit being associated with the former in most critical studies, and the more visceral hard-boiled approach being associated with the latter. As George's novels, and the development of British crime fiction from the 1970s on, demonstrate, however, this view is a restrictive one, although the early development of hard-boiled fiction did owe a great deal to the American context in which it occurred, as the following chapter will demonstrate.

3

THE HARD-BOILED MODE

Behind the buildings, behind the lights, were the streets.
There was garbage in the streets.

(McBain 2003: 1)

MURDER FOR A REASON: ORIGINS AND DEVELOPMENT

Dashiell Hammett's Continental Op in *Red Harvest* (1929) is described as a 'hard-boiled, pig-headed guy' (Hammett 1992: 85), and the term 'hard-boiled', meaning 'tough' or 'shrewd', came to describe the hero of a type of detective fiction that developed in the United States in the inter-war period. The private detective had already appeared in the shape of the New York detective Nick Carter, a character originally created by John R. Coryell in the 1880s, but it is John Daly's Race Williams who is generally acknowledged as the first hard-boiled detective hero. Williams is a large, tough, violent man, and is clearly the prototype for many hard-boiled heroes, from Raymond Chandler's Philip Marlowe to Mickey Spillane's Mike Hammer, although as a model he was quickly superseded, and has been all but forgotten. It was Hammett, more than any other author, who set the foundation for a type of fiction that was characterised, among other things, by the 'hard-boiled' and 'pig-headed' figure of the private investigator around which the sub-genre developed, a threatening and alienating urban setting, frequent violence, and fast-paced dialogue that attempted to capture the language of 'the streets'. These are the same streets that Chandler refers to in his famous description of the hard-boiled private eye in *The Simple Art of Murder*:

> But down these mean streets a man must go who is not himself mean, who is neither tarnished nor afraid. The detective in this kind of story must be such a man. He is the hero; he is everything. He must be a complete man and a common man and yet an unusual man. He must be, to use a rather weathered phrase, a man of honour.

(Chandler 1988: 18)

Both Chandler and Hammett, whom Chandler consciously emulated, began their careers in the pulp magazines by publishing short stories in *Black Mask* magazine, the most influential and successful of the pulps, before publishing novels. The 'pulps', as they were pejoratively termed because of the cheap paper on which they were printed, were inexpensive, weekly publications with lurid and garish covers intended to catch the attention of a reading public weaned on the sensational stories typical of the 'dime novel'. The dime novel, which first began to appear during the American Civil War, and which, like its literary descendant the pulp magazine, played an enormous part in creating popular literary tastes in the United States, printed sensational stories targeted at a large and rapidly growing reading audience. John Coryell's New York detective Nick Carter first appeared in the dime novel, anticipating the pattern of relocating the frontier hero of the Western into an urban environment that is generally credited to Hammett.

In Britain, there is a similar relationship between the earlier 'penny dreadfuls' and 'shilling shockers', which printed sensational stories in the same vein as the dime novel, and magazines such as the *Strand*, in which Conan Doyle's Sherlock Holmes appeared in short story form in 1891. Revealingly, the split form of Conan Doyle's early novels, such as *A Study in Scarlet* and *The Sign of Four*, contains within it the sort of adventure story that was common in the dime novel, and it is significant for hard-boiled fiction that the Western adventure story began with the dime novel, and was also a staple of pulp magazines such as *Black Mask*. The 'mask' of the title, in this way, can be read as a reference to the tradition out of which hard-boiled fiction developed, from the disguises of champions of the weak, such as Zorro, to the raised neckerchief of the Wild West outlaw (Priestman 1998: 52). Hard-boiled fiction translated the romanticism of the Western into a modern urban setting, and this movement from the Western frontier to a hostile urban environment was accompanied by an abrupt shift from the artificial gentility of the classical detective story to the creation of a fictional world of social corruption and 'real' crime (Mandel 1984: 35).

It is for these reasons that hard-boiled fiction is typically identified as a distinctively American sub-genre, and such an identification is reinforced by three elements that characterise most of the early fiction. First, the Californian setting of most of the early hard-boiled novels, and many of the later ones, is a direct extension of the frontier stories of the Western genre, and underlines the identification of the private eye as a quick-fisted urban cowboy, who, when he speaks at all, speaks in the tough, laconic American vernacular. The American vernacular, the second of these characteristics, is the same language of the 'mean streets' identified by Chandler, 'the kind of lingo', he says of the American reading audience, that 'they imagined they spoke themselves' (Chandler 1988: 15). The third distinctly American characteristic is the portrayal of crimes that were increasingly becoming part of the everyday world of early twentieth-century America.

Ernest Mandel notes that the pulp magazines 'developed more or less simultaneously with the rise of organized crime' in the United States (Mandel 1984: 34), and identifies the rapid encroachment of crime during Prohibition, from 1919 to 1933, from the fringes to the very centre of bourgeois society and existence. The Great Depression, in turn, lent impetus to crime of all sorts, but it was organised crime, in particular the violent and systematic takeover of bootlegging, prostitution, and gambling that depended on the sort of capital investment that went hand in glove with the political and police corruption which features in most early hard-boiled fiction (Mandel 1984: 31). W.R. Burnett's *Little Caesar*, published in the same year as *Red Harvest*, dealt with the reality of gangsterism and gangland violence in a cautionary tale redolent of the *Newgate Calendar* stories, but by the time of Chandler's first novel, *The Big Sleep* (1939), published just ten years after *Little Caesar*, bootlegging had already become a romanticised backdrop in the pasts of characters such as Rusty Regan.

Chandler, however, was writing in the shadow of Hammett, whose first novel, *Red Harvest*, appeared in the same year as the Wall Street Crash and firmly established many of the defining characteristics of the genre. These include the centrality of the character of the private eye, the existence of a client, along with the detective's evident distrust of the client, an urban setting, routine police corruption, the *femme fatale*, an apparently 'neutral' narrative method, and the extensive use of vernacular dialogue. But it was Hammett's casting of the genre in the realist mode that Chandler most admired, and in *The Simple Art of Murder* Chandler links this realism to Hammett's use of American vernacular dialogue. According to Chandler:

> Hammett gave murder back to the kind of people that commit it for reasons, not just to provide a corpse; and with the means at hand, not hand-wrought duelling pistols, curare and tropical fish. He put these people down on paper as they were, and he made them talk and think in the language they customarily used for these purposes.
>
> (Chandler 1988: 14)

Chandler's insistence on the realism of the genre is not unique, but despite the various claims for the realism of hard-boiled fiction, the shift from the analytical certainties and reassuringly stable social order of classical detective fiction to the gritty realism of the 'mean streets' of hard-boiled fiction disguised a certain continuity, in Chandler, at any rate, with the idealistic quest for truth and justice characteristic of romance, and its reincarnation in the indigenous American tradition in the Western. At the centre of this quest for truth and justice is the figure of the private investigator, whose wisecracking cynicism, besides providing an outlet for vernacular dialogue, often hides an inner compassion and sentimentalism quite at odds with his tough, taciturn exterior. However, as the word 'private' in the term 'private investigator' suggests, this combination of cynicism and romanticism, which Chandler discusses in *The Simple Art of Murder*, characterises many hard-boiled private eye heroes.

A SHOP-SOILED GALAHAD: THE PRIVATE EYE HERO

In *The Simple Art of Murder*, Chandler argues that the classic detective story is characterised by a primacy of plot over character, claiming that '[i]f it started out to be about real people [. . .] they must very soon do unreal things in order to form the artificial pattern required by the plot' (Chandler 1988: 12). While Hammett's lean prose and emphasis on colloquial dialogue had the effect of seeming neutral and objective, Chandler's adoption of Hammett's tough-guy tone is tempered by a romantic individualism constructed around the viewpoint of his private eye hero, Philip Marlowe. In Chandler's words, 'He is the hero; he is everything' (Chandler 1988: 18). By making Marlowe's own responses and judgements the key to unlocking the narrative, the plot, which Chandler always admitted was difficult for him to construct, is decentred. As the term 'private eye' suggests, it is the viewpoint of the detective that forms the focus of the narrative, and Chandler's plots are often nothing more than frameworks upon which to hang Marlowe's values and through which to emphasise his viewpoint (Knight 1980: 140–1).

As the term 'private eye' illustrates, the various terms used to refer to the hard-boiled detective reveal significant details about the sub-genre that grew up around this figure. The term 'private detective', as the word 'detective' suggests, identifies the hard-boiled hero as the linear descendant of the Golden Age detective. Unlike classical detective fiction, however, in the hard-boiled model that Hammett laid down in *Red Harvest* there is little or no analysis of clues and associated analytic deduction. Rather, the hard-boiled detective's investigations, involving direct questioning and movement from place to place, parallel the sort of tracking down of a quarry that is characteristic of frontier romance and the Western (Mandel 1984: 36). Similarly, the term 'private investigator', or 'PI', is also significant. The word 'private' is an indicator of the PI's most obvious trait: his private nature. This private nature is further indicated in the first-person 'I' of the term 'PI'. The hard-boiled private eye is a private 'I', a loner, an alienated individual who exists outside or beyond the socio-economic order of family, friends, work, and home. Hammett's nameless 'Operative' for the Continental Detective Agency 'has no commitment, personal or social, beyond the accomplishment of his job' (Willett 1992: 11), and Chandler's Marlowe is perhaps the best example of the alienated, 'outsider' status of the PI:

> He lives alone, in rented flats or houses. He works alone, in a cheap, comfortless office. He drinks and smokes a lot: a single, masculine

> lifestyle. He is choosy about his work, never showing much interest in money. In general, he has dropped right out of the normal family and financial patterns of modern culture.
>
> (Knight 1988: 78)

The decision to 'drop out of' normal family and financial patterns is emphasised by the self-employed status of the private eye, which both links and sets him or her apart from Golden Age detectives. Unlike the Miss Marples, Hercule Poirots, Peter Wimseys, and Gideon Fells of classic detective fiction, the hard-boiled private eye is no longer an eccentric or wealthy amateur. The private eye is a professional investigator who works for a living, and, more significantly, who works for him- or herself. Even Hammett's Continental Op, who is nominally an operative for the Continental Detective Agency, sets his own rules and follows his own agenda, claiming that '[i]t's right enough for the Agency to have rules and regulations, but when you're out on a job you've got to do it the best way you can' (Hammett 1992: 117). The private eye answers to nobody but him- or herself, and it is this independence and self-sufficiency, inherited from the frontier hero, that contributes to the hostility that the private eye typically displays for the forces of law and order.

The most common term used to refer to the hard-boiled detective, however, is potentially the most revealing. The term 'private eye', a development of the term 'PI', is primarily suggestive of covert surveillance, and, in this respect, the term calls to mind the staring eye logo of the Pinkerton detective agency, for whom Hammett worked as an agent. The notion of covert surveillance, besides emphasising the private, or secretive, nature of the private eye, is a decidedly passive one. Hammett's Op, for example, is presented as a 'direct, neutral observer', who provides 'minimal interpretation and analysis for the reader' (Willett 1992: 10). The Op employs a curiously passive investigative procedure that involves 'stirring things up', and then, significantly, keeping his eyes open 'so you'll see what you want when it comes to the top' (Hammett 1992: 85). Marlowe, similarly, does little or no active detection, such as gathering facts, and takes a more passive approach. He talks to suspects, witnesses, and clients, often 'stirring them up' in a manner similar to the Op, and then, again like the Op, he watches and listens, waiting for the truth to come to him rather than actively seeking it out (Knight 1988: 84).

Such investigative methods have the effect of decentring the plot, and emphasising the centrality of the private eye, and this is emphasised further in Chandler's novels by his use of first-person narration. Marlowe's first-person narrative voice makes him the ideological and narrative centre of the novels, but as Knight observes, it is a centre that is fundamentally divided by Marlowe's two distinct voices. According to Knight, 'the voice of Marlowe's reverie, both subtle and ironic, is quite different from the voice he uses to other characters', which, as Knight further comments, 'is uniformly tough and insensitive' (Knight 1988: 81). Later critics have expanded on Knight's insight by drawing a distinction between tough talk and wisecracks on the one hand, and the 'hard-boiled conceit' on the other (Christianson 1989: 156). Tough talk 'is fairly terse, always colloquial, and often vulgar'. More importantly, '[o]ne can only crack wise – be a wise guy – for an audience' (Christianson 1989: 152, 156). The hard-boiled conceit, on the other hand, is part of the narrative voice used by the detective when communicating directly with the reader in order to reveal his 'complex sensibility' (Christianson 1989: 157), and in this way functions to emphasise the 'private' identity of the private eye.

Such arguments, of course, only serve to reinforce the view of the private eye as a fundamentally divided figure. He (since in the majority of hard-boiled texts until the 1980s the private eye is male) has two voices, and each voice reveals a side to the private eye that is incompatible with the other. He is tough, but sensitive. He is intelligent, but resorts to physical violence and coercion to achieve his goals. He is conspicuously hostile to the forces of law and order, but yet, nominally, at any rate, he shares their aim to restore and maintain the social order. The famous opening of Chandler's first novel, *The Big Sleep*, emphasises the paradoxical combination of tough-talking cynicism and romantic sensibility by ironically identifying Marlowe with the heroes of romance narratives. Marlowe is calling to the Sternwood mansion, whose stained-glass window over the entrance doors forms the focus of his description:

> Over the entrance doors [. . .] there was a broad stained-glass panel showing a knight in dark armour rescuing a lady who was tied to a tree and didn't have any clothes on but some very long and convenient hair. The knight had pushed the vizor of his helmet back to be sociable, and he was fiddling with the knots of the ropes that tied the lady to the tree

and not getting anywhere. I stood there and thought that if I lived in the house, I would sooner or later have to climb up there and help him. He didn't seem to be really trying.

(Chandler 1993: 3)

The tone – ironic, acerbic, and laconic – is characteristic of the hard-boiled mode, but it is the ironic identification between the figure of the knight and the private eye, who imagines himself 'climb[ing] up' into the knight's position to do his job for him, and in this way literally putting himself in the knight's position, that reveals most about Chandler's fiction.

Marlowe is an idealised figure, a questing knight of romance transplanted into the mean streets of mid-twentieth-century Los Angeles. Like the questing knight, Marlowe's is a quest to restore justice and order motivated by his own personal code of honour, and in this respect, Marlowe's credentials are water-tight: in an earlier incarnation, in the short story 'Blackmailers Don't Shoot', he is called 'Mallory', in this way identifying Sir Thomas Mallory's *La Morte d'Arthur* (1470) as the text from which the inspiration for the character of Marlowe was drawn. The parallels with the grail quest and with knights of legend are alluded to throughout Chandler's novels in names such as 'Grayle' and 'Quest', and even in the title of the novel *The Lady in the Lake* (1944). At one point in *The High Window* (1943) Marlowe is referred to as a 'shop-soiled Galahad' (Chandler 1951: 174), and the description encapsulates the conflict between romance and realism that characterises Chandler's fiction in particular, and the hard-boiled mode in general. Marlowe might be a knight, but his armour, far from being shining, is 'shop-soiled', and his honour, it is implied, is equally compromised.

Hammett's private eye heroes, however, are more obviously compromised, and Sam Spade, in *The Maltese Falcon* (1930), and the Continental Op, who features in both *Red Harvest* and *The Dain Curse* (1929), have been described as 'rough people doing dirty work' with their own 'crude code of ethics' (Symons 1993: 153). The difference between Chandler and Hammett lies in the literary heritages that they drew upon to create their detective heroes. Hammett is generally credited with bringing the independence and self-sufficient morality of the old frontier hero of the Western into the urban criminal environment of modern America (Knight 1980: 135), and the shadow of the Western is most evident in *Red Harvest*.

The novel begins, like a stereotypical Western, with the arrival of a tough loner to a frontier town corrupted by crime and violence. In Hammett's novel, the anonymous Continental Op arrives in Personville ('Poisonville' to the Op and to many of its inhabitants), an ugly mining-town as polluted by the smelting chimneys that helped to found it as it is by the gunmen and gangsters who control it. The Op soon takes on the task of cleaning up the 'pig-sty of a Poisonville' (Hammett 1992: 42) by turning the criminal and corrupt elements of the city against each other.

While the Op's intention of 'opening Poisonville up from Adam's Apple to ankles' (Hammett 1992: 64) has superficial parallels with the moral righteousness and the desire for justice that characterise the frontier hero, he is as guilty and amoral as the gangsters and corrupt city officials that he exposes and helps to murder. The justice that he seeks is a vigilante justice, and he defends his personal vendetta against the city by claiming that 'there's [no] law in Poisonville except what you make for yourself' (Hammett 1992: 119). This denial of laws and regulations in favour of a personal code of justice reveals an important parallel between Jacobean revenge tragedy, with its examination of the idea of the revenger as heaven's 'scourge and minister' (*Hamlet* III.iv.176), and hard-boiled fiction. Significantly, it is the theme of vigilante justice that has been most readily borrowed in cinematic and comic book appropriations of the hard-boiled mode. Graphic novels like Frank Miller's *Sin City* series feature characters who, in their personal crusades for justice, have, like Hammett's Continental Op, 'arranged a killing or two in [their] time' (Hammett 1992: 154), and in this way have upset the balance of justice and social order that they claim to be attempting to restore. Furthermore, since the client (theoretically) pays for the detective's loyalty, hard-boiled fiction highlights the injustice of a society in which money is perceived to buy justice, further emphasising the inequities of both the dominant social order and the private eye's attempts to maintain it.

Hammett's Continental Op, however, is aware of the limitations of the vigilante justice that he brings about, and acknowledges that any victories against the crime and corruption of the modern city are short-lived. When he tells his client, Elihu Willsson, that he will have his city back 'all nice and clean and ready to go to the dogs again' (Hammett 1992: 203), the Op highlights the fact that, unlike the tidy resolutions of Golden Age detective fiction, small, local, and temporary victories are all that the hard-boiled private eye can ever hope to achieve in a corrupt world. There is, as Mandel notes, a certain naivety in the idea of a tough 'hard-boiled' individual fighting single-handedly against gangsterism, organised crime, and political and police corruption (Mandel 1984: 36). Whatever their methods, however, it is this naivety that Chandler's Marlowe and Hammett's detectives have in common, and it is the figure of the tough loner on a crusade against social corruption, above all else, that characterises the hard-boiled mode.

LAST CHANCES AND NEW BEGINNINGS: THE MYTH OF THE FRONTIER

The figure of the tough loner on a crusade against social corruption is an acknowledgement of earlier American literature and culture, in particular the stoicism and self-reliance of frontier adventure heroes like James Fenimore Cooper's Hawkeye in *The Last of the Mohicans* (1826). The identification of the frontier hero as the archetype of the private eye is well established, and the two figures share a number of characteristics that are central to the hard-boiled mode. These include 'professional skills, physical courage affirmed as masculine potency, fortitude, moral strength, a fierce desire for justice, social marginality and a degree of anti-intellectualism' (Willett 1992: 6), although this list is not prescriptive, as various of these characteristics undergo some degree of transformation in the works of different authors. The 'moral strength' associated with the frontier hero, for example, is not lightly carried by characters like the Op or Sam Spade, despite their fierce adherence to a personal code of honour. However, their professional skills are never in question, and in Hammett the central focus is the detective at his job. In particular, the Op's prime motivation is always to finish the job, come what may, even when his client attempts to call him off the case, as Elihu Willsson does in *Red Harvest*.

Physical courage and fortitude are central to the figure of the private eye, who, in many ways, is defined by his ability to both inflict, and stoically endure, physical punishment. The violence associated with the tough-guy private eye is often associated, in turn, with the anti-intellectual stance that seems to characterise certain private eye heroes. Mickey Spillane's Mike Hammer, the most violent, right-wing, misogynistic, and anti-intellectual of the private eye successors to Chandler and Hammett, is the most obvious example, although less extreme examples provide more interesting reading. The novels of James Crumley, featuring the private detectives Milo Milodragovitch and C.W. Sughrue, are set in Montana, and the setting is just one of the ways in which they acknowledge their debt to the frontier tradition. Sughrue, in *The Last Good Kiss* (1978), makes explicit the link between violence and anti-intellectualism in the American West when he declares, with typical tough-guy aplomb, that '[i]ntellectual discourse is great, man, but in my business, violence and pain is where it's at' (Crumley 1993: 303).

The violence of the world in which the private eye finds him- or herself echoes that of the great American West, 'where', according to Crumley's Milo, 'men came to get away from the laws' (Crumley 1993: 12). The American Frontier, however, was more than just a place of lawlessness and violence, and this is reflected in the hard-boiled fiction of Hammett and Chandler, as well as in the novels of writers who consciously emulate them, like Crumley. The American West, and specifically, by the beginning of the twentieth century, California, offered the promise of a new life that was the legacy of a pattern of settlement in America that is also the history of the westward movement of pioneers and new arrivals to the continent. For some, such as Leila Quest and Dolores Gonzales in *The Little Sister*, the attraction is the fame and fortune offered by Hollywood; for others, it is the promise of anonymity; while for Helen Grayle in *Farewell, My Lovely*, and Crystal Kingsley in *The Lady in the Lake*, it is the possibility of creating a new identity and beginning a new life. Significantly, almost all of Chandler's novels pivot on 'a case of mistaken, disguised, or altered identity. His characters discard their old selves, and invent new ones' (Babener 1995: 128).

The extent of such disguise and reinvention in hard-boiled fiction varies. In *The Little Sister*, Orfamay Quest, after her arrival in Los Angeles to hire a detective to search for her missing brother, soon sheds her glasses, which Marlowe appropriately calls 'cheaters', and reveals her true self-serving nature beneath the disguise. Earl, a bodyguard in *The Long Goodbye*, wears a series of costumes, including a cowboy suit and patent-leather boots which Marlowe compares to 'a Roy Rogers outfit' (Chandler 1993: 477), in this way alluding to both the influence of the Western genre on hard-boiled fiction and the fakery of Hollywood. Also in *The Long Goodbye*, Terry Lennox undergoes plastic surgery, taking the process of disguise one step further. A new identity is created to replace the old one, and a new background is created to fill the blank space of a hidden past.

In *The Lady in the Lake*, Mildred Haviland follows a similar pattern of escape from the past through reinvention in the present. The past, in Mildred Haviland's case, is a criminal past, which she escapes by renaming herself Muriel Chess, who then transforms into Crystal Kingsley, and finally, Mrs Fallbrook, and each character shift 'provokes a murder and another transmutation' (Babener 1995: 243). Similar patterns appear in other Chandler novels, as well as in Hammett's novels. In *The Dain Curse*, Maurice de Mayenne follows the same pattern by re-enacting the westward movement of the Old World immigrants from Europe to America, and specifically, San Francisco. De Mayenne, who is French, assumes various aliases, finally reinventing himself as Edgar Leggett and 'making a new place for himself in the world' (Hammett 2002: 55). However, as with most characters in hard-boiled fiction who flee from the past to the myth of the future that California offers, Leggett's past catches up with him, and he is murdered, apparently a victim of the eponymous Dain Curse. Terry Lennox, in *The Long Goodbye*, similarly attempts to erase his past, and assumes an increasing number of aliases and new identities in an attempt to stay one step ahead of a past that constantly threatens to overtake his new identity in the present. As Paul Marston, a British commando in the Second World War, Lennox also re-enacts the westward movement from Old World to New, becoming Terry Lennox, the elegant Los Angeles drunk, who quickly adopts still more assumed identities, finally becoming the Mexican Cisco Maioranos, apotheosis of a self without a centre or a past. When a disappointed Marlowe, at the close of the novel, tells him that he has 'nice clothes and perfume' and that he is 'as elegant as a fifty-dollar whore', Lennox's reply emphasises the theme of emptiness that is, ironically, the centre of Chandler's novels. '"That's just an act [. . . .] An act is all there is. There isn't anything else. In here" – he tapped his chest with his lighter – "there isn't anything"' (Chandler 1993: 659).

More than simply abandoning their pasts, these characters actively seek to destroy, hide, or bury their past lives, and in hard-boiled fiction, the return of a character's past threatens their existence in the present. It has been noted that in this respect, 'hard-boiled stories are about hauntings', in which circumstances in the present 'make evident the powerful

intervention of past experiences' (Skenazy 1995: 114). Based on this identification of the theme of 'haunting' in hard-boiled fiction, Paul Skenazy
makes a comparison between hard-boiled fiction and the Gothic novel
that is of particular significance in relation to the early origins of crime
fiction. According to Skenazy:

> The two forms share common assumptions: that there is an undisclosed
> event, a secret from the past; that the secret represents an occurrence
> or desire antithetical to the principles and position of the house (or
> family); that to know the secret is to understand the inexplicable and
> seemingly irrational events that occur in the present.
>
> (Skenazy 1995: 114)

Although the private eye's initial brief seems to be to unearth secrets,
the detective in the novels of Chandler and Macdonald is often hired
to prevent a secret from becoming known. In *The Big Sleep*, Marlowe
is hired to deal with a blackmailer, and to prevent a dark secret from
becoming public knowledge. In *The High Window*, it is gambling debts,
a bad marriage, and the discreet recovery of a stolen coin. In those novels
in which revelation, rather than concealment, is Marlowe's brief, he
is often 'unable to make full use of the truths he has exposed' (Willett
1992: 19), and is instead forced to suppress the information, as he does
with Carmen Sternwood in *The Big Sleep*, and Terry Lennox in *The Long
Goodbye*. Often, the attempt to maintain secrecy leads unwittingly to the
metaphorical (although sometimes literal) unearthing of a skeleton in the
closet. The influence of the Gothic, with its narrative structure centred
on the family with a guilty past, is evident in Chandler, in *The Big Sleep*
and *The High Window*, and in Hammett, in *The Dain Curse*. This theme
of the guilty past of a family resurfacing to threaten familial stability in
the present, more than any other, came to occupy the fiction of Kenneth
Millar, writing under the pseudonym Ross Macdonald. Macdonald began
his writing career just as the hard-boiled heyday was beginning to wane,
but drew on the thematic template set down by Chandler. Furthermore,
by choosing a variation of the name of Sam Spade's murdered partner
from *The Maltese Falcon*, Miles Archer, Macdonald also acknowledged
his debt to Hammett. The Lew Archer novels, like Chandler's Marlowe
novels, are characterised by their Californian setting, and investigate a

common theme, specifically, the notion of California as a Promised Land, offering the opportunity to escape the past and begin a new life (Speir 1995: 153).

These attempts to escape something in the past in the novels of Chandler and Macdonald are encouraged by the California Myth, where:

> [O]ne's right to create a personal identity free from social circumstances is encouraged by the new, migratory nature of the society, the open class structure, and the expanding opportunities for advancement that are found in and near Los Angeles.
>
> (Skenazy 1995: 116)

In this respect, the California Myth is a variation of the American Dream, albeit one that is sullied in early hard-boiled fiction by greed and corruption. F. Scott Fitzgerald's *The Great Gatsby* (1925), like the novels of Hammett and Chandler of which it is a contemporary, deals with a similar theme of personal reinvention beyond the Western Frontier. In the early twentieth century, however, there was nothing left of the American frontier which Frederick Jackson Turner argued, in his essay 'The Significance of the Frontier in American History' (1893), was responsible for the democratic American spirit. California, with its gold-rushes, the discovery of oil, and the arrival of the movies, was all that was left of the West, which, Jackson argued, held the democratic promise of freedom for all.

Chandler's novels, in particular, make explicit reference to the oil industry, which forms the backdrop to *The Big Sleep*, and also to Hollywood and the movies. The condemnation of the artificiality of the Hollywood movie industry, in particular, forms a recurring motif in Chandler's novels. His most damning indictment of the movies is *The Little Sister* (1949), in which the indistinction between reality and artifice and fact and fiction is a major theme, and which prompts Marlowe's cynical evaluation of the industry:

> Wonderful what Hollywood will do to a nobody. It will make a radiant glamour queen out of a drab little wench who ought to be ironing a truck driver's shorts, a he-man hero [. . .] reeking sexual charm out of some overgrown kid who was meant to go to work with a lunchbox.
>
> (Chandler 1955: 155)

This passage, in addition to identifying the frontier promise that Hollywood offered, in which 'a nobody' could reinvent themselves as a 'radiant glamour queen' or a 'he-man hero', is also a cynical identification of the important relationship between hard-boiled fiction and cinema which is responsible, in part, for the continuing vitality of the mode.

Hollywood, at the time that Chandler was writing, did not just attract those people eager to reinvent themselves in the new frontier of southern California. It is estimated that almost 20 per cent of *film noir* thrillers produced between 1941 and 1948 were adaptations of hard-boiled fiction (Krutnik 1994: 33), and this wholesale adaptation, and the money it offered, attracted many hard-boiled writers to the Hollywood movie industry. In 1943 Chandler went to Hollywood, and worked there for the movies off and on for the next five years. He worked on movies such as the adaptation of James M. Cain's *Double Indemnity* (1936), and wrote the screenplay for *The Blue Dahlia* (1946), but his distaste for Hollywood, and the five years he spent there, is clear to see in the vitriolic attack on the industry that is the foundation for *The Little Sister*.

The term '*film noir*' is derived from the French term '*roman noir*', which was used to describe the American hard-boiled fiction that was popular in France in translation, and which became an enormous influence on French writing. The word 'noir', meaning 'black', codifies the dark, shadowy atmosphere and setting of hard-boiled fiction, which is a clear indicator of the Gothic heritage of crime fiction, and *film noir* emphasised this 'darkness' both thematically and through the use of lighting techniques that emphasised or created shadows on the screen. However, the similarities between hard-boiled fiction and *film noir* go far beyond the terms used to describe them. A narrative centre of crime, often associated with desire or seduction, is typical of the *noir* film, and is a major structuring device in both hard-boiled fiction and the early crime-thrillers of James M. Cain. Cinematic flashback techniques are a visual, as well as narrative, device that recreates the relationship between the past and the present that structures hard-boiled fiction and which allows the private eye to solve the crime by uncovering the hidden relationship between past events and present circumstances. Finally, although not exhaustively, the voice-over technique that characterises much *film noir* is a direct cinematic adaptation of the first-person narrative voice of the majority of hard-boiled texts, and both techniques emphasise the alienated individual and his or her position in a threatening urban environment. This threatening urban environment is frequently alluded to in *film noir* titles (Krutnik 1994: 18) such as *Street of Chance* (1942), *Night and the City* (1950), and *Cry of the City* (1948), and it is the 'mean streets' of the threatening city that form the characteristic environment of the hard-boiled private eye.

MEAN STREETS AND URBAN DECAY: MODERNITY AND THE CITY

The modern city of hard-boiled fiction is 'a wasteland devastated by drugs, violence, pollution, garbage and a decaying physical infrastructure', and it is down the mean streets of this urban wasteland that the private eye must go in his quest to 'temporarily check the enfolding chaos' (Willett 1992: 5). The image of the modern city as a polluted wasteland emphasises the notion of a more general corruption in modern society that threatens to poison and corrupt even the private eye, and such a threat explains Chandler's insistence, in 'The Simple Art of Murder', that down these mean streets a man must go 'who is not himself mean'. The threat, however, is a powerful one. In *Red Harvest*, the Continental Op reveals to Dinah Brand his fears that the violence and corruption of the appropriately named Poisonville are beginning to infect him. 'If I don't get away soon I'll be going blood-simple like the natives', he tells her. 'It's this damned town. Poisonville is right. It's poisoned me' (Hammett 1992: 154, 157). His fears seem to be confirmed when, the next morning, he wakes to find his right hand around the handle of an ice-pick, with the 'six-inch needle-sharp blade [. . .] buried in Dinah Brand's left breast' (Hammett 1992: 164). Similarly, Marlowe, after his involvement with the Sternwood family and his decision to cover up Carmen Sternwood's murder of Rusty Regan, at the close of *The Big Sleep* acknowledges that 'Me, I was part of the nastiness now' (Chandler 1993: 164).

What is significant about the fiction of Hammett, Chandler, and Ross Macdonald is that the urban environment they depict is similar to that of T.S. Eliot's *The Waste Land* (1922) and the earlier 'The Love Song of J. Alfred Prufrock' (1915). In *The Waste Land*, the modern industrial city is depicted as a hell whose inhabitants have been 'undone' by a kind of death that is not physical, but spiritual and emotional. They are 'human engines' leading empty lives without meaning or significance, trapped in a city that is both London in 1922, and all modern cities. Eliot's fascination with detective fiction has been well documented (Priestman 1990: 204), and his depiction of the 'Unreal City' of modern existence clearly parallels the 'unreality' of Chandler's Los Angeles and Hammett's San Francisco, which are characterised by imitation, artifice, insubstantiality, fakery, and façades.

Chandler's Los Angeles, in particular, is a city characterised, above all else, by its 'unreality', and Marlowe's sustained commentary on, and analysis of, the details of architectural décor spring from his probing of the surface of this unreality. The frontier myth of California as a place of abundance and opportunity has created 'an empire built on a spurious foundation, decked in tinsel, and beguiled by its own illusory promise' (Babener 1995: 128), and this vision of Los Angeles is central to Chandler's novels. His Los Angeles has been described as 'a metropolis of lies' (Babener 1995: 128), and the description is equally appropriate for both the city's architecture and its denizens, who gravitate there in response to the city's gilded promise of forging a new identity, and leaving the past, and past identities, far behind. Marlowe's Los Angeles is a city of façades, of stucco and fake marble. It is the home of Hollywood, 'the kingdom of illusion' (Babener 1995: 127).

In this kingdom of illusion, Chandler focuses on architecture to expose the city's preoccupation with fakery and artifice. In *The Little Sister*, Mavis Weld, a B-list actress, lives in an apartment block with a mock-marble foyer, a false fireplace, and an aquatic garden made to look like the sea floor. The Grayle house in *Farewell, My Lovely* (1940) contains an imitation sunken garden 'built to look like a ruin' (Chandler 1993: 249), and doorbells that ring like church-bells. Social climbers attempt to imitate the expensive bad taste of the wealthy, evident in the Grayle house and also in the Sternwood mansion in *The Big Sleep*, which, in addition to the medieval-looking stained-glass window over the entrance, also boasts French doors, Turkish rugs, and baroque fireplaces. Such a social climber is Lindsey Marriott, who, in *Farewell, My Lovely*, 'transforms his dwelling into a tacky version of a high society saloon' (Babener 1995: 136), with pink velvet furniture, rococo decorative frills, and an unused grand piano. However, Marlowe's eyes pierce these insubstantial façades with no great difficulty, because, as he sourly notes after attempting to break down a door in *The Big Sleep*, '[a]bout the only part of a California house that you can't put your foot through is the front door' (Chandler 1993: 24–5).

The modern city of hard-boiled fiction is an insubstantial environment, lacking in depth, and populated by various fakers, frauds, and charlatans as hollow as the city in which they live. Joseph Haldorn, in Hammett's *The Dain Curse*, is an actor who has reinvented himself as the leader of a cult called, significantly, The Temple of the Holy Grail. The Temple, housed in a six-storey apartment block, uses stage magic and illusionist's tricks to con its wealthy members of their money. The fraudulent cult prefigures similar groups in later novels, such as Ross Macdonald's *The Moving Target* (1949), and is a recurring motif in contemporary hard-boiled fiction, such as James Crumley's *Dancing Bear* (1983). Similarly, Chandler's fiction is populated by charlatans, quacks, and frauds, many of whom are linked, like Joseph Haldorn in *The Dain Curse*, to the acting profession, either through their pasts or through Marlowe's descriptions of them. In *Farewell, My Lovely*, Jules Amthor, a sham psychic who preys on the wealthy, has 'as good a profile as Barrymore ever had' (Chandler 1993: 267). His sidekick, a Native American called Second Planting, speaks like an extra in a Western, until Marlowe tells him to 'Cut out the pig Latin' (Chandler 1993: 262). The eponymous Maltese Falcon, in particular, forms the most significant motif of fraud and insubstantiality in Hammett's fiction. The falcon generates the entirety of the violent action in the novel as the *femme fatale* Brigid O'Shaughnessy, 'the Fat Man' Casper Gutman, and the homosexual dandy Joel Cairo all battle for possession of what they believe to be a priceless statue. However, there is no jewelled golden statue beneath the black paint, merely a worthless lead imitation.

The fakery and artifice that characterise the modern city of hard-boiled fiction drive a wedge between what is seen and what is known, and in this way the private eye's quest to restore order becomes a quest to make sense of a fragmented, disjointed, and largely unintelligible world by understanding its connections, or, more often, its lack of connections. The various connections that the private eye makes between appearance and reality, surface and depth, past and present, and truth or falsehood, offer the possibility of making meaning, and the structure of detective fiction is a manifestation of this. The hard-boiled story is structured by a plot with a double-rhythm, advancing inevitably forward in time while simultaneously moving backward, against the narrative flow, to resolve the violence and disruption that have prompted the client to seek out the detective in the present (Skenazy 1995: 113). The private eye, in this respect, has obvious parallels with characters in *The Waste Land* like the Thames Daughter who 'can connect/Nothing with nothing', and the Fisher King with 'These fragments I have shored against my ruins'. These fragments, for the private eye, are the scattered facts and pieces of information that he brings together, or connects, in an attempt to construct a narrative that 'makes sense' as the detective 'imposes form and causality on events, and makes the meaningless significant' (Skenazy 1995: 121). This 'form and causality' is narrative in nature as, according to Steven Marcus in his introduction to Dashiell Hammett's collection of short stories *The Continental Op* (1974), the private eye has to 'deconstruct, decompose, deplot and defictionalise [. . .] "reality" and to construct or reconstruct out of it a true fiction, i.e. an account of what "really" happened' (Marcus 1983: 202).

Viewing the private eye's explanation of events as a kind of narrative, as Marcus does, reveals important parallels between detection and the act of writing. Like the private eye, an author attempts to construct a narrative that is intelligible, or 'makes sense', by imposing a narrative structure of cause and effect that can be traced from a beginning, through the middle, to an end. Such a causal structure foregrounds the act of 'making sense' through making connections, and Roger Wade, in *The Long Goodbye*, extends the making of connections from the purely structural to the linguistic and stylistic. Wade complains that with writers 'Everything has to be like something else' (Chandler 1993: 523), and by making connections through likeness, similes become an important weapon in the writer's arsenal in making sense of the world. The appearance of writers as characters in much detective fiction, such as Hammett's *The Dain Curse*, Chandler's *The Long Goodbye*, and Crumley's *The Last Good Kiss*, reinforces the parallels between writing and detection, and Paul Auster in particular makes explicit this identification of writing as a quest for meaning in *The New York Trilogy* (1987). The *Trilogy* knowingly appropriates the conventions of detective fiction, and turns them on their head, although in the postmodern world that Auster depicts the central realisation of his characters is that no world, either the real world or the fictional one, makes any sense (Priestman 1990: 178).

Perhaps more than any genre, detective fiction foregrounds the related view of *reading* as a quest for meaning, or a form of detection, and the relationship is an important one for various ideological reasons. Primary among these is that the first-person narrator of the private eye story is easily identifiable with the private 'I' of the solitary reader (Priestman 1998: 57), making the hard-boiled novel a powerful ideological tool. The ideological power of the hard-boiled mode is almost certainly one of the reasons for its appropriation on political grounds, and it is curious to note that the defining text of this most American of forms, *Red Harvest*, is, as the title suggests, a powerful socialist criticism of the relationship between capitalism and gangsterism. Hammett's imprisonment during the McCarthy period for his suspected involvement with the Communist Party only serves to reinforce such a reading. The political agendas, either overt or covert, that are evident in hard-boiled fiction range from the more right-wing paranoia and misogyny of Mickey Spillane to the increasingly liberal-reformist agenda of Ross Macdonald, and many later writers, and it is the political adaptability of the hard-boiled that accounts for its feminist appropriation in the creation of the figure of the female PI, particularly in the texts of such authors as Sara Paretsky and Sue Grafton.

Roland Barthes's identification of two kinds of text sheds some light on the openness of the hard-boiled mode to various forms of appropriation. These texts are the 'readerly' text and the 'writerly' text, and in Barthes's schema the two types of text invite distinct reading practices, with the 'readerly' text inviting a passive reader who tends to accept the text's meanings as predetermined and already made, '[p]lung[ing] him into a kind of idleness' and leaving him 'with no more than the poor freedom either to accept or reject the text' (Barthes 1975: 4). Such a text tends to reaffirm the ideology encoded in it at the same time that it attempts to pass off that ideology as natural and commonsensical. In contrast with the 'readerly' text there is the 'writerly' text, whose goal, according to Barthes, 'is to make the reader no longer a consumer, but a producer of the text' (Barthes 1975: 4). The 'writerly' text constantly challenges the reader to rewrite and revise it, and, in this rewriting and revision, to make sense of it. To this end, it foregrounds its own methods of construction, and invites the reader to become a participant in the construction of meaning.

While the whodunnit or mystery novel, with its drive towards narrative closure in the solution of the crime, does have certain of the characteristics of the 'readerly' text, it is more difficult to apply this label to the hard-boiled novel. In the hard-boiled novel the private eye achieves only partial understanding or limited and temporary success. Furthermore, the characteristic first-person narrative of the hard-boiled novel is constructed around the divided, fragmented figure of the private eye, resulting in a multivalent text that 'undermines efforts at control and closure' (Willett 1992: 9). In this way, the hard-boiled text can be identified as a 'writerly' text, whose gaps and fissures encourage the reader to enter into the production of meaning. The 'writerly' text, significantly, is usually a modernist one, plural, diffuse, and fragmented, with no determinate meaning (Eagleton 1996: 119).

Scott R. Christianson argues that the fragments of *The Waste Land*, the archetypal modernist text, 'are analogous to the episodes in hardboiled detective fiction', with the 'isolated modern hero sitting before a spectacle of modern chaos and trying to make sense of it all' corresponding to 'the posture of the autonomous and lonely hardboiled detective' (Christianson 1990: 142). The poet's attempts to order experience, mirrored in the actions of the Fisher King and Tiresias in Eliot's poem, also describe the narrative efforts of the hard-boiled private eye. 'Shall I at least set my lands in order?', pleads the Fisher King at the end of *The Waste Land*, drawing a clear link between 'making meaning' and restoring order that is central to the private eye's attempts to restore social order and justice by making sense of the crimes that have disrupted it.

However, in both hard-boiled fiction and modernist literature there are other ways of restoring or maintaining order than merely making sense of its disruption. One method, characteristic of Eliot's poetry, is the containment of the 'other' that threatens the social order, and such a strategy of containment is evident in crime fiction. Crime fiction is characterised by a hope, or an idea, of controlling crime, and this control depends, ultimately, on the containment of the criminal other, through imprisonment, banishment, or death. Crime fiction, however, like Eliot's poetry, is in many ways a revealingly defensive and paranoid genre, and no sub-genre of it more so than hard-boiled detective fiction. Reading the defensiveness of hard-boiled fiction in general, and the private eye in particular, through the lens of the strategy of containment is a rewarding exercise, and makes sense of some of the peculiarities of early hard-boiled texts.

Despite the reality of a large immigrant population, in addition to black migration from rural communities, as Knight notes, 'Chandler's southern California contains very few blacks and no Mexicans at all' (Knight 1988: 79–80). Nor does it contain Asians. Knight elaborates by observing that in the novels 'collective concepts such as class and race are quite absent' (Knight 1988: 80), suggesting a personal, rather than a social, perspective. This personal perspective is focused on the white male figure of Philip Marlowe, and the prioritisation of this perspective in the novels, as Sean McCann comments, often 'reeks of prejudice'. In particular McCann refers to the opening scene of Chandler's second novel, *Farewell, My Lovely* (1940), in which Chandler's use of racial stereotypes confirms his 'reflex racism' (McCann 2000: 160–2).

The opening paragraph of the novel, even as it acknowledges the existence of an immigrant and black migrant population, either denies these inhabitants a presence in the narrative, or hints at Marlowe's racist fear of America being 'overrun' by this population. Marlowe has been hired to find a relief barber called Dimitrios Aleidis, and his search for Aleidis has taken him to 'one of the mixed blocks over on Central Avenue, the blocks that are not yet all negro' (Chandler 1993: 167), and the beleaguered racist tone of the description, in which the block is 'not *yet* all negro' (emphasis added), is later echoed in the description of Florian's bar and its customers. One of the black customers, who is thrown from the bar by Moose Molloy, a white man looking for his lost love Little Velma, is denied a human identity by being described using the neuter pronoun 'it'. According to Marlowe:

> It landed on its hands and knees and made a high keening noise like a cornered rat. It got up slowly, retrieved a hat and stepped back on to the sidewalk. It was a thin, narrow-shouldered brown youth in a lilac-coloured suit and a carnation. It had slick black hair.
>
> (Chandler 1993: 168)

When Marlowe and Molloy enter the bar, what Molloy calls a 'dinge joint' (Chandler 1993: 168), they find themselves in 'the dead alien silence of another race' (Chandler 1993: 170), and William Marling observes that the inhabitants of the Watts neighbourhood in Chandler's novel provide 'an emblem of the inscrutability of black society to the white detective'

(Marling 1986: 98). In contrast, Walter Mosley's *Easy Rawlins* cycle of novels depicts what Chandler chooses to omit in his portrayal of Los Angeles. Mosley's hero, the black private investigator Ezekiel 'Easy' Rawlins, 'is emblematic of the passage of African Americans to Los Angeles during and after World War II' (Muller 1995: 289). He is a returning soldier, eager for work, and like most of the residents in the black Watts community in which he lives, he is a migrant 'from the country around southern Texas and Louisiana' (Mosley 1993: 15).

Chandler's omission of the black community in his depiction of Los Angeles is just one example of the strategy of containment that characterises his fiction. However, it is his depiction of women as the threatening 'other' that also characterises hard-boiled fiction in general, and the figure of the *femme fatale* is the embodiment of this apparent threat. In many ways, the *femme fatale* is the antithesis to the hard-boiled private eye, in that she reverses the normal dialectic of tough surface and sensitive depth that characterises the private eye hero. The emotional, sensitive façade of the *femme fatale*, like Brigid O'Shaughnessy in *The Maltese Falcon*, or virtually every female character in Chandler, disguises a tough, self-serving identity. The *femme fatale* uses her apparent vulnerability by appealing to the private eye's chivalry and code of honour to get close to him and, in this way, when her true nature is revealed she is in a position to threaten him personally. The personal threat posed by women is linked to a more general division between surface and depth in the hard-boiled world, and in this way, it expands to become a more general social threat, resulting in the masculinism and misogyny that are typical of much hard-boiled fiction written by men.

FALLEN ANGELS: APPROPRIATION OF THE HARD-BOILED MODE

While the detective fiction of the Golden Age is dominated by women, with only a few exceptions the majority of the Golden Age detectives are men. Considering the paucity of heroine predecessors, the hard-boiled mode, the most misogynistic of the various sub-genres of crime fiction, would seem to be an unlikely candidate to support a feminist reworking. The hard-boiled novel, however, unlike the Golden Age mystery novel, as a 'writerly' text is permeable and open-ended, and its meanings are not fixed. Its attempts to contain various threatening 'others' ultimately deconstruct it, and the general tendency of hard-boiled fiction to replicate, explore, and even interrogate its own conventions allows the entire sub-genre to be appropriated for a variety of ideological, formal, and generic purposes (Willett 1992: 7). Foremost among the ideological appropri-ations of hard-boiled fiction is the feminist counter-tradition, which began in earnest with P.D. James's *An Unsuitable Job for a Woman* (1972).

While the tone and setting of *An Unsuitable Job for a Woman* are not cast in the same mould as those of the hard-boiled fiction that preceded it, owing more to the country-house setting of classic detective fiction than they do to the mean streets of the American hard-boiled tradition, crucially the central figure in the novel, Cordelia Grey, is a private detective. The title of the novel both questions and, ultimately, endorses the male-dominated world of the private eye novel, although later writers such as Sara Paretsky and Sue Grafton were to take over the formula of the female private eye in more powerful, although not necessarily more successful, ways. Grey is an intriguing figure, literally 'inheriting' the male mantle of private eye from her late employer in the form of the private detective agency he established, and the gun that he taught her to use. A gun, of course, is an obvious metaphor for masculine potency, and it is significant that Grey never fires it, and her reluctance to do so might be read as a reaffirmation of the division between the masculine and feminine spheres of activity suggested by the title of the novel.

Sara Paretsky's V.I. Warshawski and Sue Grafton's Kinsey Millhone, in contrast, are far from reluctant to fire their guns, and Gill Plain has suggested that in Paretsky's case the attempt to mould the hard-boiled mode into a feminist narrative that still pays homage to tough-guy fiction is a project 'riven with contradictions' (Plain 2001: 142). V.I.'s name, as Plain notes, 'is important [. . .] for its calculated androgyny' (Plain 2001: 145), and this is the starting point for a number of revealing similarities to the tough-guy hero. By leaving her husband and putting her career first, she has, like Chandler's Marlowe, situated herself outside of 'the normal family and financial patterns of modern culture' (Knight 1988: 78), although she does have an alternative family structure diverse in age, gender, and ethnicity that consists of her friends, such as Lotty Herschel. Both of her parents, however, we learn in *Indemnity Only* (1982), are dead, further situating her in the sort of familial vacuum typical of the private eye of the period between the wars. Like Marlowe and the Op, V.I. is tough, and endures almost as much physical punishment as, if not more than, she delivers to others. Even the figure of the *femme fatale* has its masculine inversion in the form of what Martin Priestman terms the *homme fatal*: a man 'with whom the heroine has a sexual fling before discovering him to be deeply implicated in the murder she is investigating' (Priestman 1998: 58). In a similar fashion, Plain argues about Paretsky that in many ways, and primarily through her choice of the hard-boiled novel as the vehicle for her contribution to the feminist counter-tradition, she is 'profoundly implicated' in the patriarchal system that she opposes (Plain 2001: 144, and see also Munt 1994: 45).

However, there are other forms of ideological appropriation other than the feminist. Walter Mosley's appropriation of hard-boiled fiction is one based on racial and historical issues, in which Marlowe's xenophobia is inverted and deconstructed to reconstruct the history of black migrant experience in Los Angeles that Chandler's fiction marginalises or omits. The first Easy Rawlins novel, *Devil in a Blue Dress* (1990), appropriates the hard-boiled tradition in a knowing inversion of the opening of Chandler's *Farewell, My Lovely*. In Chandler's novel, Marlowe enters a black bar with Moose Molloy, who is searching for his old sweetheart. In Mosley's novel, a white man, Dewitt Albright, enters a black bar in the black Watts community looking for somebody who can track down a white woman, Daphne Monet, known to associate with the musicians of the Watts nightclub scene that his excessive whiteness (as the name 'Albright' suggests) prevents him from entering. In Mosley's novel, the white perspective of Chandler's fiction is reversed and it is Easy's voice that describes and controls the scene:

> I was surprised to see a white man walk into Joppy's bar. It's not just that he was white but he wore an off-white linen suit and shirt with a Panama straw hat and bone shoes over flashing white silk socks. His skin was smooth and pale with just a few freckles. One lick of strawberry-blond hair escaped the band of his hat.
>
> (Mosley 1992: 9)

Gay and lesbian appropriation of the hard-boiled mode marks another form of the ideological appropriation to which the sub-genre is open, and

Joseph Hansen's private eye fiction has been described as a 'medium-boiled' transitory stage between the heritage of the hard-boiled mode and the various products of its future appropriation (Plain 2001: 97). The overt corporeality of hard-boiled fiction, particularly as it manifested itself in the physical fortitude of the 'tough-guy' hero, is appropriated in Hansen's fiction in order to position the specifically male body at the site of the deconstruction and re-evaluation of various concepts of masculinity. The figure of the middle-aged homosexual insurance investigator Dave Brandstetter, the series detective, offers unique possibilities to examine, and ultimately expose, the myth of white heterosexual family life, although in many ways this is less an appropriation than an extension of the undermining of the notion of the family that is central to the Lew Archer novels of Ross Macdonald.

The male body as object of desire, central to Hansen's fiction, is also a central, if unintended, component of one of the best-known formal appropriations of the hard-boiled mode, *Magnum P.I.* In many ways, to extend Plain's identification of the Brandstetter novels as examples of 'medium-boiled' fiction, it might be more accurate to define *Magnum P.I.* as an example of a 'soft-boiled' mode appropriated from its tougher, more existential ancestor as a more 'appropriate' form for prime-time television. Like other examples of the televisual form, such as *The Rockford Files*, private eye series such as *Magnum* are typically cast in a light-hearted comedy mode, quite at odds with the hard-boiled tradition in general, and with the tough, uncompromising sound of their private eyes' names: Rockford (strong and tough like a rock), and Magnum (big and dangerous like the pistol with the same name). Furthermore, in the case of *Magnum*, there are homoerotic undertones to the name that are reinforced by the various elements that conspire to present the figure of Magnum as the male object of desire. The series is set in Hawaii, and the P.I. lives close to the beach, both of which provide opportunities to present the male physique to the desiring gaze. He drives an open-top sports car (not his own), which again provides the opportunity to display the figure of the actor, Tom Selleck, whose casting in the role reinforces the objectification of the male body.

The presentation of the male body as object of desire in *Magnum P.I.* parallels an increasingly similar presentation of the male body on the big screen. While the cinematic gaze is generally identified as a 'male' gaze, in which the female body is framed and presented as an object to be looked at and desired, there is a growing body of mainstream cinema in which the male body is similarly framed and presented. The *Die Hard* series, featuring the lone police detective John McClane, has many parallels with hard-boiled fiction. The first film, in a conscious acknowledgement of the hard-boiled tradition, is set in Los Angeles, and central to the series is an alienated detective hero characterised by his wisecracking, his antipathy towards the organised forces of law and order such as the Los Angeles Police Department and the FBI, and his physical toughness. It is McClane's physical toughness, clearly alluded to in the titles of the films in the series, that is central to the representation of the male body in the series, which offers 'an image of the male body as raw power and indestructibility' (Jarvis 1997: 227). The clearest example of such framing is towards the end of the first film in the series, *Die Hard* (1988), when McClane confronts the leader of the terrorists who have taken over the Nakatomi building. He appears, stripped to the waist, bloodied and bruised and with a single bullet left in his gun, back-lit by bright arc-lighting that frames his indestructible body in a halo of white light.

Christopher Nolan offers a similar presentation of the male body to the cinematic gaze in his knowing appropriation of the hard-boiled mode in *Memento* (2000). The detective hero of the film, Leonard Shelby, is an insurance investigator. In a break-in to his home, in which his wife is murdered, he is injured, resulting in the loss of his short-term memory. Unable to create new memories, and, therefore, to create the connections between past and present upon which the private eye's solution of the crime depends, Shelby tattoos his body with the information he needs to hunt down his wife's killer. In this way, through various cinematic devices that frame his body, Shelby's body also becomes a text that can be read, emphasising the relationship between detection and reading that is crucial to hard-boiled detective fiction. Furthermore, the narrative is ordered in short sections in reverse chronological order in order to recreate for the viewer the sort of temporal dislocation that the private eye is subject to in general, and which characterises Shelby's existence in particular. In this film, the living body becomes a text requiring decipherment, just as the dead body has traditionally been the catalyst for the narrative movement of detective fiction.

Memento is just one example of how cinema, primarily through the Hollywood tradition of *film noir*, has a long tradition of the adaptation and appropriation of hard-boiled texts. Direct cinematic adaptations of hard-boiled novels range from the novels of Chandler, with Howard Hawks's version of *The Big Sleep* (1946) normally being singled out for special praise, to adaptations of Mosley's *Devil in a Blue Dress* (1995) and Paretsky's *V.I. Warshawski* (1991). Lesser-known adaptations include Alan Parker's *Angel Heart* (1987), an adaptation of William Hjortsberg's *Falling Angel* (1979). Hjortsberg's novel is a hybrid of two genres, the hard-boiled mode and the supernatural fantasy, in which the private eye Johnny Angel is hired by a mysterious client, who turns out to be Satan, to find a man who disappeared twenty years before, and who turns out to have been Johnny Angel himself before he suffered amnesia and reinvented himself. This narrative reversal, in which the detective turns out to be searching for himself, makes explicit the sort of divided identity that often characterises the figure of the private eye, and which manifests itself in the figure of the *alter ego*, as happens most famously in an early crime novel, Stevenson's *The Strange Case of Dr Jekyll and Mr Hyde*.

Other cinematic appropriations of the hard-boiled mode that merit special mention include *Chinatown* (1974), Roman Polanski's homage to the hard-boiled Los Angeles of the 1930s, and Ridley Scott's *Blade Runner* (1982). *Blade Runner*, based on the Philip K. Dick science fiction novel *Do Androids Dream of Electric Sheep?* (1968), is another example of the sort of generic appropriation that the hard-boiled mode is receptive to, in which distinct genres, such as science fiction and the hard-boiled, are drawn together into a coherent whole. In the case of *Blade Runner*, and in the later *Angel Heart*, the generic appropriation is then appropriated still further by being adapted to the screen. The central figure in Scott's film is a bounty-hunter, or blade runner, whose job it is to hunt down renegade androids in the future metropolis of Los Angeles. Despite the huge digital advertising hoardings and the constant rain, the mean streets of *Blade Runner* are the same mean streets that Chandler refers to in his famous description of the detective, and Rick Deckard is the archetypal private eye. He is a tough loner with a gun and a mission who drinks like a suicide who has lost his nerve and is conspicuously bloody-minded towards the forces of law and order for which he works. His voice-over echoes the first-person narrative of much hard-boiled fiction and *film noir*, and the character of Rachel Rosen, who, initially, does not realise that she is an android, is, in the early stages of the film at any rate, an unwitting *femme fatale*.

Other forms have appropriated the characteristics and iconography of the hard-boiled mode, including computer games such as the revealingly entitled *Gabriel Knight* role-playing games, and private eye/supernatural thriller hybrids in the mould of *Angel Heart* such as *Alone in the Dark*, the title of which emphasises the position of the alienated individual in a dark, threatening environment that is generally characteristic of the hard-boiled mode, and whose storyline hinges on the uncovering of the dark past of a mysterious family. Another form that has been remarkably receptive to the ideology and iconography of the hard-boiled mode is the graphic novel, such as Frank Miller's *Sin City* series. As the series title suggests, the *Sin City* stories unfold in a fictionalised Basin City that is characterised, above all else, by crime and violence, and the individual titles in the series are clear indicators of their hard-boiled heritage. *Booze, Broads and Bullets* (1998), in its defiantly politically incorrect use of the word 'broads', is a knowing nod to the tough-guy world and misogynistic dialogue of Chandler and Hammett. *A Dame to Kill For* (1994), whose title echoes the hard-boiled slang of *Booze, Broads and Bullets*, opens with a knowing appropriation of the opening of Polanski's *Chinatown*, and features a private eye called Dwight who appears, in varying degrees, in most of the other titles in the series. In *A Dame to Kill For*, he is seduced into murdering the eponymous dame's wealthy husband, and, once he has served his purpose, she shoots him four times. In a comic book appropriation of tough-guy dialogue, Dwight's right-hand man, named Marv, tells him: 'You're damn lucky all that dame had was a .32 . . . We wouldn't even be having this conversation if she'd used a real gun on you. Even so, getting shot in the face isn't high on my list of how to have a good time.' Dwight survives, and after extensive plastic surgery he returns to exact his revenge, in an ironic reversal of the title, on the 'dame to kill for'.

Another comic book appropriation of the hard-boiled mode is Martin Rowson's *The Waste Land* (1990), a knowing parody of both hard-boiled detective fiction (specifically *The Maltese Falcon*) and T.S. Eliot's *The Waste Land*, in which a Los Angeles private eye called Chris Marlowe, searching for his dead partner's killers, 'is lured into a web of murder, deceit, lust, despair and, coincidentally, a frantic quest for the Holy Grail' (back cover). The case that Marlowe follows neatly dovetails the plot of *The Maltese Falcon* with the thematic concerns and motifs of Eliot's poem, emphasising the previously discussed parallels between modernism and hard-boiled fiction. When Marlowe first appears, he is reading a copy of *The Big Sleep*, with a client in his doorway 'coming in like a mean martini mixed from cold memory and old desire'. The rest of the story parodies both Eliot and the hard-boiled tradition in both words and images, although, significantly, Marlowe's overriding concern, expressed to Eliot in the notes at the end of the story, is 'to know what the hell's been going on!', emphasising the underlying drive of both modernism and the hard-boiled narrative.

Significantly, it is the ease with which the hard-boiled mode is appropriated that has led to the development of two distinct sub-genres in crime fiction, besides the hard-boiled itself. Priestman, following a similar claim by Julian Symons, argues that since the heyday of hard-boiled writing, the genre has split into two strands (Priestman 1990: 177). The first strand is what Priestman usefully terms the 'crime-thriller', the main focus of which is the crime, and the criminal committing it, rather than any appeal to the containment of crime or the solution of a mystery. Early examples include the novels of James M. Cain, which exploit the sort of relationship between crime and passion that Chandler always avoided, and the strand has developed further, and in different directions, in the novels of Patricia Highsmith, Elmore Leonard, and Thomas Harris. The second strand is that of the police procedural, which replaces the individual and self-employed private eye hero with a police team, and whose focus is the functioning of the group as a team. Early examples include the 87th Precinct novels of Ed McBain, but more recent examples are returning to a focus on a single individual, albeit a police detective, that has obvious parallels with the private eye hero. It is to the police procedural, in all its various manifestations, that this study will now turn.

4

THE POLICE PROCEDURAL

'You can't understand. How could you? – with solid pavement under your feet, surrounded by kind neighbours ready to cheer you or to fall on you, stepping delicately between the butcher and the policeman, in the holy terror of scandal and gallows and lunatic asylums.'

(Conrad 1974: 70)

THIN BLUE LINES: FICTION AS IDEOLOGICAL STATE APPARATUS

Another Marlowe, in this case Charlie Marlow, the narrator of Joseph Conrad's *Heart of Darkness* (1902), observes that Western civilisation controls its criminal and asocial impulses only by 'stepping delicately between the butcher and the policeman, in the holy terror of scandal and gallows and lunatic asylums' (Conrad 1974: 70). Marlow's narration of Kurtz's story of moral decay, and his own engagement with it, suggest that it is only the twin regulatory powers of the butcher and the policeman, rather than any inherent restraint or moral sense, which keep 'civilised' man on the straight and narrow. Specifically, the police procedural, as it began to develop in the second half of the twentieth century, foregrounds and is structured around 'a dominant Western symbol of social control: the policeman' (Winston and Mellerski 1992: 2).

The police, in this way, become the focus for the 'holy terror' of social scandal and judicial punishment, and '[b]ecause bourgeois civilisation is characterised by various forms of discipline' it remains civilised only through the fear of punishment articulated by Conrad's Marlow (Winston and Mellerski 1992: 1). Mandel identifies these various forms of discipline, aside from the police and the judiciary system, as being disseminated 'by the hidden hand of market laws, by the iron rules of factory discipline, and by the despotism of the nuclear family, authoritarian schools, and repressive sexual education' (Mandel 1984: 69). Significantly, the discipline they impose, in Mandel's Marxist analysis, tends to be handed down from above. In this way, despite Mandel's suggestion that the mass culture, and by extension crime fiction, is escapist, it is clear that the procedural is as much a part of the ideological state apparatus of control as the thin blue line of the police force is.

Mandel himself perhaps unintentionally suggests such a function of crime fiction when he observes that '[r]eading about violence is an (innocent) form of witnessing, and enjoying, violence – albeit perhaps in a shuddering, shameful and guilt-ridden way' (Mandel 1984: 68). It is this shuddering, shameful, guilt-ridden response to crime fiction that bears out Mandel's point that laws are respected not out of conviction or a belief in them, but simply out of fear of punishment (Mandel 1984: 69). Furthermore, there is a clear parallel here with Frederic Jameson's argument that mass culture, of which the popular market of crime fiction forms a part, can be understood as a means of 'managing', if not controlling, sublimated audience desires (Winston and Mellerski 1992: 1). The police procedural works on its audience 'to diffuse the potential for violent transgression' by foregrounding the police and the wider judiciary system, and in doing so, the procedural becomes, over the course of its development, one of the most effective means of policing a society governed not by morality, but by fear of scandal, fear of punishment, and by fear of its own capacity for criminal and amoral action (Winston and Mellerski 1992: 2).

PRIVATE EYE TO PUBLIC EYE: THE DEVELOPMENT OF THE PROCEDURAL

In its emphasis on regulatory authority and social control, there is a sense in which the lineage of the police procedural stretches back as far as the Old Testament stories from the Book of Daniel, or at least to the *Newgate Calendar* stories, but the more usual critical consensus is to identify Georges Simenon and Émile Gaboriau as its earliest practitioners. Gaboriau's hero, Monsieur Lecoq, as the similarity between the surnames suggests, is based on the figure of François Eugène Vidocq, first head of the Parisian Sûreté, and his novels, particularly the earlier *L'Affair Lerouge* (1866), are often identified as proto-procedurals. Symons says of Gaboriau's crime stories that 'they are rooted in sound knowledge of police procedure' (Symons 1993: 55), but there are faults to be found with his identification as the first proceduralist. Like Wilkie Collins, Gaboriau's crime stories are at times strait-jacketed by the conventions of the sensationalist novel, and Knight states that they are 'basically sensational crime adventures with a little police work' (Knight 2004: 48). His influence on Collins, however, was significant, and he paved the way for further developments of the procedural, with the baton next being taken up by another French-speaking author, the Belgian Georges Simenon.

Simenon's Inspecteur Maigret is a policeman, but there is little interest in police procedure and cooperation in the Maigret novels. More than this, however, and despite Ian Rankin's suggestion that Maigret was the first procedural police detective (Rankin 1998: 9), it is Maigret's excessively individualistic heroism, like that of Lecoq before him, that Knight sees as the most troubling impediment to such an identification (Knight 2004: 160). Crucially, it is the individualism of Maigret, like that of the hard-boiled private investigator, which disqualifies them from the ranks of the procedural in most critical studies of the sub-genre, in this way stressing the importance of *collective* and cooperative police agency to the procedural.

For this reason, and others, the first police procedural is generally acknowledged as being Hillary Waugh's *Last Seen Wearing . . .* (1952). Its dialogue, its attention to the details of police procedure, and the uncertain success of the final resolution of the crime establish a pattern which, according to Knight, is characteristic of subsequent examples of the sub-genre, however uncharacteristic its predominantly rural setting might be (Knight 2004: 154). While urban settings are generally considered more typical of the procedural, primarily due to its debt to realism and to the urban environment of hard-boiled fiction, later procedurals such as Tony Hillerman's Joe Leaphorn and Jim Chee novels, set on the Navajo reservation that straddles the states of Arizona, Colorado, New Mexico, and Utah, mark a commitment to rural settings that is absent throughout much of the development of the sub-genre. The process of this development includes the novels of John Creasey (writing as J.J. Marric) featuring Commander George Gideon, which introduced into the developing sub-genre the 'multiple focus of characters and crimes' that Knight considers to be the basis of the procedural (Knight 2004: 155).

In America, the procedural proper is acknowledged as starting in the late 1950s and in the 1960s with Ed McBain's 87th Precinct novels, which draw together the various separate developments of the sub-genre into a cohesive whole. Significantly, McBain both identifies with, and distances himself from, the hard-boiled tradition in various ways that will be discussed later, and the title of the first 87th Precinct novel, *Cop Hater* (1956), is an example of this, commenting in passing, as it does, on the condescending attitude to the police that characterises crime fiction in general, from Conan Doyle to Agatha Christie, and from Poe, significantly, to Chandler (Knight 2004: 153). Crucially, however, in relation to a consideration of the early development of the sub-genre, the opening of *Cop Hater* emphasises, among other things, a concern with vision and perception that is also central to hard-boiled fiction: 'From the river bounding the city on the north, you saw only the magnificent skyline. You stared up at it in something like awe, and sometimes you caught your breath because the view was one of majestic splendour' (McBain 2003: 1). Furthermore, the use of the second-person 'you' implicates the reader in the pan-urban surveillance that the 87th Precinct novels portray.

The social monitoring and control of the police procedural is a wider-reaching form of that which is evident, on a smaller scale, in the hard-boiled tradition and, to some extent, the fiction of the Golden Age. In the hard-boiled tradition it is the individual private eye who safeguards society and attempts to restore the order disrupted by criminal activity, and it is this relationship between the individual detective and society at large, crystallised through the matrix of criminality, that finds its sharpest focus in the police procedural. In the procedural, it is the police detective as part of the state apparatus of the police force who safeguards society through vigilant and unceasing surveillance, in this way replacing the often questionable vigilante justice of the PI. The transition from hard-boiled fiction to police procedural is, therefore, a transition from the *private* eye, in the sense of personal, small-scale, and often self-serving investigation, to the *public* eye, in the sense of civic, large-scale policing that serves society as a whole. It is a transition whose process is evident in the Pinkerton National Detective Agency, founded in 1850, for whom Dashiell Hammett worked and which served as the model for the Continental Detective Agency he created in his fiction.

Specifically, it is the Pinkerton symbol of the open eye and the motto 'We Never Sleep' that consolidate the notion of unceasing surveillance, and its relationship with social discipline (Messent 1997: 10). Foucault identifies such a relationship in Bentham's Panopticon, whose prefix 'pan-', meaning 'all', or 'referring to a whole', and root-word 'optic', meaning 'of the eye or sight', emphasise the notion of general, universal surveillance which in Foucault's view is the sign of a 'disciplinary' society (Foucault 1991: 209). The police procedural, in this way, becomes a sort of textual Panopticon, and the transition to the police procedural, as a mechanism of such a disciplinary society, is significant. The frequency of the serial form in the procedural, furthermore, is suggestive of its place in the larger machine of indefinite, unceasing surveillance and discipline (Winston and Mellerski 1992: 8). The increasing frequency of Internal Affairs investigations in the police procedural, such as Ian Rankin's *Resurrection Men* (2001), furthermore, is an echo of Miss Marple's self-surveillance, and emphasises the perceived need for Panoptical discipline at every level of society, including within the police, by asking the question '*Quis custodiet ipsos custodes?*' or 'Who watches the watchmen?'

However, what is perhaps most significant about the transition from hard-boiled fiction to police procedural is that the majority of criticism identifies it simultaneously as a more general transition to realism, echoing Chandler's identification of the transition from the clue-puzzle form to hard-boiled fiction in the same terms. Knight, for example, contends that the transition to the procedural arose from a 'pressure for greater verisimilitude' (Knight 1980: 169), and in this he is echoed by Priestman, who questions the credibility of major crimes being solved by single individuals, be they part of the police force or not (Priestman 1998: 32). In a similar vein, Peter Messent argues that the development of the police procedural 'has been prompted by a recognition that the marginal position and limited perspective of the PI hero or heroine makes for an ineffectual, and even irrelevant, figure as far as the representation of criminal activity and its containment goes' (Messent 1997: 2).

However, despite the almost unanimous criticism of the improbability of the lone PI investigating murders, and the accompanying emphasis on his or her marginality within the broader social process of containing and controlling crime, the police procedural frequently features as its 'central' characters police detectives who occupy similarly 'marginal' positions to the lone PI of hard-boiled fiction. Ian Rankin's John Rebus, for example, is an unorthodox, anti-authoritarian, alcoholic divorcee police detective, while James Lee Burke's Dave Robicheaux is a similarly marginalised alcoholic whose methods are as unorthodox as those of Rankin's Rebus. Both of them conform more to the hard-boiled model of the rule-bending individualist than they do to the idea of police officer working as part of a team. Tony Hillerman's Navajo Tribal Police officers Joe Leaphorn and Jim Chee, in various ways, fall between the white (*Belacani*) world of pickup trucks, short-wave radios, and police procedure, and the Navajo (*Dinee*) world of ritual and folklore, as well as poverty, alcoholism, and white racism (Willett 1992: 48–9). In this way, they are doubly marginalised: 'white but not quite', as Homi Bhabha identifies the situation (Bhabha 1994: 86), which Chee echoes in *The Ghostway* (1984) when he dourly says of his own identity that 'Halfway was worse than either way' (Hillerman 1992: 10).

Hillerman's police procedurals, specifically his Navajo Tribal Police procedurals, are just one example of how the apparent limits of the 'white, heterosexual, male' perspective of hard-boiled fiction in America are challenged through the police procedural (Ogdon 1992: 84). The various racial, ethnic, and gendered appropriations of the procedural, which will be discussed in detail later in this chapter, are further testimony of the increasing trend towards realism that characterises the procedural. In Britain, by the end of the 1960s the influence of realist crime fiction from America and from television led to the appropriation of the clue-puzzle form by writers such as P.D. James and Ruth Rendell, and later by writers such as Colin Dexter. While there are certain differences between the American and British procedurals, there are also marked similarities, and it is the characteristics common to both traditions that have come to distinguish the sub-genre of the police procedural.

TEXTUAL INVESTIGATIONS: CHARACTERISTICS OF THE PROCEDURAL

The police procedural, on both sides of the Atlantic, is a type of fiction in which the actual methods and procedures of police work are central to the structure, themes, and action. Even such a common-sense definition, however, with its emphasis on the 'actual' methods of police work, reveals the significance of the move towards realism that is central to the development of the sub-genre. Realism, in this way, can be understood to be the foundation not only of the detective's investigative process, but also of the themes, characters, action, and setting. Upon such an appeal to realism, one of the earliest commentators on the sub-genre, George N. Dove, defines the procedural according to two criteria; 'First, to be called a procedural, a novel must be a mystery story; and second, it must be one in which the mystery is solved by policemen using normal police routines' (Dove 1982: 47). Dove's definition is an acknowledgement both of the debt of the procedural to the clue-puzzle, or 'mystery', form, and of the realist foundation of the sub-genre implied in the identification of 'normal' police procedure.

In the British procedural, Priestman suggests that appropriation of the clue-puzzle form is more evident, despite its emphasis on the appeal of down-to-earth, hard-working police detectives, rather than the individualism of the Golden Age detective, often characterised by his eccentricity, his outsider status, or his upper-class origins (Priestman 1998: 26). The whodunnit foundation of the British procedural, in Priestman's analysis, is clear to see in the various substitutes for the elements of what constituted the notion of 'upper-class' before the Second World War (Priestman 1998: 26). One of these substitutes is culture, and just as the cultural distancing from the masses of P.D. James's Superintendent Adam Dalgliesh is indicated by the fact that he is a published poet, the police detective Kate Miskin who works with Dalgliesh in *A Taste for Death* (1986) is a painter, and Colin Dexter's Inspector Morse achieves this cultural distancing through his love of classical music and opera. The

Italian series hero of Michael Dibdin's procedural novels, Aurelio Zen, who is an investigator for the Criminalpol section of the Italian Ministry of the Interior, is identified as 'cultured' for an Anglophone reader simply by virtue of his 'Italianness', as signified through his fine clothes, his espresso drinking, and his baffled disdain for the advance of mass culture in contemporary Italy. Ironically, as a Venetian, Zen is subtly alienated by 'native' Italians, and this alienation is further emphasised by his parallels with Rankin's Rebus and Burke's Robicheaux as rule-bending individuals rather than conformist team-players.

Perhaps more significant for this study is Priestman's insightful identification of a shift in setting from the whodunnit of the Golden Age to the police procedural of welfare-state Britain, particularly in James's fiction (Priestman 1998: 26). In James's fiction, the settings are often the semi-public workplaces of an increasingly urban society, as befits the public face of the police that forms their centre, rather than the stately homes and bucolic village communities of the Golden Age. Significantly, however, many of these semi-public spaces, such as the training hospital in *Shroud for a Nightingale* (1971) and the publishing house in *Original Sin* (1995), are converted from the stately homes that often form the setting for the Golden Age whodunnit (Priestman 1998: 26). In *The Pale Criminal* (1990), Philip Kerr identifies a similar conversion process in Germany during the Third Reich, identifying how the building that houses the headquarters of the Nazi Security Service, for example, was once 'the summer house of the first Friedrich Wilhelm' (Kerr 1993: 303). The clumsy architectural conversions in James's fiction parallel, if not in quality then at least in kind, the appropriation of the whodunnit by the police procedural in Britain in the latter half of the twentieth century.

Setting, as Priestman's analysis demonstrates, is central to the police procedural, although it is sometimes portrayed and explored in different ways on either side of the Atlantic. In the British procedural, the focus on a relatively localised beat during its development is still echoed in contemporary procedurals. Kingsmarkham is the beat of Ruth Rendell's Inspector Wexford, while the larger Oxford and Edinburgh are the stomping grounds of Dexter's Morse and Rankin's Rebus, respectively. The change is not just one of a shift to larger urban centres, however. Rankin, for example, characteristically juxtaposes the 'hidden' face of under-privileged Edinburgh with the 'public' face of the city. In *Mortal Causes* (1994), he paints a grim picture of Pilmuir's Garibaldi Estate, a decaying high-rise scheme characterised by poverty, unemployment, and gang warfare, which Rebus describes as 'the roughest scheme in the city, maybe the country' (Rankin 2002: 18). Rebus's investigations draw him from the Gar-B, as it is nicknamed, to the touristic face of the Edinburgh Festival, the Castle, the Royal Mile, and Prince's Street Gardens, in this way emphasising the sharp social and economic divides of modern Britain.

The localised beats of the British procedural, from real or fictional small-town Britain to the contemporary reality of large urban centres, are an element of the realism of the procedural, in particular in the portrayal of crime as an everyday occurrence arising from the tensions of modern life. In America, the idea of a localised beat is suggested in the series title of McBain's 87th Precinct novels, in which the policing of large urban centres is divided between distinct precincts, mirroring a larger national concern in the United States with federal and state jurisdiction. McBain's 87th Precinct is a precinct in the fictional city of Isola, whose name neatly evokes the sense of isolation and alienation that is characteristic of modern urban life. Furthermore, with New York as its obvious model, the fictional Isola becomes a symbol of the contemporary metropolis in general, and the contemporary American metropolis in particular (Knight 2004: 156). This conflation of particularised localism and generalised universalism in the American procedural is also evident in the novels of Tony Hillerman. While at first the sheer size of the Najavo reservation seems to contradict the idea of a 'localised beat', covering as it does approximately 28,000 square miles and straddling four states, the sense of an extended community bound by shared beliefs and familial ties localises Joe Leaphorn's and Jim Chee's beat not in a spatial sense, but rather in a social and cultural sense.

The urban realism of the procedural is central to its commitment to social, structural, and thematic realism. The characteristic use of third-person narration in the procedural demonstrates this commitment at a narrative level, with the appearance of objectivity that the third-person narration creates distancing the procedural from the first-person narratives of hard-boiled fiction, in which the often alienated subjectivity of the PI hero is central to its structure, ideology, and success. The stress on the methods and procedures of police investigations that characterises the police procedural is another example of this commitment to realism, as is the celebration of teamwork. Central to the development of Rankin's John Rebus novels, for example, is the growth of a team of police officers who both function collectively to solve crime, and serve as a foil for Rebus's rule-bending and intuitive investigations. The character of Siobhan Clarke, often sourly identified by her superiors as 'another John Rebus', mediates between the twin poles of collective and individual agency, as well as allowing for an examination of the position of women in the workplace.

Characteristic of the 87th Precinct novels is a substantial police team which, unlike Rebus's 'tartan noir' novels, as they have been called, is representative of the multicultural nature of the modern American city. Steve Carella, the obvious leader of the team, is of Italian origin, while the titular Chief is of Irish stock, perhaps emphasising the Irish-American contingent of New York law enforcement, itself reflected in the pseudonym 'McBain'. Characters on the team representative of Jewish, African-American, and German origins and identities are also represented, although Hispanic police characters do not feature until later in the series, and women in general are poorly represented (Knight 2004: 156). Steve Carella's wife, Teddy, for example, is significantly deaf and dumb, and both her inability to speak and the fact that her name robs her of human subjectivity by reducing her to the status of a toy provide a focus for exposing the patriarchal ideology often associated with police forces.

The numerous members of the 87th Precinct team allow several plot lines to unfold at the same time, with different pairings of detectives investigating different crimes. The contribution to the realistic effect that such multiple plot lines create is significant, allowing for a balance of successes and failures in which not all the crimes investigated are actually solved (Priestman 1990: 177). However, it is ironic that multiple plot lines also form the foundation of the increasingly common procedural device of employing converging plot lines as a means of reaching narrative closure. Furthermore, the variety of individual characters in the team of police officers is significant for the sub-genre as a whole. It is the skills that they bring to the team as individuals which allow the team to work collectively to investigate crime, and, furthermore, it is this individualism which gives a face to collective police agency in the procedural, which 'mediates the public's fears of an overextended and inhumane police power' (Winston and Mellerski 1992: 6). It is also an example of the oscillation between the private and the collective that is evident in other areas of the procedural, such as the setting and the frequent alienation or marginalisation of central characters within the team in general.

This view of the procedural as a 'celebration' of teamwork, however, overlooks those characters who are clearly not 'team players'. Rankin's John Rebus is a loner who frequently withholds information regarding cases from his fellow officers, follows individual 'hunches' which are rarely shared with, or explained to, the other members of the investigating team, lives, and often drinks, alone, and rarely plays by the same rules as the police officers around him. In many ways, he parallels Nicholas Freeling's character Van de Valk and his frequent 'vacillations between unofficial and official methods of enquiry' (Winston and Mellerski 1992: 12), as, for example, in *The Falls* (2001), when he returns drunk, late at night, to the apartment of the missing Philippa Balfour. While he is there, Philippa's father arrives at the apartment, and his query as to what Rebus is doing there prompts a response that perfectly encapsulates Rebus's often vague, intuitive, and subjective investigative methods: 'He looked around. "Just wanted to . . . well, I suppose I . . ." But he couldn't find the words' (Rankin 2002: 16).

Often, however, it is not words, but actions, that emphasise the 'vacillations between unofficial and official methods of enquiry' in the police procedural. James Lee Burke's Dave Robicheaux, like Rankin's Rebus, is an alcoholic whose struggles with the bottle, and his own demons, are important themes. Like Rankin's portrayal of the two faces of Edinburgh, Burke portrays the conflict between the personal and the private in his juxtaposition of the New Orleans that is presented to tourists and the harsher realities of the bayou and rural Louisiana. Like Rebus, Robicheaux's methods are at times irregular. In *Purple Cane Road* (2000), he undertakes an unofficial investigation to unearth the long-hidden truth about his mother's death, teaming up with an ex-homicide officer turned PI, Clete Purcel, and at one point pushing a gun into a suspect's face in order to force information out of him. Robicheaux's partnership with the private investigator Purcel is significant, emphasising as it does the American procedural's use of hard-boiled themes and devices, such as the personal involvement of the detective. Robicheaux's personal involvement, although pronounced in *Purple Cane Road*, is by no means unusual in the series, and is clearly evident in many contemporary American procedurals.

In Patricia Cornwell's *Postmortem* (1990), for example, the close identi-fication between the series heroine Kay Scarpetta, Chief Medical Examiner for Richmond, Virginia, and one of the victims, Lori Peterson, is typical of hard-boiled fiction. Scarpetta's niece reinforces the parallels when she says of the victim, "'She was a doctor, Auntie Kay [. . . .] You're a doctor, too. She was just like you, then'" (Cornwell 2001: 47), and the improbability of such repeated personal involvement within the 'realistic' framework of the procedural serves to point out the limits of the sub-genre as a whole (Symons 1993: 232).

The hard-boiled legacy is clear to see in the marginal and alienated detectives of the procedural, such as Rebus, Robicheaux, Zen, Leaphorn, and Chee. Their marginal status, however, does not prevent them from serving the interests of the dominant social order, even when they are painfully aware of how repressive and unjust the order whose interests they serve can actually be (Messent 1997: 8). Michael Dibdin, for example, within the structure of the procedural, adds a deeper level of social criticism within which his detective Aurelio is tangentially included. In the Zen novels, plots unfold in locations across Italy from Rome (*Cabal* (1992)), to Naples (*Cosí Fan Tutti* (1996)), Sicily (*Blood Rain* (1999)), Sardinia (*Vendetta* (1990)), Perugia (*Ratking* (1988)), Tuscany (*And Then You Die* (2002)), Piedmont (*A Long Finish* (1998)), Venice (*Dead Lagoon* (1994)), and Verona (*Medusa* (2003)), according to where politics and intrigue deposit Zen. It is precisely this world of Machiavellian back-stage manoeu-vring and political (and sometimes actual) backstabbing that is ultimately to blame, either directly or indirectly, for the crimes that Zen investigates. Zen, however, is often as guilty of doctoring evidence, concealing infor-mation, and rubber-stamping 'official' verdicts to protect himself as those that he investigates are. Dibdin's Italian setting is significant here, as it clearly draws on the image of Italy formed by early-modern revenge tragedy as a place of corruption, betrayal, and Machiavellian conspiracy.

In an entirely different setting, and in different ways, Ian Rankin also emphasises how even an anti-authoritarian loner like John Rebus ulti-mately serves the interests of the dominant social and political order. *Set in Darkness* (2000) takes place just as Edinburgh is preparing to house the first Scottish Parliament in almost three hundred years, but the process is threatened by the murder of a Member of the Scottish Parliament. Rebus's investigations, in this way, serve not only to restore the social order disrupted by the crime of murder, but also to maintain Scottish political stability and credibility. Philip Kerr's historical hard-boiled novels echo the processes evident in Dibdin and Rankin in a more disturbing way, taking place as they do in Germany under the Third Reich. In the second of the three novels, *The Pale Criminal*, Kerr's series detective Bernhard Gunther is reinstated as a Kriminalkommissar in Kripo (the Berlin Kriminal Polizei) in order to find a serial killer who is murdering teenage girls who all conform to the blonde Aryan stereotype. In this way, the hard-boiled mode is transformed into a procedural of sorts, and it is the forces of National Socialist law and order, of which in this novel Gunther is effectively a part, that are behind the murders that he is investigating. He discovers that the murders are an attempt by a division in the SS to stir up anti-Semite aggression in order to start a pogrom, and despite the fact that he solves the case, the pogrom still occurs. At the close of the novel, Gunther walks through a city that is being torn apart, broken by the realisation of his own part in the political regime responsible for the destruction, despite the image he has of himself as an opponent of the Nazi regime: 'Further on, at the corner of Kurfürstendamm, I came across an enormous mirror that lay in a hundred pieces, presenting images of myself that ground and cracked underfoot as I picked my way along the street' (Kerr 1993: 519).

Kerr's novels, and Dibdin's and Rankin's as outlined above, in this way oscillate between the public and the private, combining outward social plausibility with an emphasis on inner human subjectivity. Crime in the procedural, but particularly in the American procedural, happens to ordinary people, and although plots are often based on personal crises, it is the inherent realism of the sub-genre of which this is a part that makes it the ideal vehicle for interrogating both the social order and the structures that support it. While the lone operator of hard-boiled fiction characteristically interrogates the social order, he or she can barely make a dent in its structures. The procedural, significantly, while it directly interrogates the social order, also has the capacity to finally affect it in noticeable, if not meaningful, ways. As an extension of this point, Knight suggests that the procedural 'implies an audience and a set of writers who can, at last, trust the police – or some of them – to be credible operatives against crime' (Knight 2004: 161).

SOCIAL PLACEBO: THE MAGIC BULLET OF PROCEDURAL REASSURANCE

Through a project of realism that presents the police as 'credible operatives against crime', the police procedural becomes a powerful weapon of reassurance in the arsenal of the dominant social order. The discipline and cooperation of the police force, it is implied, is just one part of a more general social discipline and cooperation whose aim is to identify and eradicate the threat of social disruption that crime represents. Unlike the easily contained, and, therefore, easily managed, criminal threat within a closed circle of suspects that is characteristic of Golden Age fiction, the criminal threat in the police procedural is just one person among the population at large. What the procedural offers, however, in all its variant forms from the forensic pathologist novel to the psychological profiler novel, is the reassurance that 'even the anonymity of the city offers no shelter' (Priestman 1998: 32) from the forces of law and order, and that organised and cooperative police procedure will always contain the threat.

Patricia Cornwell's *Postmortem* underlines the social need for reassurance by describing the rising panic, particularly among the single, career women who fit the serial killer's victim profile, caused by irresponsible media coverage of the investigations, which Scarpetta observes sourly 'went far beyond serving the useful purpose of warning the city's citizens' (Cornwell 2001: 7). When the sister of Abby Turnbull, the lead journalist in the coverage of the killings, herself becomes a victim, Abby cooperates with Scarpetta, effectively becoming part of the team that ultimately succeeds in apprehending the killer, and in this way emphasising the power of collective agency. However, it is another member of the team, the police sergeant Pete Marino, who delivers the final 'magic bullet' of social reassurance – or, more accurately, the *four* magic bullets from his .357 revolver – by shooting the killer 'dead as dog food' (Cornwell 2001: 388) as he is attempting to add Scarpetta to his list of victims. Scarpetta, too, plays her own part by leaving the killer's body where it falls, without checking for a pulse or attempting to stop the bleeding, although the extent of her complicity in his death is left uncertain, as Marino claims that the killer was dead before he hit the floor.

The final and violent expulsion of the threat to social order in *Postmortem* is a salve for the insidious nature of the threat that the killer poses in the novel. While he is not a policeman, he still works for the police as a communications officer, answering emergency calls that ironically enable him to identify potential victims. The line between the criminal and the police is further blurred when Scarpetta realises during the course of the investigation that Pete Marino himself fits the profile of the killer, and by blurring this thin blue line to include police officers as possible suspects, the identification of the entire society as possible suspects is complete. It is a possibility acknowledged in various procedurals in which Internal Affairs investigations are depicted, such as Rankin's *Resurrection Men*, in which Rebus is sent to the Scottish Police College for 'retraining' as a cover for him to investigate the suspected corrupt activities of a group of police officers. Such narratives are an example of how the procedural does not always conclude with the restoration of order, a return to the status quo, and a vindication of the methods employed in getting there.

The blurring of the thin blue line in this way creates disturbing grey areas in the portrait of an ordered and orderly society, and as a response various developments in the procedural reinstate the clarity and certainty of an idealised black and white world in which realistic shades of grey are erased. While images of corruption and infection typically characterise hard-boiled fiction, images of monstrosity have become central to the police procedural (Messent 1997: 16). The reduction of criminality – specifically, murderous tendencies – to a pure and inexplicable monstrosity, as occurs in the figure of Hannibal Lecter in Thomas Harris's *The Silence of the Lambs* (1989), in James Patterson's *Kiss The Girls* (1995), and of course in Cornwell's *Postmortem*, has two important effects. First, it isolates such criminal and murderous instincts 'from all social, political, or economic causes' (Messent 1997: 16), exonerating the social order of all responsibility regarding its 'deviant' citizens. Secondly, it returns to the clarity of black and white distinctions in which evil, unlike the unsettling abject 'other' of Julia Kristeva's theory (Kristeva 1982), with its distinctly uncertain boundaries, is a pure 'other' that is uncomplicatedly monstrous and inhuman. *Postmortem* reinforces this *reductio ad absurdum* in an exchange between Scarpetta and her niece Lucy, to whom she explains that '"There are some people who are evil"', underlining the 'animalistic' nature of the killer by significantly linking him to Marino's reduction of him to a corpse as 'dead as dog food' by continuing: '"Like dogs, Lucy.

Some dogs bite people for no reason. There's something wrong with them. They're bad and will always be bad"' (Cornwell 2001: 49).

The device of reducing the killer to something purely evil or animalistic restores an ideal status quo, and is a corresponding validation of the social order that is specifically not responsible for social aberration. Although this device is common in the procedural, the relationship between the dominant social order and the individual detective as part of a team that is a microcosm of that social order can also be used to interrogate, and even challenge, dominant values, structures, and stereotypes – in short, the dominant ideology (Messent 1997: 17). Examples of such interrogatory procedurals include those from, or describing, different cultures, such as Dibdin's Zen novels. Procedurals interrogating the dominant social order from racial and ethnic perspectives include the novels of Chester Himes and Tony Hillerman, while various feminist appropriations of the sub-genre also importantly interrogate the position of women within the predominantly white, male, heterosexual world of the procedural that is the legacy of hard-boiled fiction.

ARRESTED DEVELOPMENTS: APPROPRIATIONS OF THE PROCEDURAL

The most significant point to emerge from contemporary criticism of crime fiction is an acknowledgement of the *variety* of modern crime fiction and, more importantly, a realisation of the flexibility of its 'generic boundaries' (Messent 1997: 1). Perhaps the most obvious development is to focus on characters other than police officers and detectives who are still essential members of an investigative team, such as forensic pathologists, psychological profilers, and forensic scientists and crime-scene investigators. Many of these figures are embodiments of post-industrial, information-age responses to crime, and therefore offer reassurance that developments in science, technology, and medicine are more than adequate to contain and control even post-industrial, information-age criminal activity.

The forensic pathologist procedural is a popular variant of the police procedural, and the novels of authors such as Patricia Cornwell and Kathy Reichs are examples of the way in which the contemporary procedural uses the procedures and devices of the whodunnit, such as the idea of the corpse-as-signifier, in order to identify the criminal and restore social order.

In this sense the forensic procedural is a reinvention of both the police procedural *and* the Golden Age clue-puzzle, and in this way overlaps with the forensic science procedural. The crime-scene analysts and scientists of the forensic science procedural broaden the scope of the signifying field beyond the corpse to consider the crime scene as a whole, and success depends on both science and the procedures of police investigation. In *C.S.I.*, a televisual development of the forensic science procedural, the use of fingerprinting, DNA profiling, ballistics, scanning electron microscopy, blood splatter patterns, forensic entomology, post-mortems, shoe- and tyre-treads, psychological profiling, and more, as well as police and FBI records and computer databases, emphasises the importance of following strict procedures in investigating crime. Furthermore, at every turn it is the importance of the collective cooperation of the *C.S.I.* team that is underlined.

The position of Kay Scarpetta, Patricia Cornwell's series hero, is a clear indication of the roots that the series has in the police procedural. Although Scarpetta is a forensic pathologist, and not a police officer, she both works with, and uses the resources of, both the local police of Richmond, Virginia and the FBI. Quite apart from clearly being a member of a larger team that also includes Police Sergeant Pete Marino and FBI profiler Benton Wesley, her investigative methods *depend* on her official status as Chief Medical Examiner, which gives her access to, among other things, local and federal databases.

Another member of the investigative team, increasingly featuring as the focus of procedural novels, and represented by the character of Benton Wesley in Cornwell's Scarpetta novels, is the psychological profiler. Psychological profiling is a technique that involves analysing details about a crime, including specific scene-of-crime details, in order to build up a 'psychological profile' of the criminal in an attempt to narrow the field of suspects. Profiling is used primarily in serial-killer investigations, and can provide indications as to the approximate age of the killer, their gender and sexual orientation, their physical characteristics, their occupation, education, marital situation, and general personality, as well as the reasons why they kill, and why they kill in the way that they do. Most usefully for the procedural, particularly for narrative reasons, profiling can also provide some idea about the killer's likely future actions, and this allows the investigating team to anticipate the killer's actions in order to intercept, and ultimately apprehend, her or (usually) him. In *Postmortem*, the psychological profiler is an FBI agent, while in the novels of Val McDermid it is Dr Tony Hill, who in *The Wire in the Blood* (1997) is the head of a National Profiling Task Force, emphasising the importance of the profiler in modern police procedure. In Thomas Harris's *Silence of the Lambs*, which will be discussed later, the profiler is another doctor, but in this case it is the serial killer Dr Hannibal Lecter, whose name, roughly translating as the verb 'to read', but also implying a person who undertakes the action of reading, is a metaphorical description of what Lecter does.

Frequently, these developments go hand in hand with various appropriations of the sub-genre dealing with issues of gender, race, and ethnicity. James Patterson's procedural series, featuring the black police officer and psychological profiler Alex Cross, is a case in point, and it is the very flexibility of the procedural that allows it to be appropriated in these ways. However, the dearth of female police officers, particularly in comparison to the sheer number of feminist appropriations of hard-boiled fiction, such as in the novels of Sara Paretsky, Sue Grafton, and Liza Cody, suggests a certain resistance in the police procedural 'to female, and particularly feminist, revision' (Reddy 1988: 73). Although female police officers appear in various procedurals, such as Siobhan Clarke and Gill Templer in Rankin's Rebus novels, and they are promoted through the ranks as the series develops, there are few police procedurals written by women that actually interrogate the position of women, rather than tacitly accepting it by 'becoming one of the guys' in order to succeed in the still largely male world of law enforcement (Reddy 1988: 70, 72).

There are, and there should be, certain gender issues associated with placing women within the hierarchical and traditionally masculine world of the police, and Patricia Cornwell's Scarpetta novels investigate these issues in different ways. The less obvious way is by paralleling the victimisation of women in the workplace – and particularly the traditionally masculine workplace – with the more obvious and fatal victimisation of women by a serial killer who is specifically a man murdering women for sexual reasons (Priestman 1998: 32). Scarpetta's realisation that Sergeant Marino fits the killer's profile is therefore doubly significant, as it highlights the fact that he chauvinistically victimises and belittles Scarpetta throughout the course of the series simply for being a woman, although his attitude does improve with time. The killer's occupation as a communications officer for the police, in a similar way, disturbingly parallels his hidden identity as a serial-killing victimiser of women, emphasising the sexism of patriarchy still further.

The more obvious, but no less effective, way of investigating the position of women in the workplace is the way in which the procedural presents and examines the notion of social validation through work in a way that hard-boiled fiction, with its emphasis on a lone operator, cannot (Priestman 1998: 32). What is particular about the world of the procedural is that it is a *social* world, both in terms of the broader picture of concerning itself more obviously than Golden Age or hard-boiled fiction with the social concerns of modern urban life, and in terms of its focus on the way that a team of individuals, separated by age, experience, gender, race, and ethnicity, work collectively to restore and maintain social order. The notion of social, and also personal, validation through work is evident in James's *A Taste for Death*, in which Kate Miskin says of her time working for James's series hero Adam Dalgliesh that "'I've learnt a lot'" (James 1987: 494). According to Maureen T. Reddy, Kate 'has learned about investigative techniques, but also and more importantly about her job's meaning to her, her life, her past, and her self' (Reddy 1988: 85), and in this she echoes Charlie Marlow in *Heart of Darkness* when he says 'I like what is in the work, – the chance to find yourself' (Conrad 1974: 41).

It is this opportunity to 'find yourself' in the teamwork of police procedure that opens the procedural to racial and ethnic interrogation. The novels of Tony Hillerman, for example, feature two officers in the Navajo Tribal Police, Lieutenant Joe Leaphorn and Officer Jim Chee. As an Anglo writing about Native Americans, Hillerman's position is a difficult one to defend, and to his credit he avoids the pitfall of 'turning the Navajo characters into mysterious "others" or versions of noble savage of Vanishing American' (Murray 1997: 135). He generally avoids, for example, despite the obvious opportunity, mapping onto his Navajo detectives the concept of the detective as literal hunter or tracker following the criminal's footprints. As their university degrees in anthropology suggest, Leaphorn and Chee are involved in a process of reading social and cultural signs, and their knowledge of Navajo culture, society, and beliefs is as important an element in their investigations as their knowledge of, and adherence to, *Belacani* police procedure. As Navajos, of course, this process becomes self-reflexive, and during the course of their investigations they learn as much about themselves, and their place in Navajo society, as they do about the crime they are investigating. Like Charlie Marlow, it is in the work that they find themselves.

Achieving self-knowledge, however, comes at a price, and frequently Leaphorn and Chee are forced to 'professionally uphold laws unrelated to, or in conflict with, Navajo sensibility and culture' (Willett 1992: 48). They are cross-cultural figures, frequently trapped with one foot in the *Belacani* world and the other in the *Dinee* world, and in this they resemble those other marginalised figures who feature in appropriations of the procedural: black police officers like Alex Cross in the white world of American law enforcement; lesbian police officers, like Katherine V. Forrest's Kate Delafield, in the heterosexual world of law enforcement; and female detectives, like the pathologist Kay Scarpetta, in the masculine world of law enforcement. All of these characters, and others, serve to expose the dominant ideology of white heterosexual masculinity through a textual hijacking of one of its principal vehicles: crime fiction.

5

THE CRIME THRILLER

O my greatest sin lay in my blood.
Now my blood pays for't.
> (Webster, *The White Devil*,
> V.vi.238–9)

OUTLINING THE CRIME THRILLER

Hard-boiled themes, structures, and devices have had an enormous influence on the development of the genre of crime fiction, from the police procedural to what is often broadly termed the crime thriller, the main focus of which is the crime, and the criminal committing it. The relationship between hard-boiled fiction and the crime thriller is an important one, and John G. Cawelti underlines this when he identifies the emergence, in the 1920s, 'of two major formulaic figures in the literature of crime: the urban gangster and the hard-boiled detective' (Cawelti 1976: 59). The observation is a significant one, for various reasons. It was in 1929, the year of the Wall Street Crash and the beginning of the Great Depression, that two of the most sharply defined examples of the urban gangster and the hard-boiled detective appeared in fiction, the former in the figure of Cesare Bandello in W.R. Burnett's *Little Caesar* and the latter in the figure of the nameless Continental Op in Dashiell Hammett's *Red Harvest*. Furthermore, Cawelti's identification of both these figures as 'formulaic' echoes the prevalent literary view of the crime thriller *as a genre*, as formulaic popular literature populated with cardboard characters and employing conventional and well-worn themes, structures, and devices (Glover 2003: 135).

This negative view of the crime thriller has a long heritage, however. As early as 1924 R. Austin Freeman, the author of the Dr Thorndyke stories and novels, distinguished between detective fiction, 'which finds its principal motive in the unravelment of crimes or similar intricate mysteries' (Freeman 1992: 7), and what he calls 'the mere crime story', in which 'the incidents – tragic, horrible, even repulsive – form the actual theme, and the quality aimed at is horror' (Freeman 1992: 9). The 'mere crime story' in Freeman's terminology corresponds to the modern crime thriller, and the sole aim of such 'highly sensational' fiction, in Freeman's view, 'is to make the reader's flesh creep' (Freeman 1992: 9). The terms of his criticism echo Mary Shelley's description of her intentions in writing *Frankenstein* (1818/1831). According to Shelley, in her author's Introduction to the 1831 edition of the novel, she wanted to write a story 'to make the reader dread to look around, to curdle the blood, and quicken the beatings of the heart' (Shelley 1994: 7–8), and this underlines important parallels between the Gothic novel and the modern crime thriller.

In this respect, the line of the modern crime thriller can be traced from the Gothic novel (and even from revenge tragedy, as will be discussed later), through the novels of Charles Dickens and on to the Victorian 'sensation fiction' of the 1860s and 1870s, at which point, in Britain at least, 'the glamorous or sympathetic criminal now largely disappears from popular fiction' (Priestman 1998: 38). It is at this point, however, that such figures reappear as the focus of a type of fiction that would now be recognised as the crime thriller. The lineage of the crime thriller is an important one, as it has appropriated and adapted clearly identifiable characteristics from its predecessors, the most obvious of which is 'an interest [in] crime and its outcome' (Symons 1993: 198). From the Gothic novel, a concern with secret or hidden knowledge and the narrative and thematic spectre of social disintegration (Botting 2001: 5) are evident, while an interest in the criminal underworld is clearly drawn from such novels as Charles Dickens's *Oliver Twist* (1838). From the 'sensation fiction' of the 1860s and 1870s, such as Wilkie Collins's *The Woman in White*, comes the 'disturbing treatment of crime, mystery and betrayal' (Glover 2003: 136) that the twentieth-century crime thriller was to develop in its sensational, and often shockingly frank, depictions of sex and violent death.

For this reason, while it has often been argued that what sets the crime thriller apart from the detective story is its focus on the crime, rather than its investigation, David Glover argues that, rather, 'the thriller was and still is to a large extent marked by the way in which it persistently seeks to raise the stakes of the narrative, heightening or exaggerating the experience of events by transforming them into a rising curve of danger, violence or shock' (Glover 2003: 137). The difference, then, would seem to be one of narrative effect and narrative structure, both of which go hand in hand in Priestman's identification of one of the central aspects of the crime thriller: that it emphasises present danger rather than reflecting on, or investigating, past action (Priestman 1998: 43). Furthermore, in order to create this danger in the present the protagonist of the crime thriller must be threatened, or believe him- or herself to be threatened, by powerful external forces of some form or another (Priestman 1998: 43). In this respect there are again, of course, certain parallels with the Gothic novel, whose focus on the notion of evil and villainy finds its twentieth-century manifestation in the crime thriller's overriding concern with criminality, its causes, and its aftermath.

Symons's outline of what he terms the 'crime novel', but which for the sake of clarity will be referred to in this discussion as the crime thriller, also depends on drawing distinctions with the detective story. The most significant of Symons's points for the present study are:

1   That the crime thriller is based on 'psychology of characters – what stresses would make A want to kill B? – or an intolerable situation that must end in violence' (Symons 1993: 191).
2   The fact that, unlike hard-boiled fiction or detective fiction, there is often no detective, or, when there is, he or she plays a secondary role (Symons 1993: 192).
3   The fact that setting, as with hard-boiled fiction, is often central to the

atmosphere and tone of the story, and frequently is inextricably bound up with the nature of the crime itself (Symons 1993: 193).

4 That the social perspective of the story is often radical, and questions some aspect of society, law, or justice (Symons 1993: 193).

5 The observation that characters form the basis of the story. According to Symons, 'The lives of characters are shown continuing after the crime, and often their subsequent behaviour is important to the story's effect' (Symons 1993: 193).

Of course, crime thrillers do not always display all of these characteristics. In fact, it is the omission or inclusion of various of these characteristics that can account, in part, for the bewildering variety of different 'versions' of the crime thriller. These include legal thrillers, spy thrillers, racing thrillers, psychological thrillers, futuristic thrillers, political thrillers, cyberpunk thrillers, gangster thrillers, serial killer thrillers, heist thrillers, and more, but the majority of them can be discussed under two broader groupings identified by Priestman as the *noir* thriller and anti-conspiracy thriller (Priestman 1998: 34).

THE *NOIR* THRILLER

At the dark heart of the *noir* thriller, in Priestman's outline, is a protagonist who 'consciously exceed[s] the law' (Priestman 1998: 34), and according to such a defining characteristic there is a sense in which the *noir* thriller stretches back as far as Herodotus's story of King Rhampsinitus and the thief, although a more illuminating starting point would be English drama of the early-modern period. Plays such as *Macbeth*, *Richard III*, *The Changeling*, and *The White Devil* all have at their narrative and thematic centre characters who consciously transgress legal and social boundaries for their own personal gain, be it sexual, monetary, or political. For all their criminality, and even amorality, these characters are compelling figures, and our fascination with their inevitable fall neatly parallels the fascination exerted by the *Newgate Calendar* stories, and their like, so that from the revenge tragedies of the first half of the seventeenth century there is a certain continuity of interest into the eighteenth century, and into novels such as Daniel Defoe's *Moll Flanders* (1722). The full title of Defoe's novel clearly advertises this morbid fascination with crime, and the link to the *Newgate Calendar* tradition: 'The Fortunes and Misfortunes of the Famous Moll Flanders, Etc. Who was born in Newgate, and during a life of continu'd Variety for Threescore Years, besides her Childhood, was Twelve Year a Whore, five times a Wife, (whereof once to her own brother), Twelve Year a Thief, Eight Year a Transported Felon in Virginia, at last, grew Rich, liv'd Honest, and died a Penitent'.

The central focus on a protagonist who consciously exceeds the law, and on the social and economic context portrayed as contributing to the transgression, found its clearest early expression in W.R. Burnett's *Little Caesar*. Published in the year of the Wall Street Crash, *Little Caesar* articulated the growing realisation that urban poverty and national economic depression, for some, made a life of crime appear to be an attractive proposition. Urban gangster fiction, as a strand of the *noir* thriller, delved into the underworld of urban gangsterism, and in its charting of the rise, and inevitable fall, of the gangster hero there were certain parallels with the over-reaching hero of early-modern tragedy, such as Macbeth. Furthermore, as Cawelti notes, it made protagonists 'out of lower-class figures characterised by crudeness, aggressive violence, and alienation from the respectable morality of society' (Cawelti 1976: 61).

The focus on lower-class protagonists, and particularly protagonists trapped by poverty, was not confined to gangster fiction, but was also common in much Depression-era literature, ranging from the novels of John Steinbeck and John Dos Passos to the hard-boiled fiction of Raymond Chandler and the *noir* thrillers of James M. Cain. The audience of the pulps, and specifically *Black Mask*, with whom Chandler began his writing career, was the urban working class (McCann 2000: 147), and time and again, as Sean McCann notes, 'Chandler's most villainous figures are the decadent elite of the non-producing class' (McCann 2000: 153). Cain's contribution to crime fiction, despite Chandler's distaste for his novels, was, according to Richard Bradbury, 'to recognise the potential afforded by writing from within the "criminal's" perspective' (Bradbury 1988: 89), although it is interesting that, as an unemployed drifter, Frank Chambers, the protagonist of Cain's *The Postman Always Rings Twice* (1934), is a member of a non-working class of a different kind. In a general criticism of detective fiction as a genre, Cain maintained that murder is always written about from 'the least interesting angle, which was whether the police would catch the murderer'. Instead, he chose to write from the point of view of the effect of crime – in particular, murder – on those who commit it, and according to Cain '[t]hey would find [. . .] that the earth is not big enough for two persons who share such a dreadful secret, and eventually turn on each other' (Cain 1944: xii).

The rapid decay of human relationships due to suspicion and mistrust in the wake of the crime of murder is central to Cain's two most famous novels, *The Postman Always Rings Twice* and *Double Indemnity* (1936). Both novels are characterised, among other things, by their sense of inevitable doom, and along with Fyodor Dostoyevsky's *Crime and Punishment* (1866), which charts the mental disintegration of the student Raskolnikov in the wake of the double-murder of a pawnbroker and her simple-minded sister during a bungled burglary, they are a clear influence on a novel written sixty years after, and a world away from, the poverty and hopelessness of the Depression: Donna Tartt's *The Secret History* (1992). Tartt's novel examines the growing tension among a group of classics students at Hampden College, Vermont, caused by their complicity in not just one, but eventually two murders, the first of which is frenzied, brutal, and bacchanalian but the second of which is the coldly rationalised and cruelly considered murder of one of their own number in an attempt to prevent him from revealing the initial crime.

The sense of inevitable doom and the unravelling of relationships and of sanity in the wake of violent crime represent, in Cain's novels, 'an unhesitating, if ambivalent, confrontation with sexuality and violence in an almost completely amoral universe' (Bradbury 1988: 88). The 'amoral' universe of the *noir* thriller, as Richard Bradbury describes it, clearly has much in common with the world of revenge tragedy, and the conjunction of sex and violent death in the tragedies of blood reinforces the parallels still further. Just as the conjunction of violence and sex is 'integral to the working-out of the narrative' in the *noir* thrillers of Cain (Bradbury 1988: 91), so too is it clear in revenge tragedy, in which the ties between the 'blood' of sexual passion and of physical violence and death provide the narrative engine. De Flores, in Thomas Middleton and William Rowley's *The Changeling* (1622), agrees to murder Beatrice Joanna's suitor, Alonzo de Piracquo, in order to clear the way for her union with Alsemero, the new object of her desire. He does so, however, only in the belief that his reward will be sexual union with Beatrice. The original murder, as in the *noir* thriller, spawns further murder, deception, and betrayal, until

Beatrice's defiant claim to a shocked Alsemero that 'your love has made me/A cruel murd'ress' (V.iii.64–5), and the final murder-suicide of De Flores and Beatrice, tied to each other through murderous passion and death. Similarly, as Bradbury observes of *The Postman Always Rings Twice*, while Frank and Cora murder Nick in order to be together, 'this together-ness degenerates into the claustrophobic suspicion that the other is about to confess', ultimately ending in their deaths (Bradbury 1988: 91).

John Webster's *The White Devil* (1612) in some ways also mirrors the criss-cross murders at the heart of Patricia Highsmith's *Strangers on a Train*. Vittoria Corombona and the Duke of Brachiano arrange the murders of their respective spouses in order to clear the way for their marriage, but as in the *noir* thriller, the deaths of the two lovers spring inevitably from the original murders. Vittoria succinctly describes the union of sex and violent death at the heart of revenge tragedy as follows: 'O my greatest sin lay in my blood./Now my blood pays for't' (V.vi. 238–9), and blood and violence, too, are characteristic of Frank and Cora's union in another Cain novel, *The Postman Always Rings Twice*. When Frank first sees Cora, he says that 'her lips stuck out in a way that made me want to mash them in for her' (Cain 1997: 2). Two days later, after Frank persuades Cora's wife Nick to go into town to buy a new sign for the filling station, he kisses her, 'mash[ing] [his] mouth up against hers' until she shouts at him to bite her: 'I bit her. I sunk my teeth into her lips so deep I could feel the blood spurt into my mouth. It was running down her neck when I carried her upstairs' (Cain 1997: 9).

While David Fine observes that 'murder always curdles love into hate in Cain's fiction' (Fine 1995: 51), it is clear from the passage discussed above that in Cain's fiction love and hate are just flip-sides of the same coin, and that in the Depression-era setting of the novels it is money and the promise of a better life that are the holy grail for which his protagonists search. While it is true that Frank and Cora murder Nick in order to be together, there is another motive: the filling station worth $14,000 and the $10,000 from his life-insurance policy. In this way, as Bradbury notes, '[t]he urge for financial gain, for access to the means of acquiring material fulfilment, is welded to the urge for sexual fulfilment' (Bradbury 1988: 90), and in this respect the Southern California setting of Cain's novels is significant. David Fine, for example, identifies Frank Chambers in *The Postman Always Rings Twice* as 'a drifter and a con man with a criminal trail stretching across the country' (Fine 1995: 48), and this identification of a criminal trail 'stretching across the country' is linked to the Frontier myth of Southern California as a land of golden opportunity where Frank's 'drifting' eventually takes him. However, as Fine observes, '[t]he ironic vision which informs all of [Cain's] L.A. novels is that of the dream-come-true turning into nightmare. Driven by sexual passion or a passion for wealth, or both, Cain's protagonists commit desperate acts, experience a taste of victory, and then lose everything' (Fine 1995: 55).

Despite Priestman's suggestion that the crime thriller, and the *noir* thriller in particular, lacks the 'moral safety-net of detection' (Priestman 1990: 177), the tragic ironies of Cain's fiction offer an implied moralising judgement on the actions of the protagonists that echoes that of the 'irony of revenge' that is played out in revenge tragedy (Tomlinson 1964: 88). Fine identifies a recurrent pattern of ironic doubling and repetition in *The Postman Always Rings Twice*, at the centre of which is Cora's death. As Fine observes, 'Frank and Cora bash in Nick's head on a road in the mountains [. . .] and Cora, in a grotesque rebound is killed in a bloody crash on the Pacific Coast Highway, not far from the murder site' (Fine 1995: 50). The irony of this 'grotesque rebound' is compounded when Frank is condemned to death for what is judged to be the murder of Cora, but which, in reality, is Frank's first and only act of compassion or kindness. Frank is rushing a pregnant Cora to hospital when he overtakes a truck on the inside and the car crashes into a culvert wall, killing Cora instantly. Frank narrates the story, we learn only in the final chapter, from his prison cell as he awaits execution.

As a first-person confessional novel, *The Postman Always Rings Twice* seems to be the perfect vehicle for an examination of motivation: in Symons's analysis, to attempt to identify 'what stresses would make A want to kill B'. The first-person *noir* thriller, then, might be termed a *whydunnit*, by focusing on the reasons behind the act, rather than a *whodunnit*. However, as Bradbury notes of Cain's novels in general, and *The Postman Always Rings Twice* in particular, they never offer the sort of self-analysis that the first-person narrative structure seems to offer, and the dialogue-heavy narrative offers little access 'to the internal mechanisms of the protagonist's mind' (Bradbury 1988: 96–7). When one of the other inmates offers this access by telling Frank that it was his subconscious that killed his brother, Frank's refusal of the very notion of the subconscious mirrors the broader narrative refusal to provide any access to the internal workings of Frank's mind. 'To hell with the subconscious', says Frank. 'I don't believe it. It's just a lot of hooey' (Cain 1997: 117).

Another first-person confessional narrative that claims to offer such access, but subsequently refuses it in far more elliptical ways than Cain's novel, is Vladimir Nabokov's *Lolita* (1955). Many of the patterns and devices of Cain's novel are employed in *Lolita*, such as the retrospective first-person confessional narration discussed above and the use of doubling and mirroring. Humbert's full name, Humbert Humbert, clearly advertises the thematic and narrative centrality of doubling and mirroring, and this is emphasised at the end of the novel. After killing his double, Clare Quilty, Humbert drives away, and decides that 'since I had disregarded all laws of humanity, I might as well disregard the rule of traffic'. He crosses to the 'queer mirror side' of the highway, where he continues to drive until he is stopped by the police (Nabokov 1995: 306). The automobile, furthermore, as a key symbol of the freedom associated with the democratic promise of the American Dream, is central to both novels. In *Lolita*, Charlotte Hayes is providentially killed by a car, allowing Humbert Humbert, the narrator, to claim the young Lolita as her legal guardian and hold her captive to his paedophilic desires. Their wanderings by car across the 'crazy quilt' of America undermine the notion of the freedom of the road by depicting them each as captive to the other: Lolita to Humbert through his position as her legal guardian, and Humbert to Lolita through his obsessive and illicit desire for her. Furthermore, their travels across America mirror Frank's similar 'drifting' through America before his arrival in Southern California at the Twin Oaks Tavern. Cora, however, is unimpressed by the picture of life on 'the road' that Frank paints for her, and wants to use the insurance money from her husband's death to make the Twin Oaks Tavern into a commercial success. The tavern, as Frank describes it when he first sees it, is 'nothing but a roadside sandwich joint [. . . .] There was a lunch-room part [. . .] and off to one side a filling station' (Cain 1997: 1), and in this way even Cora's dream of commercial success and stability depends on passing automotive trade. Furthermore, as Fine notes, 'The perversity of Cora's dream of respectability and mothering domesticity, grounded in a brutal murder, is blatant' (Fine 1995: 50).

The uneasy relationship between commercial success and social respectability, and the violence and illegality on which it is based, is characteristic of another development of the gangster thriller: the Mafia story. Mario Puzo's *The Godfather* (1969) set in place most of the characteristic features of gangster fiction, a model still evident in the cinema and in television series such as *The Sopranos*. Cawelti notes that the central symbol of Puzo's novel is 'the family' (Cawelti 1976: 52–3), and he notes that the image of the family is linked, in Mafia narratives, with the development of organisational power, rather than its destruction, typical of early gangster stories such as *Little Caesar* (Cawelti 1976: 62). Central to this tracing of the development of a 'family's' organisation is the figure of the Mafia Don, particularly in relation to the presentation of the Mafia organisation as a form of business, and Knight echoes this point when he identifies the Mafia as 'the quintessential corporation' (Knight 2004: 142). The defining characteristic of Mafia Dons, like Don Vito Corleone in *The Godfather*, is 'a ruthless and brilliant professionalism' (Cawelti 1976: 67), although the insistence on physical bravery that Corleone's name ('lionheart') seems to emphasise suggests a certain continuity with the figure of the frontiersman in the Western, and the hard-boiled private detective. Knight also comments on the presentation, and perception, of Mafiosi as businessmen (Knight 2004: 148), and the Don's 'ruthless and brilliant professionalism' is clearly the underworld flip-side of the requirements for 'legitimate' business success in America.

The professional criminal, one example of which is the Mafia Don, is in Cawelti's view 'a man who applies the cool and detached rationalism of the professional specialist to matters of extreme violence and illegality' (Cawelti 1976: 67), and in this respect there are certain parallels with James Bond, to be discussed later, and the frontier hero of the Western. This criminal professionalism is evident in the novels of Elmore Leonard, in which the line between ruthless professionalism and sadistic pragmatism is often blurred in the characters of professional criminals and assassins. In *Killshot* (1989), a hitman called the Blackbird wears a suit on the job, remarking that '[h]e had to feel presentable. It was something he did for himself' (Leonard 1990: 14), and as Barry Taylor remarks of Leonard's novels, 'dress sense is one of the key indicators by which the reader is invited to form judgements of character' (Taylor 1997: 23). In this way, the Blackbird's professionalism is encoded in the attention he pays to his appearance, while his ruthlessness is evident in his rule never to leave living witnesses to a hit, and his sadism is evident in his memories of his childhood, when he and his brothers would shoot at 'dogs, you know, cats, birds' with their twenty-two rifle (Leonard 1990: 13).

Insights like these into the thoughts and background of murderers, while they are central to certain variations of the crime thriller, are often combined in Leonard's fiction with what Priestman identifies as 'a more reassuring narrative' featuring a policeman (Priestman 1990: 177), albeit a policeman flirting with the kind of criminality that is always present in Leonard's narratives. It is important to note, however, that the police narrative is rarely a procedural one in Leonard's fiction, focusing as it does on the individual actions of the policeman who, as Priestman notes, 'finally bests the villain in something resembling a Wild-West shoot-out' (Priestman 1990: 177). This is no doubt in part a hangover from Leonard's early career writing Westerns, but there is a significant parallel with the Western motifs in James Crumley's hard-boiled fiction, and particularly their examination of vigilante justice. In Leonard's novels, it is the policeman's own legal and moral ambivalence that makes their vigilante actions a necessary evil, and in this respect there are important parallels with the Continental Op in Hammett's *Red Harvest*, who has much in common with the hero of the crime thriller (Glover 2003: 138).

Despite Leonard's interest in, and even fascination with, criminality, there is in his novels, as Glover remarks, 'a marked lack of interest in criminal psychology' (Glover 2003: 149). In their examination of the mechanics of crime, rather than the motivation for it, they might be termed *howdunnits*, rather than *whydunnits*. In contrast, the novels of Patricia Highsmith examine murder as developing from 'ordinary' behaviour and motivation, and in this respect are concerned with the 'why' of crime and criminality, far more than Leonard's 'how' (Priestman 1990: 177). Knight, in the same vein, identifies Highsmith's novels as what he terms 'psychothrillers', which take place in the 'mundane world' and outline 'the criminality of ordinary people' (Knight 2004: 146–7). In particular, according to Symons, she is interested in 'the attraction exerted on the weak by the idea of violence' which normally leads, in Highsmith's fiction, to characters finding themselves 'linked to each other by the idea of crime' (Symons 1993: 196–7). This finds its most famous articulation in Highsmith's *Strangers on a Train* (1949), in which one of the two eponymous strangers, Charles Bruno, offers to kill the separated wife of the other stranger, Guy Haines, if Guy will kill Bruno's father in turn. Since neither of the two men has any connection with the victim, they have no motive for the crime, and will therefore be beyond suspicion. Guy's horror when Bruno follows through on his part of the plan, and murders Guy's wife, is compounded when Bruno then forces Guy to play his own part. Their complicity in the two murders leads eventually to Bruno's death and Guy's surrender to the authorities.

This idea of a chance meeting between two strangers that leads to murder, and eventually condemns them for the crime, is also a good thematic summary of Cain's novels, and is frequently adapted for the screen, as evident in films such as *Body Heat* (1981) and *U Turn* (1997). However, it is Highsmith's Ripley novels that best articulate what Knight terms the 'banality of evil' that springs from criminality, and in particular, murder, as an everyday activity (Knight 2004: 148). In *The Talented Mr Ripley* (1955), the first of the series, Tom Ripley hatches a plan to murder the man he has been living off, and 'become Dickie Greenleaf himself' (Highsmith 1999: 87), and what characterises the various parts of the plan, including the murder itself, is not their cleverness or ingenuity, but rather, their casualness, their selfishness, and their marked lack of cunning (Knight 2004: 148). As with the professional criminal or the Mafia Don, Tom Ripley lives out the flip-side of the 'legitimate' American Dream by displaying ambition, selfish ruthlessness, and a lack of moral baggage in order to become rich and successful. In this respect, the Ripley novels are 'a conscious rejection of the simplistic Christie-esque notion that murderers were essentially evil' (Knight 2004: 150).

The notion of evil, however, does find expression in the notion of 'monstrosity' that is the thematic centre of the serial killer novel. In a sense, the prevalence of the serial killer motif in contemporary crime fiction, including the police procedural and the crime thriller, is the logical conclusion of a process of criminal escalation in the genre, from Poe's purloined letter and the swindles and robberies of the Sherlock Holmes stories, through the single murder of the Golden Age whodunnit and the multiple murders of hard-boiled fiction, to the serial killings of late twentieth-century crime fiction. Knight argues that it was the widely recounted serial murders of Ted Bundy, Ed Gein, and Jeffry Dahmer that accounted for the development of serial killer fiction, at the forefront of which was Thomas Harris's *Red Dragon* (1981). Harris is the creator of the most famous serial killer, cannibalistic psychiatrist Doctor Hannibal Lecter, and although he is mentioned in the earlier *Red Dragon*, it is in *The Silence of the Lambs* (1989) that he comes to the fore, and in being brought in to advise FBI agent Clarice Starling in the investigation of another serial killer, he upstages her, transforming what might otherwise have been a relatively straightforward procedural investigation of a serial killer, as in Patricia Cornwell's *Postmortem*, into what Knight identifies as an 'anti-procedural' (Knight 2004: 203).

What is striking about the portrayal of Hannibal Lecter is the apparent division in his personality, on the one hand identified with animals by being caged, by his almost feral sense of smell, and, of course, by his eating habits, but on the other hand being acknowledged by the FBI as a 'genius psychologist', the two opposing sides of his personality, the animalistic and the intellectual, seeming to be at odds with each other. Of course, as in the case of Dr Jekyll, this is part of what makes him monstrous. Far more than just being somebody who breaks the taboo of cannibalism, he is a doctor, and in the same way that Doctor Sheppard's medical vocation in Christie's *The Murder of Roger Ackroyd* makes his crime of murder even more abhorrent, so too is Lecter perceived as being doubly monstrous. The influence of the extreme violence of the novels on future developments of crime fiction remains to be seen, and Carl Malmgren, for one, has posed the question whether the extreme visceral violence of the Lecter novels will act as 'vaccine or virus' on the violent excess that often characterises the crime thriller (Malmgren 2001: 190).

THE ANTI-CONSPIRACY THRILLER

In Priestman's outline of the anti-conspiracy thriller, the protagonist is pitched against a powerful conspiracy without recourse to the forces of law and order (Priestman 1998: 34), and Marty Roth suggests that it is the threatening presence of the enemy that separates the thriller from the adventure story (Roth 1995: 226). However, as it shares many of the characteristics of the adventure story, it is worth setting the anti-conspiracy thriller within this context in order to illuminate various of its central characteristics. Cawelti identifies the hero – either a group or an individual

– at the centre of the adventure story, 'overcoming obstacles and dangers and accomplishing some important and moral mission' (Cawelti 1976: 39). Such a description, of course, covers both hard-boiled fiction *and* the crime thriller, further emphasising, if further emphasis were needed, the relationship between the two.

It is Roth's identification of the three forms that the underworld of crime fiction can take, however, that allows the pattern of the anti-conspiracy thriller to be identified, without necessarily subscribing to Roth's restrictive framework. In Roth's outline, there are two worlds in detective fiction. One of these is the world as it seems, and as we would like it to be. The other is the world that is revealed when the thin veneer of civilisation is removed, and, according to Roth, the first form of this world of crime fiction, the world as it really is when the façade is stripped away, is a *conspiratorial* world, intent on disrupting the order of the ordinary world (Roth 1995: 226). This conspiratorial aspect characterises the fictive world as a world of conspiracies, and many of the Sherlock Holmes stories reflect this view of the world. The Mormon conspiracy that delineates the dual narrative structure of *A Study in Scarlet*, for example, was borrowed from Robert Louis Stevenson's *The Dynamiter* (1885), while of the sixty published Holmes stories, eleven of them, as Priestman notes, are secret society stories (Priestman 1990: 76).

Despite the evident anxiety regarding secret societies in Doyle's fiction, of the various forms that this second world can take in crime fiction, according to Roth, '[t]he spy thriller is the most overtly conspiratorial' (Roth 1995: 226). It is significant that in its first phase, in the last quarter of the nineteenth century, the spy thriller developed 'the racist and nationalistic pattern of true Britons confounding the anti-imperial wiles of foreigners of all kinds' (Knight 1990: 173), since imperial adventure motifs are frequently evident in the early development of the thriller (Glover 2003: 139–40). The timing of this development of the spy thriller is significant, and Symons suggests that it was linked to the inventions and technological developments that appeared in the years following the Industrial Revolution, and which played a major role in the expansion of the British Empire (Symons 1993: 259). When British Imperial power came under the very real threat of being undermined through the theft of technological secrets or through sabotage, stories of political and military intrigue focused around the figure of the spy began to develop, such as

Rudyard Kipling's *Kim* (1901), Erskine Childers's *The Riddle of the Sands* (1903), and John Buchan's *The Thirty-Nine Steps* (1915).

It was the approach of the First World War, however, that in Britain focused the attention of the reading public both on the figure of the spy (Priestman 1998: 45) and on the nature of the threat to the security of the nation. In Britain, the identification of Germany as the principal threat at this time emphasises how the spy thriller, more than any other sub-genre of crime fiction, is a clear response to the political and military climate within which it is produced. This point is reinforced by the fact that in the wake of the Russian Revolution of 1917, the Soviet Union quickly took over from Germany as the new enemy in the spy thriller. Graham Greene's spy novels are important in this respect, covering, as they do, the transition from a pre-Second World War perspective to a post-war perspective in which the black-and-white certainties of earlier spy thrillers, and particularly the James Bond novels of Ian Fleming, blur into an uncertain, disorienting, and far more treacherous grey (Priestman 1998: 45–6).

These shades of grey are embodied in a figure characteristic of Cold War spy thrillers: the double- (or even triple-) agent. The double-agent, as the term suggests, is characterised not only by a sense of divided loyalties, but by a fundamental division of subjectivity, and Magnus Pym, the double-agent in John le Carré's *A Perfect Spy* (1986), exemplifies this well. The name Pym is a clear reference to Edgar Allan Poe's *The Narrative of Arthur Gordon Pym* (1838), and the reference is an important interpretative clue. Poe's narrative foregrounds issues of interpretation which are also central to *A Perfect Spy*, as le Carré's Pym attempts to reconstruct 'the authentic account of his life' (Barley 1990: 152). The narrative slippage in the novel, from first-person to third-person narration, mirrors the fundamental slippage of subjectivity that characterises the double-agent, and there are clear distinctions between the first-person Pym and the third-person Pym. The I-narrator is the Pym who has sought 'the confined privacy of a rented seaside guest-room' in order to recon- struct the authentic account of his life, and in this way, to reconstruct his fractured identity. The third-person Pym is the 'plural, refracted Pym who exists *only* within social interactions' (Barley 1990: 153), which, of course, are denied him by the enforced isolation that the I-narrator has contrived.

The end of the Cold War in 1989 did not put an end to the spy thriller, but rather, as Priestman notes, it gave rise to variations on the spy thriller which exploited its after-effects, such as 'small-state nationalism' and arms-dealing (Priestman 1998: 48). In some ways, however, the legal thriller is a development of the spy thriller, and represents a shift from political and military espionage to corporate espionage. As Nick Heffernan notes, 'legal expertise [is] overwhelmingly dedicated to the protection and extension of corporate power' (Heffernan 1997: 191), and in the legal thriller proficiency and professionalism in espionage are replaced with legal professionalism, which represents a socially acceptable and palatably legal alternative to the modes of professionalism characteristic of the gangster thriller. However, the paranoid reading that the conspiratorial world of the anti-conspiracy thriller promotes irrevocably yokes the two modes of professionalism together, as, for example, in John Grisham's *The Firm* (1991), in which Mitch McDeere, the lawyer hero, discovers that the law firm for which he works is, in fact, a money-laundering outfit owned by the Mafia.

The paranoid suspicion that any one of us might be hand in glove with the devil, and not know it, is made manifest in *The Firm* in the notion of a Mafia-owned law firm. In the film *The Devil's Advocate* (1997), another legal thriller, albeit a supernatural one, this is literally the case, as the young lawyer discovers that his employer, as with Johnny Angel's employer in *Angel Heart*, is Satan himself. *The Firm*, however, articulates a far more secular kind of paranoia, and McDeere's discovery forces him to choose between complicity, and the privileged lifestyle that the job offers, and 'his responsibilities as a professional and a citizen' (Heffernan 1997: 193). He chooses professional and civic responsibility, of course, which leads to him making an agreement with the FBI in order to bring the firm down. Significantly, the agreement is made against the backdrop of the Washington Monument and the Vietnam Veterans Memorial, in this way linking McDeere's choice to 'the patriotic and martial ideas of honour, duty and sacrifice' (Heffernan 1997: 195), which in turn reinforces the legal thriller's direct lineage from the spy thriller with the end of the Cold War. Furthermore, that McDeere has been chosen for the task because he is identified by the FBI as 'self-reliant and independent' (Grisham 1991: 204–5), clearly identifies him as the direct heir of the hard-boiled hero, once more reinforcing the developmental links of crime fiction.

These developmental links reinforce the view of crime fiction as a repository of various themes, structures, and devices whose appropriation and re-appropriation over the history of the genre account for the broad diversity of crime fictions evident today. Historical crime fiction, in particular, often wears its heart on its sleeve in this respect, and clearly advertises its debt to the texts, characters, settings, plots, and devices that precede it, as the following chapter will demonstrate.

6

HISTORICAL CRIME FICTION

I prepare to leave on this parchment my testimony as to the wondrous and terrible events that I happened to observe in my youth, now repeating verbatim all I saw and heard, without venturing to seek a design, as if to leave to those who will come after (if the Antichrist has not come first) signs of signs, so that the prayer of deciphering may be exercised on them.

(Eco 1998: 11)

WRITING HISTORY AND INTERPRETING THE PAST

Common to the majority of the critical studies of historical crime fiction is the identification of significant parallels between the detective and the historian. The methods of William of Baskerville, the detective figure in Umberto Eco's *The Name of the Rose* (1980, first published in English in 1983), for example, have clear parallels with the approach of the modern historian: he weighs up evidence and attempts to establish a chain of cause and effect in order to construct a narrative of the past (Ford 2000: 97). Not just literary critics, but historians, too, have recognised the parallels, and the historian Robin Winks comments on the similarities between the work of historians and that of fictional detectives as follows: 'The historian must collect, interpret, and then explain his evidence by methods which are not greatly different from those techniques employed by the detective, or at least the detective in fiction' (Winks 1968: xiii). What is significant about both Winks's observation and William of Baskerville's methods is that in both cases the task of both the historian and the detective is implicitly identified as an interpretative one.

This subjectivity of the interpretative act is clearly at odds with the apparent neutrality and objectivity normally associated with historical research, and most modern historians recognise 'that history is less a science than an art, in which certain facts are selected from a much larger body of data to serve the historian's biases, hunches, and theories' (Jacobs 1990: 71). This process of selection is crucial to understanding that 'meaning and structure are imposed on history by narrative devices' (Lee 1990: 44), and is one of the reasons that Foucault, like Jacques Derrida, rejects a representational or mimetic 'reconstruction' of history (Marshall 1992: 148), or what Adso, in *The Name of the Rose*, describes as 'repeating verbatim all that [he] saw and heard, without venturing to seek a design' (Eco 1998: 11). No 'telling' or 'repetition' of history is pure fact, free of individual perception, interpretation, or selection. As Paul Cobley observes, '[t]hat the historical record is itself a discursive entity made up of signs means that it offers a re-presented, thoroughly selective account of what actually happened' (Cobley 2001: 30).

Such views of history are clearly mined from the same vein as Hayden White's description of the writing of history as a 'poetic process' (White 1976: 28), which Alison Lee elaborates on by identifying history as a 'discursive practice' (Lee 1990: 35). According to Lee, 'narrating *makes* things real. There is no way to know "facts" outside the telling/writing of them' (Lee 1990: 45), and in this way narrative discourse is the bridge between individual or private history, in which historical events are registered as direct experience for *someone* (for example, Adso in *The Name of the Rose*), and collective or public history, which is composed merely of stories relayed through discourse to everyone else (the readers of Adso's chronicle) (Lee 1990: 45).

In the traditional historical novel, and in the social, historical, and political context of the nineteenth century which produced it, history is viewed predominantly as a group of facts which exists 'extra-textually', and its ability to represent the past 'as it really was' is never questioned (Lee 1990: 35). Since historical research, however, like investigation, is an interpretative act, our engagement with history, at least in the postmodern moment, will always be through various 'readings' or interpretations. First, history must be read *through* the discourse within which historical texts are produced, and secondly, it must be read *within* the particular social, historical, and political context of its production (Marshall 1992: 148). In other words, history must be read as a text, and it must also be read as a text that both reflects, and is influenced by, the particular social, political, and historical context in which it is produced.

Such interpretative frames, or the ways in which a text attains meaning as part of a discursive act, correspond to Foucault's identification of 'discursive formations': that is, the historical, social, and cultural contexts within which the discursive and interpretative acts take place (Marshall 1992: 149). The interpretative aspect of history, therefore, emphasises the question of *how* we know history, and in relation to the historical crime novel, this is a significant point. According to the postmodern theorist Brian McHale, 'Classic detective fiction is the epistemological genre *par excellence*' (McHale 2002: 147), and in McHale's analysis this means that it is fiction organised 'in terms of an epistemological dominant' whose structure and devices raise issues concerning the accessibility, transmission, and reliability and unreliability 'of knowledge about the world' (McHale 2002: 146). However, for the reasons outlined above in relation to the idea of history as a 'discursive practice', historical crime fiction is also, or at least has the potential to be, organised in terms of an 'ontological dominant' (McHale 2002: 147). The formal strategies of this kind of fiction, which Linda Hutcheon has termed 'historiographic metafiction' (Hutcheon 1984: xiv), raise issues concerning 'the mode of being of fictional worlds [. . .] whether "real", possible, fictional, or what-have-you' (McHale 2002: 147).

'Historiography' is the writing of history, and the term immediately questions the transmission of historical 'fact' as unproblematic and objective, and calls into question both our knowledge of the past, and the methods of transmitting that knowledge. In other words, the term links the epistemological and ontological aspects of writing history. Fiction organised in terms of an epistemological dominant, such as Golden Age detective fiction, or even hard-boiled fiction, McHale identifies as Modernist, while fiction organised in terms of an ontological dominant he identifies as Postmodernist (McHale 2002: 146–7), and these identifications both derive from the idea of 'historiography'. Therefore, historical crime fiction, in various ways, has the potential to be organised in terms of both an epistemological dominant *and* an ontological dominant, and in this way refuses an unproblematic identification as either Modernist or Postmodernist.

CRIME, HISTORY, AND REALISM

Broadly speaking, there are two types of historical crime fiction, although within each type various permutations are evident. The first, and increasingly the most common, type is crime fiction that is set entirely in some particular historical period, but which was not written during that period (Murphy 2001: 247). So while the novels of Raymond Chandler and Walter Mosley take place in the same place and at roughly the same time – Los Angeles in the 1940s and 1950s – since Chandler's novels were written contemporaneously with their setting, they do not qualify as historical crime fiction, whereas Mosley's, written in the present moment, do. The second type of historical crime fiction has a contemporary detective investigating an incident in the more or less remote, rather than very recent, past. This type of fiction is often termed 'trans-historical crime fiction' (Murphy 2001: 247), as it is characterised by transitions from the present to the past, although as we shall see there is also a sense in which all crime fiction is trans-historical.

What is clear from these brief descriptions of the two types of historical crime fiction is that, just as with the majority of crime fiction, their settings are crucial to their success. Whereas the spatial setting is integral to the fiction of Christie or Chandler, for example, in historical crime fiction it is the temporal setting that usually takes centre stage, such as the Ancient Roman setting of Lindsey Davis's Falco novels, the medieval setting of Ellis Peters's Cadfael novels, the Elizabethan setting of the novels of Patricia Finney, the Victorian setting of the novels of Anne Perry and of Peter Lovesey, and the mid-twentieth-century settings of the novels of James Ellroy, Walter Mosley, and others. However, a closer examination reveals that the spatial settings of historical crime fiction are equally important. In the novels of Anne Perry and of Peter Lovesey, for example, setting the action specifically in Victorian London allows the authors to draw on the influence of the Sherlock Holmes stories on the popular imagination in their descriptions of the cramped gas-lit streets, dense fogs, and simultaneous grandeur and squalor of the metropolis. Lindsey Davis's Falco novels are not all confined to the city of Rome, but in Falco's movement throughout the series to the far corners of the Empire, the sheer scale of Roman influence, and the central importance of the city of Rome to the Empire, are emphasised. Furthermore, as with the Victorian London setting of Perry and Lovesey, the Roman Empire has certain associations in the popular imagination that are extremely useful to the crime novelist. Besides requiring a crime, 'the whole world of the detective novel is one of corruption, immorality, ruthlessness, and, most important, false appearances. The Roman Empire has special attractions to an author trying to evoke this atmosphere' (Hunt 2000: 32).

It is not enough, however, to rely on perceptions of other times in the popular imagination, and historical crime fiction is invariably furnished with a wealth of period detail. 'To be credible, crime fiction has to be authenticated by details' (Browne and Kreiser 2000: 4), and the authenticity of the various periods is constructed through descriptions of daily life, clothes, foods, houses, transportation, social activities, and more. Usually, this detail is deployed in the service of verisimilitude, and in this respect there are important parallels between historical crime fiction and the police procedural, which structures its themes, motifs, and characters within a realist framework. The pursuit of verisimilitude, however, causes particular problems for the historical crime writer. Historical fidelity to the beliefs and values of a radically different time and culture can result in characters who are unsympathetic, and even repugnant to modern readers. For this reason, the law of verisimilitude is often bent, and depictions of past places and cultures will often lie somewhere along a line that stretches from the realistic, but alien, to the palatable, but anachronistically modern (Hunt 2000: 37).

There are various devices employed by historical crime writers to create the appearance of verisimilitude which simultaneously undermine the realist foundation on which such fiction is often constructed. The most obvious of these is the presence of recognisable historical figures in the fictional narrative, and in the nineteenth-century historical novel, as developed by Sir Walter Scott, '"real" people, places, and events were included or alluded to in order to convince the reader of the "truth" of fictional ones' (Lee 1990: 52). However, the device of using historical figures in 'fictional' narratives was not new even in the nineteenth century. Significantly, it was a standard device in early-modern revenge tragedy, to which modern crime fiction owes a great debt. John Webster's *The White Devil* (1612), for example, is based on actual events which began in Italy in 1580, involving Paolo Giordano, Duke of Bracciano, his wife Isabella de' Medici, and a married gentlewoman, one Vittoria Accoramboni, the focus of Bracciano's violent desire. Bracciano's desire led him to murder Isabella's husband to clear the way for his union with Isabella, but when she still refused him, he then murdered his own wife, after which she gave in to his advances. The various murders were then revenged, resulting in the deaths of both Bracciano and Isabella.

While there was clearly sufficient lust and violence in the historical events, and all the central characters for Webster's play existed in history, Webster made various changes to his source material in order to satisfy both narrative demands and the popular demands of the theatre-going audience (Luckyj 1996: xii–xiii). Such appropriation of history is also common to crime fiction, and much historical crime fiction, including trans-historical crime fiction, has been based on famous, and sometimes less famous, murder cases. The most commonly appropriated incidents include the Whitechapel murders of Jack the Ripper, the death of the playwright Christopher Marlowe (another Marlowe) in Deptford on 30 May 1593, and the various theories about the assassination of John F. Kennedy, as examined in James Ellroy's *American Tabloid* (1995), and in cinema in Oliver Stone's *JFK* (1991).

Christopher Marlowe's death is examined in Martha Grimes's *The Dirty Duck* (1984), Judith Cook's *The Slicing Edge of Death* (1993), Anthony Burgess's *A Dead Man in Deptford* (1993), and Charles Nicholl's *The Reckoning* (1992), and although this last title is not fiction, it does raise interesting questions about the nature of 'truth' and 'reality', and the relationship between history and fiction. While Nicholl claims that he has not 'invented anything', he does acknowledge that the historical facts 'are only part of the story', and that *The Reckoning* is an attempt 'to fill in the spaces: with new facts, with new ways of seeing old facts, with probabilities and speculations and sometimes guesswork', in an attempt to 'get some meaning out of what remains' by telling a story (Nicholl 1993: 3).

The murders of Jack the Ripper in the Whitechapel area of London in 1888 and 1889 are perhaps the world's most famous unsolved murders, and for this reason have attracted a great deal of literary, cinematic, and televisual attention, in both factual form, in documentaries and historical analyses, and in fictional form. The appeal of the Jack the Ripper mystery clearly allows it to be appropriated by different media, and Alan Moore's graphic novel *From Hell* (1999) clearly illustrates the point. However, besides being appropriated in and of itself, the Jack the Ripper story is also taken as material to be woven into fictional pastiches, particularly by linking the details of the murders to the Sherlock Holmes mythos. In Michael Dibdin's *The Last Sherlock Holmes Story* (1978), for example, Holmes is brought in to solve the murders and bring Jack the Ripper to justice. Nicholas Meyer's *The West End Horror* (1976) similarly involves Holmes in the Jack the Ripper investigations, and is just one example of his use of characters from fiction alongside figures from history. Meyer's *The Seven-Per-Cent Solution* (1974) sees Watson tricking Holmes into travelling to Vienna in order to be cured of his cocaine addiction by Sigmund Freud.

Umberto Eco observes that '[w]hen fictional characters begin migrating from text to text, they have acquired citizenship in the real world and have freed themselves from the story that created them' (Eco 1994: 126), and the 'borrowing' of fictional characters in the pastiches discussed above is one example of the fluidity of the sub-genre. Brian McHale discusses such interpenetrations of fictional worlds as 'the violation [. . .] of an ontological boundary', and identifies the use of real-world authors to populate fictional worlds as an extreme example of such ontological disruption (McHale 2002: 153). Stephanie Barron's series of historical novels featuring Jane Austen as the detective are a case in point. However, even as Barron's use of the real-world Jane Austen as a fictional detective blurs the ontological boundaries between the fictive and the real, it also derives from the narrative impulse to 'fill in the gaps' that motivates both detectives and historians. Barron situates her Jane Austen novels, beginning with *Jane and the Unpleasantness at Scargrave Manor* (1996), between the years 1800 and 1804, a period of Austen's life characterised by a lack of epistolary evidence and of literary production. Barron accounts for these missing years by fictionalising a series of mysteries which Austen investigates, situating these fictional mysteries within the larger historical mystery surrounding the events in Austen's life at that time. In this way, 'the overarching mystery nests a series of fictional mysteries which Jane Austen solves' (Vickers 2000: 213).

By accounting for Austen's 'missing years', Barron is involved in an attempt to interpret the past by constructing it as a narrative, and the same impulse structures the historical crime writer's appropriation of real-world historical incidents. There are three ways to appropriate the past in historical crime fiction, all of which involve the interpreting of the past in narrative terms. One way is to relocate historical cases in the present by updating and fictionalising them, an approach which Edgar Allan Poe initiated as early as 1842 in 'The Mystery of Marie Rogêt'. The second way to appropriate historical cases employs a trans-historical framework, in which actual cases from the past are 're-opened' by detectives in the present, a device employed most famously by Josephine Tey in *The Daughter of Time* (1951), in which her detective, Inspector Alan Grant of Scotland Yard, investigates the involvement of Richard III in the deaths of the princes in the Tower of London in a feat of armchair (actually, hospital-bed) detection that parallels the work of the historian. A more recent example of the re-opening of actual historical cases is Colin Dexter's *The Wench is Dead* (1989), in which Inspector Morse takes a fresh look at the unsolved case of a woman found dead in an Oxford canal, and whose use of the word 'wench' in the title advertises both its trans-historical focus, and what Gill Plain has identified as an inherently sexist stance in the series (Plain 2001: 185–6). Arturo Pérez-Reverte's *The Flanders Panel* uses a medieval painting of a game of chess, and the clues it hides to the murder of one of its subjects, as the means of mirroring the clues to a contemporary murder in the art world of modern Madrid.

The third method of appropriating actual historical cases is the use of 'straight' historical fiction, although, as we shall see, the reliability and 'straightforwardness' of the mimetic representation of history suggested by Adso in *The Name of the Rose* is simultaneously undermined by its historiographic framework. James Ellroy's *The Black Dahlia* (1987) is the first book in his *L.A. Quartet*, which has been described as 'a four-volume narrative of the city's secret history from the mid 1940s to the late 1950s' (Pepper 2000: 26). Everything about *The Black Dahlia*, and the *Quartet* as a whole, conspires to emphasise the appropriation of history: both factual and literary, and collective and personal. The title *The Black Dahlia* is a clear appropriation of the title of George Marshall's *film-noir* classic, *The Blue Dahlia* (1946), scripted by Raymond Chandler, in which a murdered woman also forms the focus of the narrative. In *The*

Black Dahlia, the central murder is the unsolved Black Dahlia murder case of 1947, onto which, as his autobiographical *My Dark Places* (1996) makes clear, Ellroy mapped the murder of his mother, Jean Ellroy, on 23 June 1958, when Ellroy was ten years old. This mapping of personal history onto the collective historical register is central to *The Black Dahlia*, which by exposing familial corruption serves as the springboard for 'a sustained ransacking of Los Angeles's corrupt historical past' (Glover 2003: 148). The Los Angeles setting, in this way, is appropriated from its perception in the popular imagination and its depiction in hard-boiled fiction from Chandler to the present. Even the descriptive narration is a pastiche of Chandler's hard-boiled style, suggesting both a continuity with, and a development of, hard-boiled fiction in the procedural framework that Ellroy employs (Cohen 1997: 172). Dwight Bleichert, one of the policemen assigned to investigate the murder of Betty Short, remarks:

> The district's main drag [. . .] spelled 'postwar boom' like a neon sign. Every block from Jefferson to Leimert was lined with dilapidated, once grand houses being torn down, their facades being replaced by giant billboards advertising department stores, jumbo shopping centres, kiddie parks and movie theatres.
>
> (Ellroy 1993: 77)

The reference to advertising billboards and movie theatres is an indication of how the image of Los Angeles, and in particular the lure of Hollywood to figures like Betty Short, drawn there by the promise of stardom, is disseminated. The brutality of Betty's murder, however, and the deep-rooted corruption that its investigation reveals, exposes the gulf between fiction and reality, and, by extension, also exposes the apparent gulf between fiction and history in the realist aesthetic. Reading historical crime fiction from a realist perspective, there is a tendency to distinguish between literature, which is subjective and somehow 'untrue', and history, which is objective and 'true' (Lee 1990: 29). This results in a fundamental conflict at the heart of historical crime fiction. On the one hand, a premium is placed on verisimilitude and 'realism', while on the other hand fictive demands are evident in such realist devices as a reliable narrator, a well-structured plot, converging story-lines, and a tidy narrative transition from beginning to end that echoes, in its narrative order, the restoration of the social order initially disrupted by crime.

This fundamental conflict reveals that what historical fiction aims for is not reality, but the illusion of reality, and historical crime fiction creates and reinforces various levels of illusion and reality through the use of three primary devices (Lee 1990: 33). The first of these is the narrative device, common in modernist fiction, of framing one story within another story. The device is employed in Eco's *The Name of the Rose*, in which Adso's story is contained within the framing story of an unnamed narrator, clearly a historian, who comes across an eighteenth-century translation of the fourteenth-century manuscript of Adso of Melk that tells of the events of a single week in the year 1327. The narrative framing device is common in trans-historical fiction, and is evident, for example, in Josephine Tey's *The Daughter of Time*, Robert Wilson's *A Small Death in Lisbon* (1999), A.S. Byatt's *Possession* (1990), and Arturo Pérez-Reverte's *The Dumas Club* (1993, first published in English in 1996). The second device, often associated with the sort of narrative frames described above, is the device of the fictional editor, evident again in *The Name of the Rose*, and also evident in a crime novel of sorts, Vladimir Nabokov's *Lolita*, in which the foreword of the fictional editor, John Ray Jr., frames Humbert Humbert's confessional story of paedophilia and murder. Stephanie Barron also employs this device in her Jane Austen novels by using the convention – almost a cliché, now – of her fictional editor discovering a manuscript in an old trunk (Vickers 2000: 215). The third device is the use of footnotes, or endnotes, giving details of 'real' historical events, used most ingeniously by José Carlos Somoza's *The Athenian Murders* (2000, first published in English in 2002), in which, contained in the footnotes to the story of the murder of Tramachus, a student at Plato's academy, is yet another mystery that the modern-day translator – and by extension the reader – must unravel. The mystery is a metafictional one, as the characters in the historical mystery begin to suspect that their actions are predetermined, and as the events in the contemporary story contained in the footnotes begin to mirror those in the central story. All three devices, while apparently reinforcing the 'reality' of the historical details, simultaneously emphasise its illusory quality.

The illusion of reality, or what Conrad's Marlow might call a 'great and saving illusion', is necessary because it is often argued that factual accuracy 'produces only a shallow realism like that of the figures in a wax museum, which, though accurate to every measurement and every mole, are too rigid and static either to convince or inform' (Jacobs 1990: xvii). The waxworks analogy is a significant one, and it illustrates that even apparently 'mainstream' historical crime fiction, such as the Sergeant Cribb novels of Peter Lovesey, can interrogate, in its plots, themes, and backgrounds, the fictive and historical relationship between the past and the present. Lovesey's *Waxwork* (1978) is a case in point. The relationship between the present and the past, and between reality and fiction, forms a powerful theme in this novel, in which the portrayal of Madame Tussaud's Wax Museum allows Lovesey to place dynamic, living and breathing fictional characters alongside perfectly accurate, but 'rigid' and 'static' representations of real-world personages. That Madame Tussaud's has always been aware of the public fascination with crime and the spectacle of punishment only adds to the self-referential aspect of the novel.

This sense of *mise-en-abyme*, or the paradoxical mirroring '*within* the fictional world *of* the fictional world itself' (McHale 2002: 155), is not particular to *Waxwork*, or to Lovesey's novels in general. *A Case of Spirits* (1974), for example, opens with a séance in a police station, and in addition to being an accurate depiction of the Victorian obsession with spiritualism and the search for proof of life after death (Foxwell 2000: 289), the theme clearly echoes the historiographic nature of the novel, and suggests a parallel between mediums and historical novelists. Naomi Jacobs identifies the historical novelist as a 'medium who contacts the spirits of the dead' (Jacobs 1990: xviii), and in this respect the historical novelist also has clear parallels with the figure of the fictional detective.

What this implies, of course, is that the sense of *mise-en-abyme* in historical crime fiction is unavoidable: it is integral to the sub-genre. However true this might be, novels like Anne Perry's *The Face of a Stranger* (1990) deliberately foreground this self-referential mirroring in various ways. The first novel in Perry's William Monk series, *The Face of a Stranger*, introduces the series hero by describing him awakening in hospital suffering from amnesia, with no recollection of his past, or his identity. As the series progresses, Monk's 'official' investigations as a police detective, and, later, as a private detective, run alongside his own personal investigations into his own past, and his own identity, in an attempt to overcome his amnesia. The parallel is made clear in this first novel of the series, in which Monk, on leaving hospital, is assigned to investigate the murder of a Crimean war hero and gentleman, Major the Honourable Joscelin Grey. Soon after he begins his investigations, Monk becomes aware of the parallels between them: 'Grey's life was as blank an outline as his own, a shadow man, circumscribed by a few physical facts, without colour or substance' (Perry 1994: 70). With no memories, Monk lives in a perpetual present, with no links to his past other than the ones that he unearths through a process of investigation, and this thematic and structural motif running through the series mirrors the historical novelist's own relationship with the historical past.

Caleb Carr's *The Alienist* (1994), set in turn-of-the-century New York, foregrounds the same sort of links between present and past, and between the living and the dead, by opening with a description of a burial. The burial is that of Theodore Roosevelt, twenty-sixth president of the United States of America, on 8 January 1919: a verifiable historical event which signals not only the co-existence of 'real' and fictional characters, but also the retrospective narration of the novel (Tallack 2000: 254). That the story of a series of murders in New York in 1896 is being narrated retrospectively is emphasised by the fact that even Roosevelt's burial is being narrated 'after the fact', as the narrator, John Schuyler Moore, and Laszlo Kreizler, the alienist of the novel's title, discuss it over dinner in a restaurant frequented by the group during the events of 1896, and which Moore observes sadly is 'on its way out like the rest of us' (Carr 2002: 7). The relationship between the past and the present, crucial to both historiography and detection, is further developed in *The Alienist* in the image of two cities, one laid on top of the other, that Carr creates. By revealing the traces of past events, the group of detectives unearths 'a different, hidden city [. . .] beneath the everyday city', a city delineated in space and time by the dates and locations of the murders that the detectives are investigating (Tallack 2000: 261). There are clear parallels here with Carr's own fictional project, in which the traces of the historical city and the historical past are revealed beneath the surface of the modern one, situating the historical crime writer, like the detective, in an uneasy position between the present and the past, and between surface and depth.

The historical mysteries of Peter Tremayne, featuring the seventh-century Irish investigator Sister Fidelma of the religious community founded by St Brigid in Kildare, in Ireland, are similarly concerned with the relationship between the past and the present. Fidelma's background and position are carefully detailed by Tremayne in order to depict a society in transition, and Fidelma's own position at a transitionary period between old and new is a metafictional comment on the fiction in which she appears. Fidelma belongs to the royal family of Munster, and has studied for eight years at a bardic school in Tara (Luehrs and Luehrs 2000: 45). The bardic schools, which taught poetry, science, medicine, and law, were the direct descendants of druidic schools in Celtic Ireland, and in this way, as a member of the Catholic religious community, Fidelma's Celtic heritage is 'a blend of old beliefs with the new concepts of Christianity' (Luehrs and Luehrs 2000: 46). The use of historical figures in the Fidelma stories, particularly figures like Archbishop Ultan of Armagh, or King Oswy of Northumbria, who might not be immediately recognisable to most modern readers, is significant. Rather than simply being a device to convince the reader of the 'truth' of the fictional characters, as is the case with recognisable historical figures, for those readers who interrogate the historiographical aspect of the stories, these real-world figures are an effective way to maintain the 'simultaneous awareness of past and present' (Jacobs 1990: 74–5) that Fidelma embodies.

The simultaneous awareness of past and present evident in historical crime fiction seems to offer a means of gaining a new perspective on the present through the lens of the past. While the Foucauldian project resists attempts to make sense of the past 'through the present' as the past is only ever accessible to us as a discursive construct (Marshall 1992: 150), at the same time any attempts to make sense of the present 'through the past' are based on an unstable teleological premise, in which the present moment is viewed as the *telos*, or end, to which all human history has been directed; such a view leads us 'to see history as a means by which to trace a movement throughout time which results in ourselves' (Marshall 1992: 164). Significantly, both of these interpretations parallel two 'ways of knowing' that lie in conflict at the heart of one of the twentieth century's most famous historical crime novels: Umberto Eco's *The Name of the Rose*.

THE CASE OF *THE NAME OF THE ROSE*

The Name of the Rose is clearly a detective story, and a detective story, furthermore, that draws greatly on the models and conventions of classic detective fiction. The Benedictine abbey, where a series of grisly murders that seem to follow an apocalyptic pattern occurs, provides the 'closed' setting and limited circle of suspects typical of the Golden Age whodunnit, and the reproduction of a map of the abbey in the text is similarly typical of the Golden Age. However, as the name of its hero, William of Baskerville, makes clear, Eco's primary intertextual model is Conan Doyle's *The Hound of the Baskervilles* (1902), and although other intertextual models are evident, including Jorge Luis Borges's 'Death and the Compass' ('La Muerta y la Brújula', 1942) and Poe's 'The Purloined Letter' (McHale 2002: 147), it is the model of the detective story established in the Sherlock Holmes stories that provides the easiest entry into Eco's novel. If, as his name indicates, William of Baskerville is the novel's Sherlock Holmes figure, then Adso of Melk, as William's foil and narrator, is clearly his Watson, and Adso's description of William early in the novel reinforces such a reading. According to Adso:

> Brother William's physical appearance was at that time such as to attract the attention of the most inattentive observer. His height surpassed that of a normal man and he was so thin that he seemed still taller. His eyes were sharp and penetrating; his thin and slightly beaky nose gave his countenance the expression of a man on the lookout, save in certain moments of sluggishness of which I shall speak.
>
> (Eco 1998: 15)

Compare this with Watson's description of Holmes in *A Study in Scarlet*:

> His very person and appearance were such as to strike the attention of the most casual observer. In height he was rather over six feet, and so excessively lean that he seemed to be considerably taller. His eyes were sharp and piercing, save during those intervals of torpor to which I have alluded; and his thin, hawk-like nose gave his whole expression an air of alertness and decision.
>
> (Doyle 1981: 20)

Not only the description of William, but even the terms and structure of the description, are clearly appropriated from Doyle's fiction. The parallels continue in the respective descriptions of William's 'moments of sluggishness' and Holmes's 'intervals of torpor', as Watson's outline of Holmes demonstrates:

> Nothing could exceed his energy when the working fit was upon him; but now and again a reaction would seize him, and for days on end he would lie upon the sofa in the sitting-room, hardly uttering a word or moving a muscle from morning to night. On these occasions I have noticed such a dreamy, vacant expression in his eyes, that I might have suspected him of being addicted to the use of some narcotic, had not the temperance and cleanliness of his whole life forbidden such a notion.
>
> (Doyle 1981: 20)

Again, Adso's description of William closely echoes Watson's description of Holmes:

> His energy seemed inexhaustible when a burst of activity overwhelmed him. But from time to time, as if his vital spirit had something of the crayfish, he moved backward in moments of inertia, and I watched him lie for hours on my pallet in my cell, uttering barely a few monosyllables, without contracting a single muscle of his face. On those occasions a vacant, absent expression appeared in his eyes, and I would have suspected he was in the power of some vegetal substance capable of producing visions if the obvious temperance of his life had not led me to reject this thought.
>
> (Eco 1998: 16)

Adso's description of William 'moving backwards', however, is an intriguing, and somewhat obvious, addition to what is otherwise a near-facsimile of Watson's description of Holmes. Initially, the image of William 'moving backwards' calls to mind the process of detection, in which the normal causal progression from cause to effect is reversed in order to solve some mystery. And sure enough, soon after this description Adso recounts William's feat of Holmesian deduction when he correctly deduces the size, colour, appearance, name, and, finally, the location, of the abbot's missing horse upon their arrival at the abbey. William's piecing together of the clues of a horse's hoof-prints in the snow, some broken twigs, and some long black horsehairs caught in the brambles of a blackberry bush, is an example of the 'science of deduction' which characteristically begins each Holmes story.

However, the image of 'moving backwards' also calls to mind both the process of historical research and of Adso's own narration, and this image is therefore an important one in the novel, linking, as it does, detection, historical research, and narration. According to Judy Ann Ford, 'William approaches the murders like a modern historian, searching for small connections in order to construct a finite chain of causality, a story whose outlines he does not know until the end of the investigation' (Ford 2000: 98). The purpose of investigation, as Ford's analysis of William's method makes clear, is epistemological, and Eco's acknowledgement of the epistemological dominant of the whodunnit is clear in the Chinese Box structure of the novel, in which one 'epistemological quest' is contained within another, and that within yet another, and so on (McHale 2002: 147). The main epistemological quest, of course, is William's quest to discover who the murderer in the abbey is, but there are others. The second quest, arising from the first, focuses on the identity of the book over which the murders are being committed, while the third is the attempt to recover the actual book itself (McHale 2002: 148).

William's method, however, is just one of two opposing epistemological approaches, or 'ways of knowing', in the novel, and these approaches correspond roughly with attempts to make sense of the past 'through the present', and to make sense of the present 'through the past'. William's method, as it has been described, is an attempt to make sense of apparently unintelligible situations in the present by working backwards to first principles. When defending his method to the abbot, he does so by questioning the teleological aspect of apocalyptic thinking favoured by the abbot, but also by Jorge, the monk responsible for the murders. As William argues:

> 'Let us suppose a man has been killed by poisoning. This is a given fact. It is possible for me to imagine, in the face of certain undeniable signs, that the poisoner is a second man. On such simple chains of causes my mind can act with certain confidence in its power. But how can I

complicate the chain, imagining that, to cause the evil deed, there was yet another intervention, not human this time, but diabolical? I do not say it is impossible [. . . .] But why must I hunt for these proofs?'

(Eco 1998: 30)

Jorge's 'way of knowing' is apocalyptic, while William's method, his 'way of knowing', is rational and scientific, drawn from the philosophies of Roger Bacon and another William, William of Ockham. Jorge's method 'begins with a narrative and sets events into it', while William's method 'begins with events and builds to a narrative' (Ford 2000: 99). Significantly, however, as the murders appear to begin to fall into an apocalyptic pattern, William begins to accept that it is possible that the murderer is engineering them that way, although this is not the case. There has been no deliberate attempt to create an apocalyptic pattern to the murders, except in the case of one of the murders where Jorge is aware of William's growing acceptance of an apocalyptic pattern and engineers one of the murders to fit this pattern as a red herring and mislead him. As a result, while William does discover the truth, he does so 'by stumbling upon it, not by a successful chain of deductions' (McHale 2002: 149), and he perceives his misinterpretation of the evidence, despite reaching the truth, as a far greater failure than not uncovering the truth at all. For this reason, Eco, in his *Postscript to The Name of the Rose* (1983), identifies the novel as 'a mystery in which very little is discovered and the detective is defeated' (Eco 1984: 54), while William describes his defeat in more specific detail:

'There was no plot,' William said [. . . .] 'I arrived at Jorge through an apocalyptic pattern that seemed to underlie all the crimes, and yet it was accidental. I arrived at Jorge seeking one criminal for all the crimes and we discovered that each crime was committed by a different person, or by no one. I arrived at Jorge pursuing the plan of a perverse and rational mind, and there was no plan [. . . .] I behaved stubbornly, pursuing a semblance of order, when I should have known well that there is no order in the universe.'

(Eco 1998: 491–2)

POSTMODERNISM AND THE ANTI-DETECTIVE NOVEL

William's failure as a detective in *The Name of the Rose* is linked to larger concerns in the novel about the impossibility of historical authenticity, as Adso's plan to 'repeat verbatim' all that he saw and heard, and his subsequent failure to do so, attest. Not only does the novel demonstrate the act of interpreting or making sense of history to be 'presumptuous, arrogant and dangerous' (Ford 2000: 95), but William's final disconsolate realisation that '"There is too much confusion here"' (Eco 1998: 493) ultimately suggests the impossibility of identifying *any* order or intelligibility in the universe. As McHale observes, 'So profoundly has the rationality of detection been compromised here that *The Name of the Rose* qualifies as an "anti-detective story"', an anti-detective story, furthermore, that undermines any assumption regarding 'the adequacy of reason itself' (McHale 2002: 150).

In this respect, the anti-detective novel, of which *The Name of the Rose* is just one example, wears its postmodern philosophy on its sleeve, rejecting, as it does, any notion of the certainty of knowledge and the unity of the human subject. The postmodern critique of mimetic representation, in particular the representation of history, is fundamental to the anti-detective novel, which demonstrates that 'We no longer are able to think about absolute and unquestionable "facts" or "truths" of history, speaking now of "histories" instead of History' (Marshall 1992: 147). This division between 'History' and 'histories' is identifiable in the postmodern distrust of Grand Narratives, which Lyotard describes as an 'incredulity' towards what he terms 'metanarratives' (Lyotard 1992: xxiv). Turning away from Grand Narratives, the postmodern project appropriates various 'local' narratives or histories from the previously unassailable edifice of 'History', and does so through a process of fragmentation and deconstruction (Lyotard 1992: 20, 22).

Walter Mosley's Easy Rawlins novels are a good example of how more apparently 'traditional' mainstream crime fiction – in this case, historical crime fiction – can employ postmodern approaches in order to appropriate canonical crime texts for its own engagement with both literary and social history. By setting his novels in post-war Los Angeles, Mosley consciously takes on, in both senses of the term, the conventions of hard-boiled fiction, and the opening of the first novel in the series, *Devil in a Blue Dress* (1990), knowingly appropriates the opening of an established classic of hard-boiled fiction, Raymond Chandler's *Farewell, My Lovely* (1940), by 'repeat[ing] the dominant white American story with a black difference' (Cullen Gruesser 1999: 240). In Chandler's novel, the white detective Marlowe enters a black bar, imposing a white narrative perspective on a black space in what is only the first of many marginalising narrative strategies in the novel. In Mosley's novel, the perspective is reversed, with the white detective, in the shape of Dewitt Albright, stopping 'in the doorway' (Mosley 1992: 9) of the bar, barred from entering, as it were, due to the excessive whiteness that his name suggests. Simultaneously, the black perspective that is marginalised in Chandler's novel is centred in Mosley's, as Easy Rawlins surveys Albright as a member of the bar's black clientele and appropriates the first-person narrative voice of the hard-boiled detective which has 'traditionally' always been white and male. In this way, Mosley's Easy Rawlins cycle is not only what Knight has described as a 'black-focused recovery of the place [Los Angeles] and the past' (Knight 2004: 200): it is also a recovery of the 'notoriously conservative' genre of crime fiction itself (Cullen Gruesser 1999: 236).

As the fragile white male perspective normally associated with hard-boiled fiction suggests, other postmodern recoveries of the genre are also possible, and the postmodern anti-detective novel is often characterised by far more radical refusals and reworkings of literary and generic conventions than Mosley's novels are. Barbara Wilson's *Gaudí Afternoon* (1990), as its title makes clear, is a conscious appropriation of Dorothy L. Sayers's *Gaudy Night* (1935) and the conventions of the Golden Age whodunnit, but in its examination of the fraught relationship between 'outer' appearance and 'inner' identity, and between gender and sexuality, it owes more to the novels of Raymond Chandler and the theories of Judith Butler, respectively, than it does to the whodunnit. Butler's view of gender as a performance (Butler 1990), central to the various corporeal transformations at the heart of *Gaudí Afternoon*'s plot, is employed to undermine sexual and gender polarities and to demonstrate how 'the "real" evades our slippery grasp' (Munt 1994: 144–5). The novel's rejection of determinacy, certain knowledge, and unified subjectivity, as with William's failure as a detective in *The Name of the Rose*, undermines the epistemological certainties that are structurally encoded in the crime genre.

These postmodern anti-detective novels, characterised by the profound questions they raise 'about narrative, interpretation, subjectivity, the nature of reality, and the limits of knowledge', have also been termed 'metaphysical detective stories' (Merivale and Sweeney 1999: 1–2). Patricia Merivale and Susan Elizabeth Sweeney favour the term 'metaphysical detective fiction' as they suggest that the term 'anti-detective fiction' is misleading, implying as it does a complete opposition to the conventions of the detective genre, when in fact the metaphysical detective story depends absolutely on those conventions for its existence and success (Merivale and Sweeney 1999: 3). Paul Auster's *New York Trilogy*, consisting of *City of Glass* (1985), *Ghosts* (1986), and *The Locked Room* (1986), for example, appropriates and deconstructs the detective fiction genre, and in so doing displays most of the characteristics of the metaphysical detective story identified by Merivale and Sweeney. These include 'the defeated sleuth', 'the world, city, or text as labyrinth', 'the purloined letter, embedded text, [and] *mise en abyme*', 'the ambiguity [. . .] or sheer meaninglessness of clues and evidence', 'the missing person [and] the double', and 'the absence [. . .] or self-defeating nature of any kind of closure to the investigation' (Merivale and Sweeney 1999: 8).

This is a great deal of intellectual and metaphysical baggage for any genre to carry, and the fact that the conventions of the detective genre can bear the burden with ease is an indication of its suitability as a foundation for the anti-detective or metaphysical detective story. However, the paradox here is that the intention of the metaphysical detective story is to overload these generic conventions in order to undermine them, and this is exactly what happens in Auster's *City of Glass*. The entry into the narrative, which appropriates and subverts the conventions of detective fiction in general, and hard-boiled fiction in particular, immediately highlights the epistemological doubt that structures the novel. 'It was a wrong number that started it', begins the novel, 'the telephone ringing three times in the dead of night, and the voice on the other end asking for someone he is not' (Auster 1992: 3). The 'someone' is Daniel Quinn, a detective fiction author writing under the pseudonym of William Wilson, a name drawn from Poe's proto-detective story, 'William Wilson' (1838). The 'someone he is not' is Paul Auster, of 'the Auster Detective Agency' (Auster 1992: 7), an identity and a profession which Quinn eventually assumes when the calls to the wrong number do not stop. The case that

Quinn takes on as Paul Auster is to follow a man named Peter Stillman, who has recently been released from prison where he was serving a sentence for his cruel treatment of his then young son. Quinn's surveillance becomes obsessive, and he purchases a red notebook in which to record the minutiae of Stillman's apparently random wanderings through New York.

The wrong number is just the first of many examples in the novel of the limits of knowledge, which reaches its apotheosis in Quinn's failure as a detective, and the narrator's failure as a detective, in turn, when despite the clues set down in Quinn's red notebook he fails to find Quinn, who has simply disappeared in the postmodern labyrinth of New York city. Quinn's entry into a city and a story 'where the reassurance of limits or ends is withdrawn [and] where circumference becomes centre' (Nealon 1999: 123) closely parallels our experiences as reader, in particular of texts like *City of Glass*. Quinn, who follows what Michel de Certeau has described as 'the thicks and thins of an urban text' that people walking through a city create (de Certeau 1984: 93), maps the ironically named Stillman's wanderings through the city, and interprets the traces of his perambulations in diagrammatic form as letters spelling the cryptic phrase THE TOWER OF BABEL. The phrase, of course, underlines two things. First, in its reference to 'the Biblical narrative of the fall into linguistic multiplicity' (Marcus 2003: 260), it emphasises not only the impossibility of a universal language, but more specifically, the impossibility of natural, unproblematic, and unmediated communication and interpretation. Secondly, Quinn's extraction of the letters OWEROBAB from Stillman's negotiation of the labyrinth of the city, and his interpretative leap to the phrase THE TOWER OF BABEL, reinforce at a metafictional level the limits that the fall of the biblical tower signifies in relation to the reader's engagement with Auster's novel itself, and with crime fiction in general.

What postmodern detective fiction emphasises at every turn are the clear parallels between reading, detection, and interpretation, and it is the ease with which crime fiction can articulate and investigate these parallels that accounts for both the profusion of postmodern, or anti-detective, novels, and the various critical and analytic responses to them. Crime narratives that are structured around the investigation of a crime are, by default, metanarratives. They are narratives about narratives, or stories about reconstructing and interpreting the story of a crime, and it is this metanarrative self-awareness that both invites critical and theoretical approaches, and creates the perfect framework within which the genre can endlessly question and reinvent itself.

Glossary

Armchair detection A method of detection in which a detective solves a crime through deductive reasoning alone. The crime is solved purely on the basis of second-hand information, without the detective ever leaving his or her armchair, as it were, to visit the scene of the crime or personally observe the evidence. *The Armchair Detective* is also a magazine devoted to the genre of crime fiction, with an emphasis on mystery and detective fiction.

Country-house mystery A sub-genre of mystery fiction typical of the Golden Age, in which a crime takes place in the restricted setting of a country house. This provides a means of containing the action within a self-contained setting and limiting the number of suspects to a closed circle of guests. Variations of the country-house mystery include the snowbound mystery, used to great effect in Agatha Christie's play *The Mousetrap* (1949), and mysteries set on board ships or trains.

Detective fiction A type of fiction centred around the investigation of a crime that focuses attention on the method of detection by structuring the story around a mystery that appears insoluble through normal investigative methods. For this reason it is also known as mystery fiction. Detective fiction, by focusing on the method of detection, simultaneously focuses attention on the figure of the methodical detective: that is, the detective who follows a particular method.

Discourse The term refers to language that is understood as communicative utterance, and which therefore implies the presence of the *subject* of the utterance (that is, the subject who speaks or writes) and the *object* of the utterance (the 'target' of the utterance, the listener or reader). The term emphasises the role of the speaker or writer in any communicative act, and in Foucault's theory, discourse always occurs in specific social and historical contexts. In this way, discourse will always reflect the ideology of its context, although it may attempt to camouflage or disguise it.

Enlightenment A term used to describe an intellectual movement in Europe from roughly 1600 to 1790. The period, sometimes referred to as the 'Age of Reason', is characterised by a faith in the power of human reason and rationality, and an intellectual questioning of religious and monarchical authority. The Enlightenment reached its political and philosophical apotheosis in the French Revolution in 1789.

Epistemology '*Episteme*' is the Greek word for knowledge, and epistemology is the theory of the methods or foundations of knowledge, and more particularly the branch of philosophy dealing with questions of knowledge and issues concerning its accessibility, transmission, and reliability. Epistemology asks the question 'how do we know what we know?', and exposes apparently commonsensical assumptions associated with ways of knowing.

Genre The term for a literary type or class, as opposed to a literary form such as the sonnet, novel, or short story. Genres in fiction include science fiction, romance, the Gothic, or crime fiction. The major classical genres, in descending order of their perceived literary value, were epic, tragedy, lyric, comedy, and satire.

Golden Age In crime fiction, the Golden Age refers to the period between the First and Second World Wars, and is usually used to refer specifically to the flowering of British talent and to the mysteries written in Britain during this time. The Golden Age is often identified as starting in 1920 with the publication of Agatha Christie's *The Mysterious Affair at Styles*.

Gothic fiction A genre of fiction that flourished from the 1760s until the late 1820s, and which still survives in various forms. Typical settings include forbidding castles, ruined abbeys, and desolate landscapes, and Gothic stories are normally dark tales of mystery, horror, and the supernatural. They are often structured around some terrible hidden secret, and in this respect, and others, they closely resemble crime fiction.

Hard-boiled fiction A type of fiction whose style is derived from the tough-guy prose associated with Ernest Hemingway, and which was developed in the **pulp fiction** of the 1920s and 1930s in America. The hard-boiled style is terse, tough, and cynical, like the hard-boiled detectives it features, and the typical hard-boiled story is one of violence, sex, and betrayal.

Historical crime fiction A sub-genre of crime fiction that can take two forms. The first is crime fiction that is set in some distinct historical period, but which was not written in that period. The second is crime fiction that has a detective in the present investigating a crime in the remote, rather than recent, past.

Locked-room mystery A type of crime story whose central mystery is that a crime (usually a murder) has occurred in a room which seems to be hermetically sealed, allowing the criminal neither entrance to nor exit from it. The locked-room mystery is most closely associated with the Golden Age.

Metafiction Fiction characterised by its tendency to step 'beyond' or 'outside' conventional fictional confines in order to comment on its own status as fiction, and on its own fictional devices. Metafiction is often associated with **postmodernism**.

Modernism A term used to refer to both a period and an artistic movement, normally identified as beginning in the last few years of the nineteenth century. While the term is a notoriously slippery one, modernism in literature can be identified as a reaction to nineteenth-century artistic thought that was characterised in modernist fiction by its break with realist narrative structure and devices, and with the view of fiction as passively and unproblematically mirroring the world.

Mystery fiction See **detective fiction**.

Narrative The showing or the telling of a series of events from a starting point to an end point neither of which need necessarily correspond to the beginning and the end of the series of events that occurred. Narrative is often referred to as **story**, but the use of the term is not exact. The series of events, or more precisely the story, is usually recounted in either the first person or the third person, and the voice that recounts the story is referred to as the narrator.

Ontology Literally translated, the branch of philosophical enquiry concerned with the nature of being. Whereas **epistemology** is the branch of philosophy dealing with questions of knowledge, and which asks the question 'how do we know what we know about the world?', ontology asks the question 'what is the nature of the world, and what are its modes of being?'

Plot The organisation of a series of events, or a **story**, which emphasises the causal links of the story but manipulates them in order to heighten meaning, suspense, or humour.

Police procedural A sub-genre of crime fiction which foregrounds the actual methods and procedures of police work in the investigation of crime. The police procedural usually features a team of police officers, often pursuing a number of different cases at the same time, and the procedures of modern police work, including forensic technology, the interviewing of suspects, and records searches, are emphasised.

Postmodernism A contentious term used to refer to developments in art, architecture, literature, theory, and philosophy since the **modernist** movement. The 'post' of the term 'postmodernism' suggests a reaction against, if not a break from, modernism, and whereas the modernist project was concerned with emphasising the distinction between 'high' art and 'popular' art, postmodernism is characterised, among other things, by a tendency to undermine such distinctions.

Pulp fiction The term originally referred to any type of fiction printed on the cheap pulpwood paper used for popular fiction magazines in America in the first half of the twentieth century. The pulps, as they were called, published adventure fiction of all sorts, as well as love stories, Westerns, science fiction, and, of course, detective fiction, with which it became most closely associated through magazines such as *Black Mask*, and writers such as Dashiell Hammett and Raymond Chandler who began their writing careers in the pulps. *Pulp Fiction* (1994) is also the name of a film by Quentin Tarantino that cinematically appropriates the techniques and devices of the genre of crime fiction which initially developed in the early pulps.

Realism In literature, realism is associated with the development of the novel in the nineteenth century, particularly regarding its concern with producing an objective and accurate representation of the world, a representation normally viewed as a kind of passive reflection in fiction of the contemporary 'world-out-there'. The majority of fiction is still governed by realist concerns.

Revenge tragedy A type of tragedy that developed in Elizabethan and Jacobean England which features a plot that is motivated by the desire for revenge. Revenge tragedies were generally written for, and performed in, the public theatres, and clearly catered for popular public tastes. These popular tastes are clear in the presence of ghosts and supernatural elements, sub-plots and mechanisms of disguise and deception, and the often violent and bloody intersection of sex and death.

Romance The early verse romances of the twelfth and thirteenth centuries were fictional stories of love, chivalry, and adventure, and the term is normally used to describe any fictional narrative featuring heroic characters and settings and action far removed from the everyday world of the nineteenth-century **realist** novel. The two best-known examples in English are *Sir Gawain and the Green Knight*, from the late fourteenth century, and Mallory's *La Morte d'Arthur* (1470).

Sensation fiction A type of fiction that owed a great debt to the **Gothic** novel, sensation fiction flourished in the 1860s and 1870s, and the best-known example is Wilkie Collins's *The Woman in White* (1860). As the term suggests, sensation fiction featured sensational and often melodramatic themes and action, often containing colourful accounts of crime and violence that prefigured those of twentieth-century crime fiction.

Serial fiction Serial fiction developed in the nineteenth and early twentieth centuries, when novels were frequently serialised in magazines aimed increasingly at a commuting middle class. The novels of Dickens, for example, were frequently serialised, but it was the serialisation of the Sherlock Holmes short stories which anticipated the serial crime novels of the twentieth century, with each story being self-contained, and linked only by the character of the detective and his faithful companion and narrator, Dr Watson.

Story The chronological order of a series of events from beginning to end which can be structured or manipulated through various **plot** devices.

Thriller A term so vague as to be almost useless without further particularisation, the thriller can refer to any narrative structured in order to maximise tension, suspense, and exciting action. The origins of the thriller can be traced back through the sensation novel to the **Gothic fiction** of the late eighteenth and early nineteenth centuries.

Suggestions for Further Reading

While the Bibliography provides a more comprehensive list of texts that are useful and relevant to anybody studying crime fiction, the following titles are either essential reading in any study of the genre, or provide useful starting points for specific theoretical approaches.

Browne, Ray B. and Kreiser, Lawrence A., Jr. (2000) *The Detective as Historian: History and Art in Historical Crime Fiction*, Bowling Green, OH, Bowling Green University Popular Press. As the only book-length study of the rapidly growing sub-genre of historical crime fiction, this book is well worth looking at, with particularly useful and incisive chapters on Peter Lovesey and Umberto Eco.

Knight, Stephen (1980) *Form and Ideology in Crime Fiction*, Basingstoke, Macmillan. Although it is now beginning to show its age, this book provides an invaluable outline of the fiction of key writers in the development of the genre, such as Conan Doyle, Christie, and Chandler, and should be in the library of every student of crime fiction.

Knight, Stephen (2004) *Crime Fiction 1800–2000: Detection, Death, Diversity*, Basingstoke, Palgrave Macmillan. This book provides a clear outline of the history, practices, and conventions of the genre which is theoretically alert and which also considers very recent developments in the genre.

Most, Glenn W., and Stowe, William W. (eds) (1983) *The Poetics of Murder: Detective Fiction and Literary Theory*, San Diego, New York and London, Harcourt Brace. Although a little dated, both in terms of its theoretical framework and in its textual coverage, this is still a very good collection of literary theoretical examinations of the genre.

Munt, Sally R. (1994) *Murder by the Book? Feminism and the Crime Novel*, London, Routledge. A useful application of feminist and psycho-analytic theory to crime fiction by women, including an interesting, if weighty, chapter on postmodernism.

Plain, Gill (2001) *Twentieth-Century Crime Fiction: Gender, Sexuality and the Body,* Edinburgh, Edinburgh University Press. This excellent book provides an examination of the construction of gender, sexuality, and the body in crime fiction, and its critical focus on corporeality considers both the corpse-as-signifier and the body of the detective as the site of various socio-cultural conflicts.

Priestman, Martin (1990) *Detective Fiction and Literature: The Figure on the Carpet,* Basingstoke, Macmillan. A comprehensive study of the genre from Oedipus to the police procedural which, despite its broad canvas, does not sacrifice analytic detail or theoretical engagement. Essential reading.

Priestman, Martin (1998) *Crime Fiction: From Poe to the Present,* Plymouth, Northcote House in Association with the British Council. Short, concise, and thoroughly readable, this is an excellent introduction to the study of the genre.

Symons, Julian (1993) *Bloody Murder: From the Detective Story to the Crime Novel,* New York, The Mysterious Press. Descriptive, rather than discursive, and lacking the theoretical alertness of other titles on this list, this book is still a useful and illuminating outline of the developmental history of the genre.

Walker, Ronald G. and Frazer, June M. (eds) (1990) *The Cunning Craft: Original Essays on Detective Fiction and Contemporary Literary Theory,* Macomb, Western Illinois University Press. A useful collection of critical essays on crime fiction, including chapters on the feminist counter-tradition, postmodern detective fiction, and the crime novel's debt to modernism. Scott R. Christianson's chapter on modernity and the hard-boiled detective, in particular, is excellent.

Willett, Ralph (1992) *Hard-Boiled Detective Fiction,* Staffordshire, British Association for American Studies. Short, concise, and engagingly written, this book provides a useful critical overview of the major hard-boiled writers, with chapters on early authors such as Chandler and Hammett, but also more contemporary authors such as James Crumley.

SELECT BIBLIOGRAPHY

TEXTS

Allingham, Margery, *The Crime at Black Dudley* (1929), Harmondsworth, Penguin, 1950.
—— *The Fashion in Shrouds* (1938), Harmondsworth, Penguin, 1950.
—— *More Work for the Undertaker* (1948), Harmondsworth, Penguin, 1991.
—— *The Tiger in the Smoke* (1952), New York, Carroll & Graf, 2000.
—— *Hide My Eyes* (1958), Harmondsworth, Penguin, 1960.
Auster, Paul, *City of Glass* (1985), in *The New York Trilogy*, London, Faber, 1992.
—— *Ghosts* (1986), in *The New York Trilogy*, London, Faber, 1992.
—— *The Locked Room* (1986), in *The New York Trilogy*, London, Faber, 1992.
Barron, Stephanie, *Jane and the Unpleasantness at Scargrave Manor: Being the First Jane Austen Mystery* (1996), New York, Bantam, 1996.
—— *Jane and the Man of the Cloth: Being the Second Jane Austen Mystery* (1997), New York, Bantam, 1997.
—— *Jane and the Wandering Eye: Being the Third Jane Austen Mystery* (1998), New York, Bantam, 1998.
Bentley, E.C., *Trent's Last Case* (1913), New York, Carroll & Graf, 1996.
Berkeley, Anthony, *The Poisoned Chocolates Case* (1929), London, Pan, 1950.
Blake, Nicholas, *A Question of Proof* (1935), London, HarperCollins, 1979.
—— *Thou Shell of Death* (1936), London, Collins, 1970.
Buchan, John, *The Thirty-Nine Steps* (1915), Harmondsworth, Penguin, 1991.
Burgess, Anthony, *A Dead Man in Deptford* (1993), London, Vintage, 1994.
Burke, James Lee, *The Neon Rain* (1987), London, Arrow, 2000.
—— *Black Cherry Blues* (1989), London, Arrow, 2000.
—— *A Morning For Flamingos* (1992), London, Arrow, 2000.
—— *A Stained White Radiance* (1992), London, Arrow, 2000.
—— *In the Electric Mist with Confederate Dead* (1993), London, Orion, 2002.
—— *Purple Cane Road* (2000), London, Orion, 2001.
—— *Last Car to Elysian Fields* (2003), London, Orion, 2003.
Burnett, W.R., *Little Caesar* (1929), London, Jonathan Cape, 1932.
Byatt, A.S., *Possession* (1990), London, Vintage, 1991.
Cain, James M., *The Postman Always Rings Twice* (1934), London, Bloomsbury, 1997.
—— *Double Indemnity* (1936), London, Orion, 2002.
Carr, Caleb, *The Alienist* (1994), London, Warner, 2002.
—— *The Angel of Darkness* (1997), London, Warner, 1998.
Chandler, Raymond, *The Big Sleep* (1939), in *Raymond Chandler: Three Novels*, Harmondsworth, Penguin, 1993.
—— *Farewell, My Lovely* (1940), in *Raymond Chandler: Three Novels*, Harmondsworth, Penguin, 1993.

—— *The High Window* (1943), Harmondsworth, Penguin, 1951.

—— *The Lady in the Lake* (1944), Harmondsworth, Penguin, 1952.

—— *The Little Sister* (1949), Harmondsworth, Penguin, 1955.

—— *The Long Goodbye* (1953), in *Raymond Chandler: Three Novels*, Harmondsworth, Penguin, 1993.

Chesterton, G.K., *Father Brown Stories*, Harmondsworth, Penguin, 1994.

Childers, Erskine, *The Riddle of the Sands* (1903), Harmondsworth, Penguin, 1952.

Christie, Agatha, *The Mysterious Affair at Styles* (1920), London, HarperCollins, 2001.

—— *Murder on the Links* (1923), London, HarperCollins, 2001.

—— *The Murder of Roger Ackroyd* (1926), London, HarperCollins, 2002.

—— *The Murder at the Vicarage* (1930), London, HarperCollins, 2002.

—— *Murder on the Orient Express* (1934), London, HarperCollins, 1994.

—— *Death on the Nile* (1937), London, HarperCollins, 2001.

—— *The Body in the Library* (1942), London, HarperCollins, 1994.

—— *A Murder is Announced* (1950), London, HarperCollins, 1993.

Collins, Wilkie, *The Woman in White* (1860), Harmondsworth, Penguin, 1999.

—— *The Moonstone* (1868), Harmondsworth, Penguin, 1986.

Connelly, Michael, *The Black Echo* (1992), London, Orion, 1997.

—— *The Last Coyote* (1995), London, Orion, 1997.

—— *A Darkness More Than Night* (2001), London, Orion, 2001.

—— *City of Bones* (2002), London, Orion, 2002.

Conrad, Joseph, *Heart of Darkness* (1902), Harmondsworth, Penguin, 1974.

Cook, Judith, *The Slicing Edge of Death* (1993), London, Simon & Schuster.

Cornwell, Patricia, *Postmortem* (1990), London, Warner, 2001.

—— *Body of Evidence* (1991), London, Warner, 2000.

—— *Cruel and Unusual* (1992), London, Warner, 2004.

—— *The Body Farm* (1993), London, Warner, 2000.

—— *Unnatural Exposure* (1997), London, Warner, 2000.

—— *The Last Precinct* (2000), London, Warner, 2004.

Crumley, James, *The Wrong Case* (1975), in *James Crumley: The Collection*, London, Picador, 1993.

—— *The Last Good Kiss* (1978), in *James Crumley: The Collection*, London, Picador, 1993.

—— *Dancing Bear* (1983), in *James Crumley: The Collection*, London, Picador, 1993.

—— *The Mexican Tree Duck* (1993), New York, Mysterious Press, 2001.

—— *Bordersnakes* (1996), London, Flamingo, 1998.

—— *The Final Country* (2001), London, HarperCollins, 2003.

Davis, Lindsey, *The Silver Pigs* (1989), London, Arrow, 2000.

—— *Shadows in Bronze* (1990), London, Arrow, 2000.

—— *Venus in Copper* (1991), London, Arrow, 1992.

—— *The Iron Hand of Mars* (1992), London, Arrow, 1993.

—— *Poseidon's Gold* (1993), London, Arrow, 1994.

—— *Last Act in Palmyra* (1994), London, Arrow, 1995.

—— *A Dying Light in Cordoba* (1996), London, Arrow, 1997.

—— *A Body in the Bath House* (2001), London, Arrow, 2002.

—— *The Jupiter Myth* (2002), London, Arrow, 2003.

Defoe, Daniel, *Moll Flanders* (1722), Harmondsworth, Penguin, 1994.

Dexter, Colin, *Last Bus to Woodstock* (1975), London, Pan, 1997.

—— *Last Seen Wearing* (1976), in *The Second Inspector Morse Omnibus*, London, Pan Macmillan, 1994.

—— *The Dead of Jericho* (1981), London, Pan, 1983.

—— *The Riddle of the Third Mile* (1983), in *The Second Inspector Morse Omnibus*, London, Pan Macmillan, 1994.

—— *The Secret of Annexe 3* (1986), in *The Second Inspector Morse Omnibus*, London, Pan Macmillan, 1994.

—— *The Wench is Dead* (1989), London, Pan, 1998.

—— *The Remorseful Day* (2000), London, Pan, 2000.

Dibdin, Michael, *Ratking* (1988), London, Faber, 1999.

—— *Vendetta* (1990), London, Faber, 1999.

—— *Cabal* (1992), London, Faber, 1999.

—— *Dead Lagoon* (1994), London, Faber, 1999.

—— *Così Fan Tutti* (1996), London, Faber, 1999.

—— *A Long Finish* (1998), London, Faber, 1998.

—— *Blood Rain* (1999), London, Faber, 2000.

—— *And Then You Die* (2002), London, Faber, 2002.

—— *Medusa* (2003), London, Faber, 2003.

Dick, Philip K., *Do Androids Dream of Electric Sheep?* (1968), London, Grafton, 1984.

Dickens, Charles, *Oliver Twist* (1838), Oxford, Oxford University Press, 1999.

—— *Bleak House* (1853), Harmondsworth, Penguin, 1996.

—— *The Mystery of Edwin Drood* (1870), Harmondsworth, Penguin, 2002.

Dickson Carr, John, *The Hollow Man* (1935), London, Orion, 2002.

Dostoyevsky, Fyodor, *Crime and Punishment* (1866), Oxford, Oxford University Press, 1998.

Doyle, Arthur Conan, *The Penguin Complete Sherlock Holmes*, Harmondsworth, Penguin, 1981.

Eco, Umberto, *The Name of the Rose* (1980), trans. William Weaver, London, Vintage, 1998.

Ellroy, James, *The Black Dahlia* (1987), London, Arrow, 1993.

—— *The Big Nowhere* (1988), in *James Ellroy: The Dudley Smith Trio*, London, Arrow, 1999.

—— *L.A. Confidential* (1990), in *James Ellroy: The Dudley Smith Trio*, London, Arrow, 1999.

—— *White Jazz* (1992), in *James Ellroy: The Dudley Smith Trio*, London, Arrow, 1999.

—— *My Dark Places* (1996), London, Arrow, 1997.

Finney, Patricia, *Firedrake's Eye* (1992), London, Phoenix, 1999.

—— *Unicorn's Blood* (1998), London, Phoenix, 1998.

Fleming, Ian, *Casino Royale* (1953), Harmondsworth, Penguin, 2002.

—— *From Russia, With Love* (1957), Harmondsworth, Penguin, 2002.

—— *Doctor No* (1958), Harmondsworth, Penguin, 2002.

—— *On Her Majesty's Secret Service* (1963), Harmondsworth, Penguin, 2002.

Forrest, Katherine V., *Amateur City* (1984), London, Pandora Press, 1987.

—— *Murder at the Nightwood Bar* (1987), London, Pandora Press, 1987.

—— *Murder by Tradition* (1991), Tallahassee, FL, Naiad Press, 1991.

—— *Sleeping Bones* (1999), New York, Berkley Prime Crime, 2000.

Gaboriau, Emile, *The Widow Lerouge* (1866), Milton Keynes, Lightning Source, 2003.

—— *Monsieur Lecoq* (1869), Mineola, NY, Dover, 1975.

George, Elizabeth, *A Suitable Vengeance* (1991), London, Bantam, 1992.

Godwin, William, *Caleb Williams* (1794), Harmondsworth, Penguin, 1988.

Grafton, Sue, *'A' is for Alibi* (1982), London, Macmillan, 1993.

—— *'C' is for Corpse* (1986), London, Macmillan, 1988.

—— *'E' is for Evidence* (1988), New York, Bantam, 1989.

—— *'G' is for Gumshoe* (1990), London, Macmillan, 1990.

Green, Anna Katherine, *The Leavenworth Case* (1878), Mineola, NY, Dover, 1982.

Grimes, Martha, *The Dirty Duck* (1984), London, Headline, 1987.

Grisham, John, *The Firm* (1991), London, Arrow, 1991.

—— *A Time to Kill* (1992), London, Arrow, 1992.

—— *The Pelican Brief* (1992), London, Arrow, 1992.

—— *The Client* (1994), London, Arrow, 1994.

Hammett, Dashiell, *Red Harvest* (1929), New York, Vintage Crime/Black Lizard, 1992.

—— *The Dain Curse* (1929), London, Orion, 2002.

—— *The Maltese Falcon* (1930), London, Pan, 1975.

—— *The Glass Key* (1931), London, Orion, 2002.

—— *The Thin Man* (1934), New York, Vintage Crime/Black Lizard, 1992.

Hansen, Joseph, *Fadeout* (1970), Harpenden, No Exit Press, 1996.

—— *Skinflick* (1979), Harpenden, No Exit Press, 1990.

—— *Gravedigger* (1982), Harpenden, No Exit Press, 2000.

—— *The Little Dog Laughed* (1986), Harpenden, No Exit Press, 2002.

Harris, Robert, *Fatherland* (1992), London, Arrow, 1993.

Harris, Thomas, *Red Dragon* (1981), London, Arrow, 1993.

—— *The Silence of the Lambs* (1989), London, Arrow, 1999.

—— *Hannibal* (1999), London, William Heinemann, 1999.

Highsmith, Patricia, *Strangers on a Train* (1950), London, Vintage, 1999.

—— *The Talented Mr Ripley* (1955), London, Vintage, 1999.

Hillerman, Tony, *The Blessing Way* (1970), in *The Leaphorn Mysteries*, Harmondsworth, Penguin, 1994.

—— *Dance Hall of the Dead* (1973), in *The Leaphorn Mysteries*, Harmondsworth, Penguin, 1994.

—— *Listening Woman* (1978), in *The Leaphorn Mysteries*, Harmondsworth, Penguin, 1994.

—— *People of Darkness* (1980), New York, HarperCollins, 1991.

—— *The Dark Wind* (1982), New York, HarperCollins, 1990.

—— *The Ghostway* (1984), New York, HarperCollins, 1992.

—— *A Thief of Time* (1989), Harmondsworth, Penguin, 1993.

—— *Talking God* (1990), Harmondsworth, Penguin, 1993.

—— *Sacred Clowns* (1993), New York, HarperCollins, 1994.

Himes, Chester, *A Rage in Harlem* (1957), London, Allison & Busby, 1985.

—— *The Real Cool Killers* (1959), London, Allison & Busby, 1985.

—— *The Big Gold Dream* (1960), Harmondsworth, Penguin, 1976.

—— *Cotton Comes to Harlem* (1965), London, Allison & Busby, 1985.

Hjortsberg, William, *Falling Angel* (1979), Harpenden, No Exit Press, 1998.

Høeg, Peter, *Smilla's Sense of Snow* (1992), trans. Tiina Nunnally, New York, Dell, 1995.

Hume, Fergus, *The Mystery of a Hansom Cab* (1886), London, Hogarth Press, 1985.

Iles, Frances, *Malice Aforethought* (1931), London, Pan, 1979.

James, P.D., *Cover Her Face* (1962), London, Faber, 2002.

—— *Unnatural Causes* (1967), London, Faber, 2002.

—— *Shroud for a Nightingale* (1971), London, Faber, 2002.

—— *An Unsuitable Job for a Woman* (1972), London, Faber, 2000.

—— *The Skull Beneath the Skin* (1982), London, Sphere Books, 1983.

—— *A Taste for Death* (1986), New York, Warner, 1987.

—— *Devices and Desires* (1990), London, Faber, 1990.

—— *Original Sin* (1995), Harmondsworth, Penguin, 1996.

Kerr, Philip, *March Violets* (1989), in *Berlin Noir*, Harmondsworth, Penguin, 1993.

—— *The Pale Criminal* (1990), in *Berlin Noir*, Harmondsworth, Penguin, 1993.

—— *A German Requiem* (1991), in *Berlin Noir*, Harmondsworth, Penguin, 1993.

—— *A Philosophical Investigation* (1992), New York, Bantam, 1995.

Kipling, Rudyard, *Kim* (1901), Harmondsworth, Penguin, 1987.

le Carré, John, *The Spy Who Came In From the Cold* (1963), London, Victor Gollancz, 1963.

—— *A Perfect Spy* (1986), London, Hodder & Stoughton, 1986.

Leonard, Elmore, *Glitz* (1985), Harmondsworth, Penguin, 1986.

—— *Freaky Deaky* (1988), Harmondsworth, Penguin, 1988.

—— *Killshot* (1989), Harmondsworth, Penguin, 1990.

—— *Get Shorty* (1990), Harmondsworth, Penguin, 1991.

—— *Maximum Bob* (1991), Harmondsworth, Penguin, 1992.

—— *Out of Sight* (1996), Harmondsworth, Penguin, 1997.

Lovesey, Peter, *Wobble to Death* (1970), London, Macmillan.

—— *The Detective Wore Silk Drawers* (1971), London, Allison & Busby, 1999.

—— *Abracadaver* (1972), London, Allison & Busby, 2000.

—— *A Case of Spirits* (1974), London, Arrow, 1991.

—— *Waxwork* (1978), London, Arrow, 1988.

—— *Bertie and the Tinman* (1987), London, Warner, 1988.

—— *Bertie and the Crime of Passion* (1993), London, Warner, 1995.

McBain, Ed, *Cop Hater* (1956), London, Orion, 2003.

—— *Killer's Choice* (1958), London, Allison & Busby, 2000.

—— *The Heckler* (1960), Harmondsworth, Penguin, 1966.

McDermid, Val, *The Mermaids Singing* (1995), London, HarperCollins, 2002.

—— *The Wire in the Blood* (1997), London, HarperCollins, 1998.

—— *The Last Temptation* (2002), HarperCollins, 2003.

Macdonald, Ross, *The Moving Target* (1949), London, Fontana, 1978.

—— *The Drowning Pool* (1950), London, Allison & Busby, 1989.

—— *The Doomsters* (1958), London, Fontana, 1971.

Marsh, Ngaio, *A Surfeit of Lampreys* (1940), London, HarperCollins, 1999.

—— *Death and the Dancing Footman* (1941), London, HarperCollins, 1999.

—— *Black As He's Painted* (1974), London, HarperCollins, 2000.

Meyer, Nicholas, *The Seven-Per-Cent Solution* (1974), New York, W.W. Norton, 1993.

—— *The West End Horror* (1976), New York, W.W. Norton, 1994.

Middleton, Thomas and Rowley, William, *The Changeling* (1622), London, A&C Black, 1999.

Miller, Frank, *Sin City* (1992), London, Titan Books, 1993.

—— *A Dame to Kill For* (1994), London, Titan Books, 1994.

—— *The Big Fat Kill* (1995), London, Titan Books, 1996.

—— *That Yellow Bastard* (1997), Milwaukie, OR, Dark Horse Comics, 1997.

—— *Family Values* (1997), London, Titan Books, 1997.

—— *Booze, Broads, and Bullets* (1998), London, Titan Books, 1999.

Moore, Alan and Campbell, Eddie, *From Hell* (1999), London, Knockabout Comics, 2000.

Mosley, Walter, *Devil in a Blue Dress* (1990), London, Pan, 1992.

—— *A Red Death* (1991), London, Pan, 1993.

—— *White Butterfly* (1992), London, Serpent's Tail, 1992.

—— *Black Betty* (1994), London, Serpent's Tail, 1994.

—— *A Little Yellow Dog* (1996), London, Picador, 1997.

—— *Bad Boy Brawly Brown* (2002), London, Serpent's Tail, 2002.

Nabokov, Vladimir, *Lolita* (1955), Harmondsworth, Penguin, 1995.

Nicholl, Charles, *The Reckoning: The Murder of Christopher Marlowe* (1992), London, Picador, 1993.

Paretsky, Sara, *Indemnity Only* (1982), Harmondsworth, Penguin, 1987.

—— *Deadlock* (1984), Harmondsworth, Penguin, 1987.

—— *Killing Orders* (1985), Harmondsworth, Penguin, 1987.

—— *Bitter Medicine* (1987), Harmondsworth, Penguin, 1988.

—— *Toxic Shock* (1988), Harmondsworth, Penguin, 1990.

—— *Burn Marks* (1990), London, Virago, 1991.

—— *Guardian Angel* (1992), Harmondsworth, Penguin, 1992.

—— *Tunnel Vision* (1994), Harmondsworth, Penguin, 1995.

—— *Hard Time* (1999), Harmondsworth, Penguin, 2000.

—— *Total Recall* (2001), New York, Dell, 2002.

Parker, Robert B., *The Godwulf Manuscript* (1973), New York, Dell, 1996.

—— *Mortal Stakes* (1975), Harmondsworth, Penguin, 1977.

—— *The Widening Gyre* (1983), Harmondsworth, Penguin, 1987.

Patterson, James, *Along Came a Spider* (1992), London, HarperCollins, 1994.

—— *Kiss the Girls* (1995), London, HarperCollins, 1996

—— *Cat and Mouse* (1997), London, Warner, 1998.

Pérez-Reverte, Arturo, *The Flanders Panel* (1990), London, Vintage, 2003.

—— *The Dumas Club* (1993), London, Vintage, 2003.

—— *The Seville Communion* (1995), London, Vintage, 2003.

Perry, Anne, *The Cater Street Hangman* (1979), London, HarperCollins, 1998.

—— *Resurrection Row* (1981), New York, Fawcett Books, 1989.

—— *Death in the Devil's Acre* (1985), New York, Fawcett Books, 1989.

—— *Silence in Hanover Close* (1988), New York, Fawcett Books, 1996.

—— *The Face of a Stranger* (1990), London, Headline, 1994.

—— *A Dangerous Mourning* (1991), London, Headline, 1994.

—— *The Hyde Park Headsman* (1994), London, HarperCollins, 1996.

Peters, Ellis, *A Morbid Taste for Bones* (1977), in *The First Cadfael Omnibus*, London, Warner, 2001.

—— *One Corpse Too Many* (1979), in *The First Cadfael Omnibus*, London, Warner, 2001.

—— *Monk's-Hood* (1980), in *The First Cadfael Omnibus*, London, Warner, 2001.

—— *A Rare Benedictine* (1988), London, Headline, 1989.

—— *Brother Cadfael's Penance* (1994), London, Warner, 1995.

Poe, Edgar Allan, *The Murders in the Rue Morgue: The Complete Crime Stories*, London, Orion, 2002.

Puzo, Mario, *The Godfather* (1969), London, Arrow, 1991.

Queen, Ellery, *The Roman Hat Mystery* (1929), London, Gollancz, 1969.

—— *The French Powder Mystery* (1930), London, Gollancz, 1970.

—— *The Greek Coffin Mystery* (1932), London, Gollancz, 1971.

Rankin, Ian, *Knots & Crosses* (1987), in *Rebus: The Early Years*, London, Orion, 2000.

—— *Hide & Seek* (1990), in *Rebus: The Early Years*, London, Orion, 2000.

—— *Tooth & Nail* (1992), in *Rebus: The Early Years*, London, Orion, 2000.

—— *Mortal Causes* (1994), London, Orion, 2002.

—— *Let it Bleed* (1996), London, Orion, 1996.

—— *Set in Darkness* (2000), London, Orion, 2002.

—— *The Falls* (2001), London, Orion, 2002.

—— *Resurrection Men* (2001), London, Orion, 2002.

Reichs, Kathy, *Deja Dead* (1997), London, Arrow, 1998.

—— *Death du Jour* (1999), London, Arrow, 2000.

Rendell, Ruth, *A Judgement in Stone* (1977), London, Arrow, 1978.

—— *The Lake of Darkness* (1980), London, Arrow, 1981.

—— *An Unkindness of Ravens* (1985), London, Arrow, 1994.

Rowson, Martin, *The Waste Land* (1990), London, Picador, 1999.

Sayers, Dorothy L., *Whose Body?* (1923), London, Coronet Crime, 1989.

—— *Unnatural Death* (1927), London, Coronet Crime, 1989.

—— *Strong Poison* (1930), London, Coronet Crime, 1989.

—— *Gaudy Night* (1935), London, Hodder & Stoughton, 1970.

Shakespeare, William, *Hamlet* (1601), ed. Harold Jenkins, London, Arden Shakespeare, 1997.

Shelley, Mary, *Frankenstein: or, The Modern Prometheus* (1818/1831), Harmondsworth, Penguin, 1994.

Somoza, José Carlos, *The Athenian Murders* (2000), trans. Sonia Soto, London, Abacus, 2003.

Sophocles, *Oedipus the King*, in *The Three Theban Plays*, trans. Robert Fagles, Harmondsworth, Penguin, 1984.

Spillane, Mickey, *One Lonely Night* (1951), London, Corgi, 1970.

—— *The Big Kill* (1951), London, Corgi, 1970.

—— *I, The Jury* (1960), London, Corgi, 1971.

Stevenson, Robert Louis, *The Strange Case of Dr Jekyll and Mr Hyde, and Other Tales of Terror*, Harmondsworth, Penguin, 2002.

Stout, Rex, *Fer-de-Lance* (1934), Harmondsworth, Penguin, 1955.

—— *The League of Frightened Men* (1935), New York, Bantam, 1995.

—— *Too Many Cooks* (1938), New York, Bantam, 1995.

—— *Not Quite Dead Enough* (1944), New York, Bantam, 1992.

—— *Death of a Doxy* (1966), New York, Bantam, 1995.

Tartt, Donna, *The Secret History* (1992), Harmondsworth, Penguin, 1993.

Tey, Josephine, *The Daughter of Time* (1951), Harmondsworth, Penguin, 1954.

Tremayne, Peter, *Absolution by Murder* (1994), London, Headline, 1994.

—— *Shroud for the Archbishop* (1995), London, Headline, 1995.

—— *The Subtle Serpent* (1996), London, Headline, 1996.

—— *The Spider's Web* (1997), London, Headline, 1997.

—— *Valley of the Shadow* (1998), London, Headline, 1998.

Tourner, Cyril, *The Revenger's Tragedy* (1607), London, A&C Black, 2000.

Van Dine, S.S., *The Benson Murder Case* (1926), London, Simon & Schuster, 1983.

—— *The Bishop Murder Case* (1929), London, Simon & Schuster, 1983.

—— *The Dragon Murder Case* (1933), London, Simon & Schuster, 1985.

Vidocq, Eugène François, *Memoirs of Vidocq: Master of Crime* (1828), Oakland, CA, AK Press, 2003.

Waugh, Hillary, *Last Seen Wearing . . .* (1952), London, HarperCollins, 1981.

Webster, John, *The White Devil* (1612), London, A&C Black, 1996.

Wilson, Barbara, *Murder in the Collective* (1984), London, Virago, 1994.

—— *Gaudí Afternoon* (1990), Seattle, WA, Seal Press, 2001.

—— *Trouble in Transylvania* (1993), London, Virago, 1993.

Wilson, Robert, *A Small Death in Lisbon* (1999), London, HarperCollins, 1999.

FILM AND TV

Angel Heart (1987: dir. Alan Parker)

The Big Sleep (1946: dir. Howard Hawks)

Blade Runner (1982: dir. Ridley Scott)

The Blue Dahlia (1946: dir. George Marshall)

Body Heat (1981: dir. Lawrence Kasdan)

Chinatown (1974: dir. Roman Polanski)

C.S.I.: Crime Scene Investigation (TV episodes: 'Chaos Theory'; 'Ellie'; '"Primum Non Nocere" AKA "Icings"'; 'Random Acts of Violence'; 'Scuba Doobie Doo'; 'Unfriendly Skies')

Devil in a Blue Dress (1995: dir. Carl Franklin)

The Devil's Advocate (1997: dir. Taylor Hackford)

Die Hard (1988: dir. John McTiernan)

Identity (2003: dir. James Margold)

Memento (2000: dir. Christopher Nolan)

U Turn (1997: dir. Oliver Stone)

V.I. Warshawski (1991: dir. Jeff Kanew)

CRITICISM

Auden, W.H. (1963) 'The Guilty Vicarage', in *Dyer's Hand and Other Essays*, London, Faber, pp. 15–24.

Babener, Liahna K. (1995) 'Raymond Chandler's City of Lies', in *Los Angeles in Fiction: A Collection of Essays*, revised edn, ed. David Fine, Albuquerque: University of New Mexico Press, pp. 127–49.

Bacon, Francis (1999) *Essays* (1598), London, Everyman.

Barley, Tony (1990) '"Loving and Lying": Multiple Identity in John le Carré's *A Perfect Spy*', in *Watching the Detectives: Essays on Crime Fiction*, ed. Ian A. Bell and Graham Daldry, Basingstoke, Macmillan, pp. 152–71.

Barnard, Robert (1980) *A Talent to Deceive: An Appreciation of Agatha Christie*, London, Collins.

Barthes, Roland (1975) *S/Z*, trans. Richard Miller, London, Jonathan Cape.

Bell, Ian A. and Daldry, Graham (eds) (1990) *Watching the Detectives: Essays on Crime Fiction*, Basingstoke, Macmillan.

Belsey, Catherine (1985) *The Subject of Tragedy: Identity and Difference in Renaissance Drama*, London, Methuen.

Bertens, Hans and D'haen, Theo (2001) *Contemporary American Crime Fiction*, Basingstoke, Palgrave Macmillan.

Bhabha, Homi (1994) *The Location of Culture*, London, Routledge.

Bird, Delys (ed.) (1993) *Killing Women: Rewriting Detective Fiction*, Sydney, Angus & Robertson.

Bloom, Clive (ed.) (1990) *Twentieth-Century Suspense: The Thriller Comes of Age* Basingstoke, Palgrave Macmillan.

Botting, Fred (2001) *Gothic*, London, Routledge.

Bradbury, Richard (1988) 'Sexuality, Guilt and Detection: Tension between History and Suspense', in *American Crime Fiction: Studies in the Genre*, ed. Brian Docherty, Basingstoke, Macmillan, pp. 88–99.

Browne, Ray B. and Kreiser, Lawrence A., Jr. (2000) *The Detective as Historian: History and Art in Historical Crime Fiction*, Bowling Green, OH, Bowling Green University Popular Press.

Butler, Judith (1990) *Gender Trouble: Feminism and the Subversion of Identity*, New York, Routledge.

Cain, James M. (1944) Preface to *Three of a Kind*, New York, Alfred A. Knopf.

Cawelti, John G. (1976) *Adventure, Mystery, and Romance: Formula Stories as Art and Popular Culture*, Chicago and London, University of Chicago Press.

Chandler, Raymond (1988) *The Simple Art of Murder*, New York, Vintage Books.

Christianson, Scott R. (1989) 'Tough Talk and Wisecracks: Language as Power in American Detective Fiction', *Journal of Popular Culture* 23 (Autumn), pp. 151–62.

—— (1990) 'A Heap of Broken Images: Hardboiled Detective Fiction and the Discourse(s) of Modernity', in *The Cunning Craft: Original Essays on Detective Fiction and Contemporary Literary Theory*, ed. Ronald G. Walker and June M. Frazer, Macomb, Western Illinois University Press, pp. 135–48.

Cobley, Paul (2001) *Narrative*, London, Routledge.

Cohen, Josh (1997) 'James Ellroy, Los Angeles and the Spectacular Crisis in Masculinity', in *Criminal Proceedings: The Contemporary American Crime Novel*, ed. Peter Messent, London, Pluto Press, pp. 168–86.

Cullen Gruesser, John (1999) 'An Un-Easy Relationship: Walter Mosley's Signifyin(g) Detective and the Black Community', in *Multicultural Detective Fiction: Murder from the 'Other' Side*, ed. Adrienne Johnson Gosselin, New York and London, Garland, pp. 235–55.

de Certeau, Michel (1984) *The Practice of Everyday Life*, trans. Steven F. Rendall, Berkeley and Los Angeles, CA: University of California Press.

Dove, George N. (1982) *The Police Procedural*, Bowling Green, OH, Bowling Green University Popular Press.

Eagleton, Terry (1996) *Literary Theory: An Introduction*, 2nd edn, Oxford, Blackwell.

Earwaker, Julian and Becker, Kathleen (2002) *Scene of the Crime: A Guide to the Landscapes of British Detective Fiction*, London, Aurum Press.

Eco, Umberto (1984) *Postscript to The Name of the Rose*, trans. William Weaver, San Diego, New York and London, Harcourt Brace.

—— (1994) *Six Walks in the Fictional Woods*, Cambridge, MA and London, Harvard University Press.

Ellroy, James (1994) *The American Cop, Without Walls*, Channel 4 TV Programme (British), 29 November.

Fine, David (1995) 'Beginning in the Thirties: The Los Angeles Fiction of James M. Cain and Horace McCoy', in *Los Angeles in Fiction: A Collection of Essays*, revised edn, ed. David Fine, Albuquerque: University of New Mexico Press, pp. 43–66.

—— (ed.) (1995) *Los Angeles in Fiction: A Collection of Essays*, revised edn, Albuquerque: University of New Mexico Press.

Fiske, John (1992) *Understanding Popular Culture*, London, Routledge.

Fletcher, Angus (ed.) (1976) *The Literature of Fact*, New York, Columbia University Press.

Ford, Judy Ann (2000) 'Umberto Eco: *The Name of the Rose*', in *The Detective as Historian: History and Art in Historical Crime Fiction*, ed. Ray B. Browne and Lawrence A. Kreiser Jr., Bowling Green, OH, Bowling Green University Popular Press, pp. 95–110.

Foucault, Michel (1980) *Power/Knowledge: Selected Interviews and Other Writings, 1972–1977*, trans. Colin Gordon and Leo Marshall *et al.*, Brighton: Harvester Press.

—— (1991) *Discipline and Punish: The Birth of the Prison*, trans. Alan Sheridan, Harmondsworth, Penguin.

Foxwell, Margaret L. (2000) 'Peter Lovesey: No Cribbing on History', in *The Detective as Historian: History and Art in Historical Crime Fiction*, ed. Ray B. Browne and Lawrence A. Kreiser Jr., Bowling Green, OH, Bowling Green University Popular Press, pp. 283–92.

Freeman, R. Austin (1992) 'The Art of the Detective Story', in *The Art of the Mystery Story: A Collection of Critical Essays*, ed. Howard Haycraft, New York, Carroll & Graf, pp. 7–17.

Gardiner, Dorothy and Sorley Walker, Kathrine (eds) (1997) *Raymond Chandler Speaking*, Los Angeles and London, University of California Press.

Glover, David (2003) 'The Thriller', in *The Cambridge Companion to Crime Fiction*, ed. Martin Priestman, Cambridge, Cambridge University Press, pp. 135–53.

Hargreaves, Tracy (2001) *Donna Tartt's The Secret History*, New York and London, Continuum.

Haut, Woody (1999) *Neon Noir: Contemporary American Crime Fiction*, London, Serpent's Tail.

Hawkes, Terence (1997) *Structuralism and Semiotics*, London, Routledge.

Haycraft, Howard (ed.) (1992) *The Art of the Mystery Story: A Collection of Critical Essays*, New York, Carroll & Graf.

Heffernan, Nick (1997) 'Law Crimes: The Legal Fictions of John Grisham and Scott Turow', in *Criminal Proceedings: The Contemporary American Crime Novel*, ed. Peter Messent, London, Pluto Press, pp. 187–213.

Hilfer, Tony (1990) *The Crime Novel: A Variant Genre*, Austin, University of Texas Press.

Horsley, Lee (2001) *The Noir Thriller*, Basingstoke, Palgrave Macmillan.

Hunt, Peter (2000) 'Lindsey Davis: Falco, Cynical Detective in a Corrupt Roman Empire', in *The Detective as Historian: History and Art in Historical Crime Fiction*, ed. Ray B. Browne and Lawrence A. Kreiser Jr., Bowling Green, OH, Bowling Green University Popular Press, pp. 32–44.

Hutcheon, Linda (1984) *Narcissistic Narrative: The Metafictional Paradox*, New York and London, Methuen.

Jacobs, Naomi (1990) *The Character of Truth: Historical Figures in Contemporary Fiction*, Carbondale and Edwardsville, Southern Illinois University Press.

Jarvis, Brian (1997) 'Watching the Detectives: Body Images, Sexual Politics and

Ideology in Contemporary Crime Film', in *Criminal Proceedings: The Contemporary American Crime Novel*, ed. Peter Messent, London, Pluto Press, pp. 214–40.

Johnson Gosselin, Adrienne (ed.) (1999) *Multicultural Detective Fiction: Murder from the 'Other' Side*, New York and London, Garland.

Klaus, H. Gustav and Knight, Stephen (eds) (1998) *The Art of Murder: New Essays on Detective Fiction*, Tübingen, Stauffenburg Verlag.

Knight, Stephen (1980) *Form and Ideology in Crime Fiction*, Basingstoke, Macmillan.

—— (1988) '"A Hard Cheerfulness": An Introduction to Raymond Chandler', in *American Crime Fiction: Studies in the Genre*, ed. Brian Docherty, Basingstoke, Macmillan, pp. 71–87.

—— (2004) *Crime Fiction 1800–2000: Detection, Death, Diversity*, Basingstoke, Palgrave Macmillan.

Knox, Ronald A. (1992) 'Detective Story Decalogue', in *The Art of the Mystery Story: A Collection of Critical Essays*, ed. Howard Haycraft, New York, Carroll & Graf, pp. 194–6.

Kristeva, Julia (1982) *Powers of Horror: An Essay in Abjection*, trans. Leon S. Roudiez, New York, Columbia University Press.

Krutnik, Frank (1994) *In A Lonely Street: Film Noir, Genre, Masculinity*, London, Routledge.

Lange, Bernd-Peter (1998) 'The Detective as Genteel Chess Player: Poe, Doyle, Dibdin', in *The Art of Murder: New Essays on Detective Fiction*, ed. H. Gustav Klaus and Stephen Knight, Tübingen, Stauffenburg Verlag, pp. 50–66.

Lee, Alison (1990) *Realism and Power: Postmodern British Fiction*, London, Routledge.

Light, Alison (1991) *Forever England: Femininity, Literature and Conservatism between the Wars*, London, Routledge.

Luckyj, Christina (1996) Introduction to *The White Devil* by John Webster, London, A&C Black.

Luehrs, Christiane W. and Luehrs, Robert B. (2000) 'Peter Tremayne: Sister Fidelma and the Triumph of Truth', in *The Detective as Historian: History and Art in Historical Crime Fiction*, ed. Ray B. Browne and Lawrence A. Kreiser Jr., Bowling Green, OH, Bowling Green University Popular Press, pp. 45–59.

Lyotard, Jean-François (1992) *The Postmodern Condition: A Report on Knowledge*, trans. Geoff Bennington and Brian Massumi, Manchester, Manchester University Press.

McCann, Sean (2000) *Gumshoe America: Hard-Boiled Crime Fiction and the Rise and Fall of New Deal Liberalism*, Durham, NC and London, Duke University Press.

McHale, Brian (2002) *Constructing Postmodernism*, London, Routledge.

Malmgren, Carl D. (2001) *Anatomy of a Murder: Mystery, Detection and Crime Fiction*, Bowling Green, OH, Bowling Green University Popular Press.

Mandel, Ernst (1984) *Delightful Murder: A Social History of the Crime Story*, London, Pluto Press.

Marcus, Laura (2003) 'Detection and Literary Fiction', in *The Cambridge Companion* to *Crime Fiction*, ed. Martin Priestman, Cambridge, Cambridge University Press, pp. 245–67.

Marcus, Steven (1983) 'Dashiell Hammett', in *The Poetics of Murder: Detective Fiction and Literary Theory*, eds. Glenn W. Most and William W. Stowe, New York, Harcourt Brace, pp. 197–209.

Marling, William (1986) *Raymond Chandler*, Boston, Twayne.

—— (1995) *The American Roman Noir: Hammett, Cain, and Chandler*, Athens, University of Georgia Press.

Marshall, Brenda K. (1992) *Teaching the Postmodern: Fiction and Theory*, London, Routledge.

Merivale, Patricia and Sweeney, Susan Elizabeth (eds) (1999) *Detecting Texts: The Metaphysical Detective Story from Poe to Postmodernism*, Philadelphia, University of Pennsylvania Press.

—— (1999) 'The Game's Afoot: On the Trail of the Metaphysical Detective Story', in *Detecting Texts: The Metaphysical Detective Story from Poe to Postmodernism*, ed. Patricia Merivale and Susan Elizabeth Sweeney, Philadelphia, University of Pennsylvania Press, pp. 1–24.

Messent, Peter (ed.) (1997) *Criminal Proceedings: The Contemporary American Crime Novel*, London, Pluto Press.

—— (1997) 'Introduction: From Private Eye to Police Procedural – The Logic of Contemporary Crime Fiction', in *Criminal Proceedings: The Contemporary American Crime Novel*, ed. Peter Messent, London, Pluto Press, pp. 1–21.

Most, Glenn W. and Stowe, William W. (eds) (1983) *The Poetics of Murder: Detective Fiction and Literary Theory*, San Diego, New York and London, Harcourt Brace.

Muller, Gilbert H. (1995) 'Double Agent: The Los Angeles Crime Cycle of Walter Mosley', in *Los Angeles in Fiction: A Collection of Essays*, revised edn, ed. David Fine, Albuquerque: University of New Mexico Press, pp. 287–301.

Munt, Sally R. (1994) *Murder by the Book? Feminism and the Crime Novel*, London, Routledge.

Murphy, Bruce F. (2001) *The Encyclopedia of Murder and Mystery*, New York, Palgrave.

Murray, David (1997) 'Reading the Signs: Detection and Anthropology in the Work of Tony Hillerman', in *Criminal Proceedings: The Contemporary American Crime Novel*, ed. Peter Messent, London, Pluto Press, pp. 127–49.

Nealon, Jeffrey T. (1999) 'Work of the Detective, Work of the Writer: Auster's *City of Glass*', in *Detecting Texts: The Metaphysical Detective Story from Poe to Postmodernism*, ed. Patricia Merivale and Susan Elizabeth Sweeney, Philadelphia, University of Pennsylvania Press, pp. 117–33.

Ogdon, Bethany (1992) 'Hard-boiled Ideology', *Critical Quarterly* 34.1 pp. 71–87.

Orwell, George (1965) *The Decline of the English Murder and Other Essays* (1944), Harmondsworth, Penguin.

Pepper, Andrew (2000) *The Contemporary American Crime Novel: Race, Ethnicity, Gender, Class*, Chicago, Fitzroy Dearborn.

Plain, Gill (2001) *Twentieth-Century Crime Fiction: Gender, Sexuality and the Body*, Edinburgh, Edinburgh University Press.

Porter, Denis (1981) *The Pursuit of Crime: Art and Ideology in Detective Fiction*, New Haven, CT, Yale University Press.

Priestman, Martin (1990) *Detective Fiction and Literature: The Figure on the Carpet*, Basingstoke, Macmillan.

—— (1998) *Crime Fiction: From Poe to the Present*, Plymouth, Northcote House in Association with the British Council.

—— (ed.) (2003) *The Cambridge Companion to Crime Fiction*, Cambridge, Cambridge University Press.

Rankin, Ian (1998) 'Heroes Doing it by the Book', *The Times*, 18 May, p. 9.

Reddy, Maureen T. (1988) *Sisters in Crime: Feminism and the Crime Novel*, New York, Continuum.

Roth, Marty (1995) *Foul and Fair Play: Reading Genre in Classic Detective Fiction*, Athens, University of Georgia Press.

Rowland, Susan (2001) *From Agatha Christie to Ruth Rendell: British Women Writers in Detective and Crime Fiction*, Basingstoke, Palgrave Macmillan.

Salgādo, Gāmini (ed.) (1969) *Three Jacobean Tragedies*, Harmondsworth, Penguin.

—— (1977) *The Elizabethan Underworld*, London, J.M. Dent and Sons.

Sayers, Dorothy L. (1992), 'Introduction to *The Omnibus of Crime*' (1928), in *The Art of the Mystery Story: A Collection of Critical Essays*, ed. Howard Haycraft, New York, Carroll & Graf, pp. 71–109.

Skenazy, Paul (1995) 'Behind the Territory Ahead', in *Los Angeles in Fiction: A Collection of Essays*, revised edn, ed. David Fine, Albuquerque: University of New Mexico Press, pp. 103–25.

Speir, Jerry (1995) 'The Ultimate Seacoast: Ross McDonald's California', in *Los Angeles in Fiction: A Collection of Essays*, revised edn, ed. David Fine, Albuquerque: University of New Mexico Press, pp. 151–62.

Symons, Julian (1993) *Bloody Murder: From the Detective Story to the Crime Novel*, 3rd revised edn, New York, The Mysterious Press.

Tallack, Douglas (2000) 'Caleb Carr: Running Away from the Darkness', in *The Detective as Historian: History and Art in Historical Crime Fiction*, ed. Ray B. Browne and Lawrence A. Kreiser Jr., Bowling Green, OH, Bowling Green University Popular Press, pp. 251–64.

Taylor, Barry (1997) 'Criminal Suits: Style and Surveillance, Strategy and Tactics in Elmore Leonard', in *Criminal Proceedings: The Contemporary American Crime Novel*, ed. Peter Messent, London, Pluto Press, pp. 22–41.

Todorov, Tzvetan (1977) *The Poetics of Prose*, trans. R. Howard, Oxford, Blackwell.

Tomlinson, T.B. (1964) *A Study of Elizabethan and Jacobean Tragedy*, London: Cambridge University Press.

Van Dine, S.S. (1992) 'Twenty Rules for Writing Detective Stories', in *The Art of the Mystery Story: A Collection of Critical Essays*, ed. Howard Haycraft, New York, Carroll & Graf, pp. 189–93.

Vickers, Anita (2000) 'Stephanie Barron: (Re)Inventing Jane Austen as Detective', in *The Detective as Historian: History and Art in Historical Crime Fiction*, ed. Ray B.

Browne and Lawrence A. Kreiser Jr., Bowling Green, OH, Bowling Green University Popular Press, pp. 213–21.

Walker, Ronald G. and Frazer, June M. (eds) (1990) *The Cunning Craft: Original Essays on Detective Fiction and Contemporary Literary Theory*, Macomb, Western Illinois University Press.

Walton, Priscilla L. and Jones, Manina (1999) *Detective Agency: Women Rewriting the Hard-Boiled Tradition*, Berkeley, University of California Press.

White, Hayden (1976) 'The Fictions of Factual Representation', in *The Literature of Fact*, ed. Angus Fletcher, New York, Columbia University Press, pp. 21–44.

Willett, Ralph (1992) *Hard-Boiled Detective Fiction*, Staffordshire, British Association for American Studies.

—— (1996) *The Naked City: Urban Crime Fiction in the USA*, Manchester, Manchester University Press.

Winks, Robin (ed.) (1968) *The Historian as Detective: Essays on Evidence*, New York, Harper & Row.

Winston, Robert P. and Mellerski, Nancy C. (1992) *The Public Eye: Ideology and the Police Procedural*, Basingstoke, Macmillan.

Index

Related titles from Routledge

Contemporary Fiction
Jago Morrison

'This is a very valuable book, particularly for undergraduate literature majors wishing to deepen their own understanding of their literary and cultural moment. An interesting, worthwhile and challenging study.'

Mark Willhardt, *Monmouth College, Illinois*

The past twenty-five years have seen an explosion of new developments in the English language novel. Jago Morrison's *Contemporary Fiction* provides a much-needed accessible account of this vital evolving field. He enables readers to navigate the subject by introducing the key areas of debate and offers in-depth discussions of many of the most significant texts. Writers examined include:

Ian McEwan, Maxine Hong Kingston, Jeanette Winterson, Toni Morrison, Salman Rushdie, Angela Carter, Hanif Kureshi, Buchi Emecheta and Alice Walker.

Tackling issues such as history, time, the body, race and ethnicity, this book is essential reading for those approaching the area for the first time.

Hb: 0–415–19455–5
Pb: 0–415–19456–3

Available at all good bookshops
For ordering and further information please visit:
www.routledge.com

Related titles from Routledge

Popular Fiction
The Logics and Practices of a Literary Field
Ken Gelder

'This is a book which other explorations into this vast and largely uncharted territory will build on. Moving from a theoretically sophisticated overview, Gelder engages – closely, uncondescendingly, and entertainingly – with a stimulating range of samples. Most importantly it's enjoyable.'

John Sutherland, *University College London*

'With a deceptive ease, Gelder breaks new ground in treating popular fiction as a distinctive cultural field with its own logic. The result is a rare combination of clarity and accessibility and challenging insight.'

Tony Bennett, *The Open University*

In this groundbreaking book, Ken Gelder offers a lively and comprehensive account of popular fiction as a distinctive literary and cultural field. Drawing on a wide range of popular novelists, from Sir Walter Scott and Marie Corelli to Ian Fleming, J. K. Rowling and Stephen King, the book describes for the first time how the field works, what its distinctive features are, and discusses the ways in which popular fiction is produced, advertised, distributed and read.

Popular Fiction provides a critical history of three primary genres: romance, crime fiction and science fiction; and looks at the role of bookshops, fanzines and prozines in the distribution and reception of popular fiction. Finally, it examines five bestselling popular novelists in detail – John Grisham, Michael Crichton, Anne Rice, Jackie Collins and J. R. R. Tolkein – to see how popular fiction is used, discussed and represented in contemporary culture.

An essential introduction to this dynamic literary and cultural field, *Popular Fiction* is ideal for all those interested in the 'culture' of popular fiction.

Hb: 0–415–35646–6
Pb: 0–415–35647–4

Available at all good bookshops
For ordering and further information please visit:
www.routledge.com

Related titles from Routledge

Science Fiction
Adam Roberts

the *NEW CRITICAL IDIOM*

Science fiction is one of the most vigorous and exciting areas of modern culture, ranging from groundbreaking novels of ideas to blockbusters on the cinema screen. This outstanding volume offers a clear and critically engaged account of the phenomenon. Adam Roberts' book:

- provides a concise history of science fiction and the ways in which the genre has been defined
- explores key concepts in SF criticism and theory, in chapters such as Gender, Race and Technology
- examines the interactions between science fiction and science fact
- anchors each chapter with a case study drawn from a short story, book or film, from Frank Herbert's *Dune* to Barry Sonnenfeld's *Men in Black.*

Introducing the reader to nineteenth-century Pulp, Golden Age, New Wave, Feminist and Cyberpunk science fictions, this is the essential guide to a major cultural movement.

Hb: 0–415–19204–8
Pb: 0–415–19205–6

Available at all good bookshops
For ordering and further information please visit:
www.routledge.com